Praise for CONC
by Patricia

"With cool, compelling prose, CONCRETE ANGEL reveals the menace that lurks beneath a mother's charming facade. An absorbing novel by an unusually fine writer."

—Meg Gardiner, Edgar Award-winning author of CHINA LAKE and THE MEMORY COLLECTOR

"(An) enthralling, dark debut novel...It's a potent and at times poignant combination. Those who enjoy suspenseful, atmospheric family drama will find much to love here."

—*Library Journal* (starred review)

"Christine's mother Eve is sharp, beautiful, charismatic... and a murderous sociopath. Their complicated and heartbreaking relationship is explored in CONCRETE ANGEL -- a riveting depiction of family ties and how they can bind, ensnare, strangle."

—Alison Gaylin, *USA Today* bestselling author

"CONCRETE ANGEL is debut novelist Patti Abbott's exquisitely rendered character study of a manipulative mother over two decades. Eve is a woman obsessed – but how will our narrator, Eve's only daughter, respond as her childhood innocence is taken away? Abbott exhibits a pitch-perfect precision with both language and setting in capturing the tragic world of a mid-century Pennsylvania family."

—Naomi Hirahara, Edgar Award winning author of SNAKESKIN SHAMISEN

"This is a gripping psychological thriller...will draw fans of the late Ruth Rendell as well as Paula Hawkins' *The Girl on the Train*."

—*Booklist*

"A fresh, original voice telling a story that's probably, in broad outline if not detail, more common than we know. But what detail! From the opening sentence, a grabber."

—SJ Rozan, Edgar-winning author (as Sam Cabot) of SKIN OF THE WOLF

"The characters in Abbott's debut novel are fully realized."

—*Kirkus Reviews*

"CONCRETE ANGEL is a culmination of her very best and is not to be missed."

—Criminal Element

SHOT
IN
DETROIT

PATRICIA ABBOTT

POLIS BOOKS

3907505074412972

The following is a work of fiction. Names, characters, places, events and incidents are either the product of the author's imagination or used in an entirely fictitious manner. Any resemblance to actual persons, living or dead, is entirely coincidental.

Copyright © 2016 by Patricia Abbott
Cover and jacket design by Georgia Morrissey
Interior design by E.M. Tippetts Book Designs

ISBN 978-1-940610-82-5
eISBN 978-1-943818-14-3
Library of Congress Catalog Number: 2016938170

First trade paperback publication: June 2016
1201 Hudson Street
Hoboken, NJ 07030
www.PolisBooks.com

POLIS BOOKS

To Josh and Megan

CHAPTER 1

"*The best photographs are often subversive,*
unreasonable, delirious."
Lisette Model

MIDWAY INTO MY mad flight to Belle Isle in the March predawn chill, a journey I undertook after a distressing evening with Ted Ernst, it occurred to me the park might not be open at six in the morning. I'd jumped into my car not thinking to check the hours. But if my memory was reliable, there was no way to close the park.

My foot tapped the brake anxiously as I stopped for the umpteenth time, the traffic light swinging jauntily in the river's breeze, a seagull perched on its top. Planting my foot on the gas pedal a second later, I wondered if Detroit's population of Canadian geese, abandoned buildings, and rusted cars would soon overtake the number of residents. In New York, they were gassing geese. Perhaps in Detroit it was people instead. Another red light a block later, and I hammered the wheel in frustration.

Today, I needed the boost that discovering I could still produce a first-rate photo would give me. Why did I feel so comfortable at Belle

Isle, a place most suburbanites found threatening, and even depressing, considering their memories of its glory days? But a huge park on the water in a spectacular state of decay could yield good results for a photographer. Ruin porn was the current phrase.

Parking on an unpaved area inside the park, I hurried through the trees and within seconds spotted a half-naked man on a park bench being serviced by a woman old enough to be on Medicare. She glanced at me smiling, perhaps seeing me as potential back-up. The missing teeth her smile revealed would add an interesting element to both a photo and the act itself. The pair was situated under a street lamp and consequently photographable. Did people on Belle Isle usually act on such desire at dawn? Not even *quite* dawn? Perhaps they'd been up for hours already and it was mid-afternoon on their cockeyed clock.

I was considering snapping a picture when the man lifted his grizzled head, spotted me, and wiggled a finger in warning. The light caught the whites of his eyes, his half-smile. Aw, I wouldn't have done it anyway. If their interest in such activity had not diminished, let 'em at it. I smiled back and moved on, looking for—well, I didn't know just what—which was precisely the problem. How would I top the scene I'd witnessed? So I snapped away as I walked, stray lights pointing out my path. This hit-or-miss strategy didn't usually pan out, but what else was there to do?

I'd barely taken half a dozen pictures when two Detroit cops, attracted by the flashes, approached. Park cops were lenient with activity inside Belle Isle up to a point. They put up with the park's semi-permanent, homeless residents as long as they behaved themselves. The randy teenagers populating the park on summer nights were also tolerated. Probably kids kept the homeless afloat with gifts of burgers, half-drunk beers, loose change: an environmental niche in action.

Certainly the homeless had it better here than the guys hovering by the freeway entrances. Months of cold and the horrible economy made opportunities for successful panhandling scant in Michigan.

Today it was the more suburban-looking photographer—me—who drew the cops' attention, and I had no idea why. I lowered my camera, trying to smile, as they approached. Cops made me tense so my smile might've been more of a leer if they could see my expression in what was still near-dark.

One of the cops shone a flashlight, one of those gadgets with the ability to light a small city, in my face, holding it the way the cops on CSI do.

"Reporter?" the burly, red-haired sergeant asked. His tone hovered between conversational and investigatory. "One of the papers send you down?"

I shook my head. "Taking a few pictures of my own."

When neither man responded, I added, "I'm a photographer," wondering if I should dig out my press pass or portfolio since the cops still didn't look satisfied. The flashlight continued to play across my face—like the lights in an interrogation room.

"Should we know your name?" the burly guy said, chuckling to himself.

"No, I'm just poking around. You know. Looking for a good subject."

I was babbling. Their noticeable lack of approval was throwing me off. How many fools ended up marking time in police stations through excessive chatter? And my teeth *were* chattering. It was damp and chilly. Having darted out my door on impulse, I was underdressed in a light jacket.

"Poking around, huh? At six in the morning and down here for some reason," the second cop said. He was African-American and his manner was brusque. "It's barely light, lady. Sure you're not here to score drugs?" Both cops looked around, alert to this possibility. "Or sell them?" He nodded toward my bag but did not ask me to open it.

Ignoring his gesture, which could have been right but wasn't, I said, "I've got the necessary lighting in there. To take good pictures, I mean."

"Lights? You've been snapping away for the last ten minutes."

"Proper pictures," I clarified. Did he really think I was up to something?

Two blank faces as they continued to see me as a potential dealer or buyer. Trying to distract them, I pointedly glanced at a nearby picnic table where a young woman was sleeping, her head pillowed on one arm, a breast poking provocatively from her half-zipped hoodie. An overturned vodka bottle rested on the bench beside her, another lay on the ground. Shouldn't they be more interested in her? At the very least, wasn't she vulnerable to assault given her inebriated state? Hadn't she probably scored drugs? Where was her dealer?

"It looks like that woman needs your help, Officers." Head gesture.

Neither bothered to follow my gaze. "Bettie's okay," the black cop said. "We got her back."

They'd seen it a million times and were unimpressed with Bettie and her errant boob. They knew how to protect her. They had her "back." I was the problem.

I pushed forward. "Photographers find inspiration in urban settings." I'd definitely have to work on my vocabulary before venturing down here again. I sounded phony, guilty, snotty, or all three.

"So it's art to you, huh?" the redheaded cop interrupted. "The people you snap don't matter more than apples on a cutting board."

This from a guy who allowed Bettie to sleep it off—her breast on the table exactly like a still life object—and up for grabs.

The cop coughed, scraping the phlegm from his throat and swallowing it back down, a common practice during the nine months of allergy season in Detroit. "But these people here," he gestured with a sweeping motion and a shrug, "well, you're not here to take pictures of their fine couture or snazzy cars for *HUM* magazine. You're looking for—more." His lips twisted as he sniffed his displeasure.

I was getting annoyed at their attempt to provoke me—to make me the villain of their morning stroll, the scenario they were insisting on writing. What if I *was* hoping for something darker, something that might upset their peace? I did feel sorry for the people in the park. Who didn't? But they'd been part of the landscape in Detroit for as long as I could remember. For decades before the Canadian geese arrived. Had it ever been any different? You'd have to go back to the fifties to find prosperity and that was long before my birth.

Anyway, was I much better off in my dreary little apartment in a blue-collar suburb a few miles away? I wasn't the suburbanite they thought I was. I lived on the fringes of Detroit life, and probably a lot more frugally than the cops.

My intentions were serious if they'd only try to understand. What I did take "seriously," as callous as it might seem, was how these people might look on film. How they'd become art in my hands if I was good enough. Occasionally I thought I was. Once in a while, someone actually said it. But the span of time between such periods was lengthening each year—the periods between days when I got that chill from what I produced. When I knew it told a truth.

"Maybe I can draw attention to what you guys see down here. Raise public awareness."

God, I sounded like a public service announcement, but I was growing desperate to win my release. I couldn't seem to stop the gush of pompous sentiments spilling from my mouth. But I did mean it. Good art was meant to do this. If I were inside the island's greenhouse or in the aquarium, these dudes would be happy. Probably setting up my lights for me. Popping quarters in the pop machine and sharing an early morning swig of Coke as they watched me work. But out here....

The black officer looked like he was choking back a laugh. "You'd better be careful," he said. "People here might not like turning up in your darkroom. This isn't exactly a pre-theater gala at the Fox Theater. Nobody's on the red carpet."

He turned to his red-haired buddy and got the obligatory laugh. Their mood had lifted a bit as the day's grayness became tinged with gold. "Don't get paid to watch the asses of ladies who should be and could be somewhere else, do we? What's your name anyway?" he said, pulling out a pad.

"Violet Hart," I told him. He scribbled it down, flipped the pad shut, and stashed it.

"Gawkers, I call them—and yes, *you*," the black cop continued. "No better than the guy who slows down to watch a fatality hauled off the freeway." He looked me over again. "Maybe you *are* here to start trouble, Ms. Hart. What d'ya think, Den? Is she here to make us sweat at six in the morning? Is the pretty lady up to no good?"

Before his partner could respond, the silver flash of the Renaissance Center, Detroit's hat tip to the architecture of the early seventies, caught our eyes as the sun began its slow ascent. Only two towers were visible and both looked more like spires of amorphous smoke than objects of steel and glass. When I turned back again, the park had become instantaneously benign, scenic—a site for a photographer seeking such a landscape—a place for joggers and cyclists in bright spandex; city workers in large gloves stabbing at yesterday's trash; two authentically suburban ladies dressed in olive-colored L.L. Bean wear, binoculars in hand.

But I couldn't imagine a moment when a woman in a canvas coat and baggy jeans would show up in my darkroom. Could an artist live right outside Detroit and not be attracted to its gloomy underbelly rather than its predictable suburbs? The possibility of getting striking shots of darker subjects, an opportunity existing only minutes earlier, had disappeared. I'd squandered those sacred moments talking to the cops, explaining what shouldn't need to be explained.

Perhaps I'd never been more than a source of early-morning amusement, a person to hassle or harass—a sort of cop's flirtation.

I went home to develop the film—the few pictures I'd snapped—but none of the photographs looked like anything special on the contact sheet. And the exposed breast of the woman looked like a rock lying on that picnic table. I turned my eyes away in embarrassment. The overturned bottles looked stagey. You could find better pictures in the free rags. Today's work joined yesterday's in the trash.

I picked up the phone and called Di's number. "Is he there?" I asked Alberto when he answered. "I need to talk to him."

"*You need*," he said sarcastically. "Can't it wait? You know what time he gets home." I could feel him consulting a clock. "Barely five hours' sleep."

"Did he hire you to monitor his calls?"

This was the kind of relationship we had. Like Grace and Jack vying for Will's attention on that old TV show.

"You like to pretend I'm hired help." He paused a minute, and when I didn't reply, sighed again and yelled, "Diogenes! Your ol' lady's on the line." This was a joke, of course, since it was Alberto who was

Di's ol' lady.

When Di got on the line, I told him I was finished. "I'm gonna be taking pictures of bar mitzvahs and sweet sixteens till I'm too old to carry my equipment. I'm no damned good."

No response. I was boring him or he'd fallen back to sleep.

"I earned less than thirty thousand dollars last year. My car's about to die. My mother hit me up for a loan last week. *My mother.* There's little hope I will ever marry, ever put a cent away for retirement, and I am no longer young enough to ignore these things. And I need new equipment for those stupid wedding pictures. But mostly, I am no damned good. And I live in Detroit—a city that makes no promises that any of that will change. Sure a few new restaurants are opening up. So what? 2011 will likely be no better than 2010."

He sighed sleepily. "What put the bug up your ass this time?"

"I can't bear to tell you."

"But you know you will. Start at the beginning." He yawned. "I need a bedtime story."

CHAPTER 2

"My photographs are intended to represent
something you don't see."
Emmet Gowin

THE NIGHT BEFORE, around eight, an hour I usually devote to a glass of cabernet and a gritty mystery novel, the landline rang. When I heard Ted Ernst recording a message on my ancient machine, I ran for the receiver, nearly tripping over a table leg in my rush. Ted Ernst owned an art gallery where ten or so of my photographs—depending on whether he'd sold any—currently filled one wall. It wasn't his best wall, the one flooded with light, but still I had a wall. Something I'd found hard to come by.

"Doing anything?" he asked, not identifying himself. Maybe he assumed I'd seen the caller ID, but probably he thought I'd remember his voice. He was that sort of arrogant prick. "Thought I might drop by since I'm in your neighborhood." I heard paper rustling. "Hazel Park. Right?"

I looked around the room, deciding whether cleaning up might be worth it. Could he respect an artist who lived in squalor? Was there any other kind? My work tended to take over any unclaimed space. But at least it covered the dust.

"Sure. Come on up." I couldn't help but add, "Anything special?"

I'd been wondering how my pictures were selling but had been afraid to check. Four weeks into a ten-week show and I hadn't heard a word since my gala opening. The free wine and cheese had brought in a fair number of guests the first night, but I wasn't the only artist. Woodcuts hung primly on the best wall, the crowd making it difficult to see them. The blue and red abstracts across the room were as lonely as a cloud though so I didn't feel too bad.

"Let's save it. Have ourselves a little face time."

Ted's jokey tone was moderately comforting. Did terrorists about to explode their flak jackets joke with potential victims? I shoved things into drawers and closets, put on some eye liner and blush, thinking that with any luck he was coming over to ask for a few more pieces. Did I have other work to give him? Optimism was not part of my normal makeup, but he'd sounded—well, not negative—if I read him right. Would he come over just to give me bad news? Reading people correctly did not top my list of talents, however.

When he'd first agreed to show my work, I took the photographs to an upscale framing store in Birmingham, a ritzy suburb. The shop did a first-rate job too—triple matting, maple frames, glare-proof glass; you could hang the damned photos in the Met. This elegant presentation added about $150 to the price of each piece. Ted was encouraging about possible sales so it seemed worth the expenditure. One he'd suggested. The unpaid bill still sat on my desk. So too the email reminder.

"No one buys quality work out of bins," he'd said. "That's for art fairs."

He stood in the foyer half an hour later, examining my African mask collection.

"Holy shit!" he muttered, stepping away from an especially severe-looking face—a dark, rotting brown mask with white slashes for features, dark red feathers for hair, the mouth: a burnt scream. It was meant to frighten, and it did. "Must've been some crazy ceremony going on." He accompanied his words with a war-dance of sorts, managing to be offensive and awkward simultaneously. God, I hated the jerk.

"That particular mask may be authentic," I said, trying to get past his rude display. "It was infested with insect larvae when I bought it at a going-out-of-business sale at a gallery in Soho. Got home and realized it ten minutes later—when I felt something crawling up my arm." Ted made the requisite face. "Had to throw the mask in the freezer for a week. Good thing I never keep food in there."

I pulled the mask down from the wall, unable to help myself. "Look at the stains inside, will you? Someone wore this baby more than once."

"Sweat, huh," Ted said, taking it from me. "But most of these are reproductions, right?"

"Yeah—or decorative art. Souvenirs for tourists." I took the mask from him, carefully replacing it. "If I sell enough of my own work, I can buy more authentic pieces."

Was this true? Would I ever be able to even afford more than groceries and heat? I thought of the ten-year-old car sitting outside at the curb.

Was a smile lurking on his lips? My stomach rose and fell like an elevator as I tried to figure him out, to keep a step ahead. Why did he feel like the enemy?

"Why masks?"

So it was to last a bit longer: the cat-and-mouse part of the evening.

"A friend gave me the first one." It'd been Bobby Allison in the nineties. "Got me hooked on them."

Bobby Allison could only make love wearing a mask. Rip the mask off and he deflated like a stuck balloon. Bobby's masks came from Venice and were much more expensive and elegant than any in my collection. Beautiful but boring to me. I still remembered the sensation of Venetian glass beads rattling over my eyes, of feathery embellishments tickling my cheeks. He wore reproductions in the bedroom. He wasn't crazy, just kooky.

"Makes for a memorable hallway."

"I like it."

Ted looked around more openly now. "Spooky, but unforgettable," he repeated, his mind elsewhere. Suddenly his eyes lit up. "Hey, I wonder if I should do a show using masks. Where did you say you got these?"

"EBay, flea markets, Ann Arbor, downtown at DuMouchelles, you know." Was this what he came up here for? Ideas for a show? "See that one over there?" I said, pointing to one that looked like a plaster cast but with a tin nose.

"Yeah."

"It's from the First World War. There were no cosmetic surgical procedures to deal with disfigurement, which was rampant. So they made masks like this one."

Zero interest. It wasn't pretty enough for Ted. So I went on.

"You know, like for a soldier who lost his nose?" No reaction. "One or two I got on a trip to the Caribbean—when I was flush once."

Now he looked engaged. "You look a little flushed now."

Oh, so that's why he was here. Not a good line, but enough to sway me when paired with the image of Bobby Allison rattling around in my head. And suddenly, we were in the bedroom. Had this been his sole intention? He was probably horny tonight and knew he had the upper hand here. But as an imperfect person in an imperfect world, I was going to let him have his way. The question was: was I easy, was I attracted to him, or was I desperate? Strike one and two. Well, at least two. Did I think a quick—and I do mean quick—roll in the hay would change my luck? I'd have the whole night if not lifetime to regret it. I could tell a fast finisher a mile away.

Along with his freckles, Ted had a pelt of reddish fur running from his neck to his ass. He looked like a fox in his reflection in the mirror over my bed. I ran my fingers through the hair on his back cautiously, not sure if he regarded his pelt as unfortunate or not.

Our activity was further punctuated by the guy who lived upstairs pounding miles out on his treadmill. Why had my neighbor decided he needed a huge piece of machinery in his apartment—a one-bedroom unit if I remembered correctly? I used to run into him at the gym. Ben—that was his name—was one of the guys who watched himself in the mirror. Maybe I could shoot a group of photos of gym patrons examining themselves with a critical but loving gaze. Fingers on the offending bulges or pictorial pecs. A sideways glance to see if anyone was watching. Damn, a good idea finally. I filed it away, betting they'd readily agree to being immortalized. But just the men, I reckoned. Women would never be satisfied enough with their body to allow it.

Ted and I tried each other on for size: sucked, kissed, moaned, traded positions, indicating preferences and dislikes. The stuff new sexual partners did, and it wasn't as quick as I'd expected. Both our bodies instinctively picked up the thumping rhythm going on above, finishing only moments after Ben walked heavily across the floor to the bathroom to pee. I'd listened to the sequence of events enough times to know his routine and anticipate the stuttering flush of an old toilet.

Ben was slower than usual tonight, perhaps diverted by the mirror over his bathroom sink. Or else he'd drunk a lot. Perhaps he'd heard us below. Did I scream? Not tonight. It was possible Ted had though. He seemed like a screamer. Maybe he'd spotted his pelt.

I was breathing heavily.

Ted, of course, credited his skill as a lover. "Good way to burn calories, huh."

I scurried him out the bedroom door as soon as it didn't look like bad manners, shutting the door behind us. He reached for seconds, but I ducked away. Afterwards was seldom more than afterwards for me.

"Is there construction going on upstairs? Funny time to be doing work."

Shrugging, I didn't bother to explain.

"So how's the show going?" I asked when we were back in the living room. "Sold much of my stuff?"

Ted frowned. It was a deeply practiced frown, and I sunk into myself as he began to speak. Was it a pity-fuck we'd engaged in or was he exacting a payment? Either way I'd been had.

THE UNSOLD PHOTOGRAPHS were neatly wrapped in brown butcher paper and sitting on his counter when I arrived later that day, well after my sojourn at Belle Isle. Nine studies of the implosion of Detroit apartment buildings along with one photo of the demise of the downtown J.L. Hudson's store, the signature Michigan department emporium for most of the twentieth century. At first, I thought the tenth photograph had sold, but there it was in Ted's white hands. Hands all over me sixteen hours earlier.

"They lack—*je ne sais quois*—" Ted said unctuously, holding the tenth picture up. "I wish I could tell you what it is, Vi. What's keeping them from selling. Maybe this subject's been done before and perhaps a bit better." He ducked his head. "FYI, I can't tell you how many photographs I've seen of the Hudson's Department Store implosion." He thrummed his fingers on the counter—like a drum roll before his final shot. "Makes you seem like an amateur to shoot such dull subjects."

The tenth photograph was a shot of the Seville Apartments on the Cass Corridor, one of Detroit's most notorious streets. I took it when the building was being dismantled, several years ago now. Part of the Seville seemed to be melting into the earth, creating a sort of lava-like concrete eruption. I'd thought it looked pretty cool back then. Still did. Making a good subject a better one was the steady stream of water directed at the building by an unseen hand, making a high arching rainbow with nothing at its end but rubble: perhaps resembling holy water emanating from the hand of God. Occasionally, I could get into spiritual stuff—when a photo captured an image I'd never noticed with my naked eye. There was otherworldly stuff out there: any photographer will tell you that. Images not there when you took the shot.

"You're giving the viewer exactly what he'd expect," Ted said, lecturing me like he was Beaumont Newhall, the art critic.

I feigned attentiveness, hoping it'd put an end to the agony, but he continued in a hectoring tone. "Too bad you didn't get into the Seville a little earlier. I hear they kept a shooting range in a back hallway. *New Jack City*—remember that movie—with a few senior citizens cringing behind plywood doors."

What an ass! An ass I'd recently had over mine.

He blinked twice and began to wrap the photo. "Maybe that's what you should aim for—getting in there before they implode. Record the final days of these buildings. Might be where the money is." He found his knife and waved it theatrically before cutting a piece of string. "Funny how often photographers have no sense of which pictures will sell," he added, mercilessly. "If I see one more picture of New Orleans after Katrina. Or the vineyards in Tuscany, for God's sake." He shook his head. "With digitals and cell phones, anyone can photograph doorways and grapes. So too, oil spills."

I looked at those soft white hands again, his impeccable eggshell suede shirt.

"Great idea—the final day thing, Ted. I'll see if I can get the demolition schedule from the city. Maybe I can beat them to the next site."

"Great," he said, missing my sarcasm. He tied the string around the picture, pushing the pile across the counter. "Guess you'll need help carrying them to the car."

His tone hissed disdain. The bastard didn't want to touch my work. It was poison; I was poison.

Ted's idea of photographing a building's final days would never work for me, I thought, as we marched to the car. I wasn't interested in photojournalism, had nothing to say—it wasn't how my mind worked. My work depended on setting up a shot, getting the right lighting, using a camera that allowed me to manipulate, experiment. Lots of time and trials. The idea of running through deserted hallways in an inner city building, chased by rats, human and otherwise, well, it wasn't going to happen. Words weren't my talent. I could go for days without using any.

Painters, sculptors, ceramicists—they were never expected to expose societal ills. Why were photographers? Why couldn't I take pictures of the ill, the poor, the disfigured, the freakish without providing a script or an apology, without starting a non-profit to go with the work? When Degas painted his lovely but prosaic dancers for the hundredth time, no one chided him for not marching out into the teeming streets of Paris where urchins panhandled to support their families. But right from the start, photography was held to a different standard.

Ted seemed to have no memory of his enthusiasm of several months ago when I brought my portfolio to him after meeting him at a cocktail party at the Omni. Back then he'd talked about my idiosyncratic vision, my honed craft—arty claptrap probably designed to get me into bed. A particular sort of arrangement, sex for favors, had happened more times than I cared to remember, but I'd also had a sense my work impressed him. Could I have read him wrong?

So after Ted used me to scratch an itch the night before, and a mere half hour after he'd dismissed my work as boring and repetitive at his gallery, I sloshed through the melting snow and found myself with Ted at Vicente's, a Cuban spot on Library Street. I was a chump, but there it was. Give a girl the slightest hint of another shot at a show and she'll follow you anywhere. Or I would at least.

After a scotch or two, Ted mellowed, especially in his critique of my work. "You're still looking for the right subject, Vi. Give it time. Talent's there."

He was all teeth, with a slight odor of wet dog hair, as he moved his chair closer so I could hear his insights over the percussive noise. "The technique's in place, the skill. What are you—thirty? You've got time to find your subject."

He was almost shouting over the music and people at the adjacent tables turned to stare at us. Ted patted my hand, and I didn't flinch at his touch. Another gallery show, a whisper about my work in the right ear, the opportunity to be in on it; for this, I could tolerate a lot of pawing. How far would I go for a few shards of success? I wasn't sure.

After my second margarita, I looked him over with renewed interest, now fueled by a possible payoff down the road, a second show when I'd found my subject. I remembered those freckles stretching from head to toe, his strangely hairy back.

Perhaps I could play it differently this time. I knew what he liked. In bed at least. And his odd smell, by now it reminded me of the seashore: a wet dog at the beach. He repeated himself when I didn't respond, breaking my trance.

"You're still a baby, Vi. You can't rush it. You'll find a marketable subject before long."

Actually, I was thirty-five, okay, thirty-nine, and had given it time, though till now, I'd never fretted much about the passing years. Someone—even if it had to be crappy Ted—had yanked me from my ennui. My dazed state.

How old was Weegee when he started following cops around? When did O'Keeffe grasp the concept that certain flowers resembled vaginas? What was the cutoff age for edgy, important work?

"Marketable? Are you saying I should turn to shtick?"

This thought woke me up. I'd always secretly, or not so secretly, thought most of the photographs people flocked to in galleries relied on shtick. Here was my confirmation.

"Good God, no," Ted said, drawing back in semi-believable alarm. "Hate the stuff. Babies dressed like caterpillars. Psychedelic tints. Yuck."

I wondered how he'd define "stuff." Were the street scenes Helen Levitt or Berenice Abbott shot almost a century ago more or less shtick too? If a photograph reflected honest life, could it still be shtick?

"But you want art that sells? Right? A moneymaker." Surely, I could figure it out. Seduce him with the right subject.

"Well, naturally, I want to eat. But hey, I love being part of the art scene. I could've run a hotel or an Applebee's if I didn't."

He massaged my hand in a way that expressed another desire. Once again, I resisted the impulse to withdraw it. He'd lost the last remnant of any respect back when he'd said "FYI." No, he'd lost it last night when he played me.

But maybe it was the moment to get serious. Perhaps taking scattershot pictures of whatever caught my interest wasn't enough. I wasn't going to fall into success like I'd always imagined. It might take more than that, but of what I wasn't sure.

I started to tell Ted about my new insights but realized he might see the panicky look in my eyes even in Vicente's dim light. So I took him home again—right after the music got loud and Latin dancing took over the floor; had there ever been any doubt?

"Ever consider hanging the masks in the bedroom?" he said as we passed through the hallway again on his way out. "Anyway, I've decided masks wouldn't be right in my gallery. I've never gone in for that primitive stuff. It's more the province of Detroit galleries."

He was down the flight of stairs in seconds, the door slamming behind him, never giving me a chance to tell him not all masks were primitive. What had he meant when he said masks were the province of Detroit galleries? Did he know these masks hadn't been made to hang in galleries any more than dinosaurs existed only to end up as fossils in a natural history museum? It sounded like a racist remark. Well, no surprise there. It was still 1967 in Detroit in most respects.

FOR THE REST of the night, I agonized over Ted's words. Was art like mathematics, where only artists under thirty produced important work? Had I gone from novice artist to spent hack without a period of fertility in between? I also wondered if Bill would understand these two occasions were work and not love related. Bill…

CHAPTER 3

Detroit News: A 26-year-old Detroit man was rushed to a Rochester hospital today after collapsing on a playing field in Rochester Hills. He was pronounced dead at 2:17 p.m. by doctors at Crittenden Hospital. The victim was identified by his rugby teammates as Rodney Jones, a Detroit attorney. Mr. Jones came to the U.S. from Manchester, England in 2009 to attend law school at the University of Michigan. He was employed as an associate with Barker, Shay & McDougal, a Detroit law firm specializing in patent and copyright law. The cause of Mr. Jones' death is still under investigation by the Rochester Police.

(March 2011)

"DID YOU HANG that up there for the aesthetics?" Bill Fontenel asked me the first time we had sex nearly two years before. He was looking up at the ornate mirror fastened to the ceiling. No one had ever raised the subject that quickly before. Most men laughed nervously when they first glimpsed their naked bodies above them, perhaps imagining I'd be hard to please or might require flourishes or tricks they'd never even fantasized. Over time, I realized Bill found the mirror comical, which made me feel foolish. Yet I didn't remove it.

My super had hung it for me amidst lewd glances and stifled smirks the week I moved in five or six years ago. My apartments in Chicago and New York had lower ceilings than this one, making the mirror more of a sexual accessory and less of the furtive, almost sinister, enhancement that it was here in Hazel Park, Michigan.

I was occasionally tempted to halt the action and reach for a camera. More than once, I had a video camera running from an alcove, but the finished product was always more pornography than art. Or some sort of sinister voyeurism. It'd take a well-thought-out script to get the proper effect and I'd never had the nerve to suggest it. I didn't know if I had such a script in me. It was that storytelling trap again. Straightforward pictures didn't make judgments. Or did they?

Despite my ambitions, notwithstanding my trips to places like Belle Isle, I supported myself with dull assignments from university presses, small publishing houses, and an occasional newspaper job. Nearly all of my subjects—local rappers, sports figures, entrepreneurs, or media celebrities—insisted on posing with a whippet or a Siamese in their Birmingham or Grosse Pointe garden, library, or three-story foyer. They'd been told an animal in the picture humanized them, I guess. Since they tended to choose animals reeking of pretention, it seldom worked.

And, of course, I mostly shot bar mitzvahs, weddings, and birthday parties. The people paying me to take these pictures were nearly always satisfied with the product; it was I who wanted to burn the photographs of perfectly turned-out brides, of virile football players, of thirteen-year-old versions of Lady Gaga. Well, actually the Lady Gaga clones were interesting. I'd more than a dozen lookalikes in my files.

Bill had no idea I took pictures the first time he came home with me.

"Hobby?" he said, running his hand over an old Leica M2 resting on the console table.

I'd met Bill for the first time earlier that day at his funeral home on Jefferson on the eastside of Detroit. I'd only been to half a dozen funerals in my life, but this one was definitely the best if you rate funerals. It was mostly due to the elegant dress Bill turned his corpse out in. No respectable navy-blue suits for Bill. The commonplace turned him off as much as it did me.

Some of my appreciation for his work may have stemmed from the fact Bill Fontenel was a terrifically handsome man. That's what made me linger in his foyer longer than was necessary. When would I ever get inside his funeral home again? I wasn't about to arrange my future funeral merely to catch his attention. But it'd been a long time between dates, and I usually had pretty good instincts about which men find me attractive. Or at least initially appealing until they spot a certain weirdness I can't hide for long.

Bill was helping an elderly man escort his wife out the door, placing a gentle hand under her frail arm as they negotiated an icy sidewalk, chatting with the two mourners as if the woman's difficulty in maneuvering the steps was nothing unusual. I watched as he helped her into the waiting car, bending over at the last minute to adjust her seatbelt, smiling. When the car finally pulled away, he turned around and grinned. So he *had* noticed me. Bill didn't miss much.

I made a few flattering remarks about the service, talked about the recently deceased: an elderly man I'd known only casually, but who'd purchased a photograph of mine at an art fair last summer. And then another two at a Christmas market where we ended up having the pancake supper together in the food hall. Anyone who'd placed faith and money in me deserved my presence at his funeral. So when I saw the notice in the newspaper, I went.

An hour later, Bill climbed the steps to my apartment. We'd gotten on the subject of the African art in the foyer of his funeral home (he had a Yombe sculpture on a sideboard) and I said I owned a few interesting pieces. It only took twenty minutes to drive to Hazel Park, where I poured wine, offered him cashews.

Geez, I'd like to stretch it out, but truthfully an hour later he was in my bed. It doesn't usually happen that fast—I am cautious if nothing else. Glancing up, I admired what I saw in the mirror. Oh, there'd been other black men in my bed, but Bill was the most photogenic. Actually there was not much contrast between the two of us, and our similar height made things line up nicely.

Afterwards, and I noticed immediately Bill liked *afterwards* more than most men, my thoughts returned to the funeral and Chester Roland.

"What an elegant man."

"Well, thank you," Bill said, looking up at our reflection with a sly grin. "My mother says the same thing."

"I meant Chester Roland—the man you buried today," I said with a laugh, poking a finger into his slightly meaty middle. "He was older than Moses but you made him look—well, like Moses." When he looked at me quizzically, I said, "Well, he looked…dignified. Like a man you'd trust to part the seas or track down wise words carved on a boulder."

"You seem to know the Bible pretty well."

"Bibles were the only thing relatives gave me when I was a kid. Books of Bible stories, recordings of the Mormon Tabernacle Choir, reprints of famous sermons, little nylon bookmarks with Bible verses on them, cheap gold-painted crosses, an actual cross necklace that turned my neck green. My aunts thought I was being raised by a heathen—and one deserted by the trumpet-player husband she should never have married. That's how they always referred to him. 'That trumpet-player Bunny married.' Lots of eye-rolling went with it." I swallowed the bile. "Look, we don't want to go there. Once you get me started…. Getting back to Mr. Roland, he looked gorgeous."

"You're flattering me in the hope of more sexual favors, aren't you? But hey, I can live with it." Bill sat up a bit, adjusting the pillows behind him. "Dead people aren't elegant, Violet. You wouldn't use the word elegant if you saw them when we pick them up. Saw the damage done to them by disease, age, poverty, other people. That's how it is before we work our magic." He massaged my hip absentmindedly. "But they're a little closer to elegance after I spend time with them. Perform a little hocus-pocus. Mr. Roland was easier to bring up to snuff than most of them though. Lucky enough to have a quick, merciful death. It hardly took the color from his cheeks."

Mr. Roland had been dressed in a pearl gray banker's pin-striped suit he'd probably never worn as the bookkeeper for a small business. A lavender shirt and tie and a dark purple vest peeked out. A slate gray fedora sat on his head.

"You gussy them up like it's the best day they've ever had. Is that your niche? Why people come to you?"

"That's my secret, yes. The ones who never looked good in life—the ugly ones, the messed-up ones, the ravaged ones—they get my best work. If they look good resting in my house, how can death be so bad? They must be going somewhere nice to look that fine."

He shook his head, walking his fingers back to my hip. The scar was a small memento from a guy in New York who liked to play rough. Ironically, it was my talisman now, a reminder of my limits, of the men

I guarded myself against. And I didn't like Bill's hand there. I eased it off.

He shook his hand like it'd been burnt. "I dress 'em up like they're going to a ball—like Mardi Gras or New Year's Eve."

"And that's what they want? What their families request?"

Personally, I didn't get the obsession about funerals. I was planning on a green funeral when the time came. I wanted the sort of burial where they bundled you in a biodegradable cloth and lowered you into the ground. No coffins, or urns. No elaborate rituals. It was the worms who were served the last supper at green funerals. I'd have to trust Di to see to this. Make him my executor if that was the name for it. I could trust him to see me off the way I wanted, and I would do the same for him if Alberto wasn't around. I wondered whom Diogenes trusted more. I wanted to be the one. I wanted to be someone's one.

"Not all of them request or even tolerate such elaborate dress. But enough do. It *is* my niche. How I got famous." He smiled.

"Did you take over the business from your dad?"

"Nope. Bought it from a little old lady. An old white woman who couldn't get enough business from black folks to survive in Detroit after a while. Folks around here may go to a white doctor or lawyer, but they want their own kind to bury 'em if that's an option." He paused. "Dad was an autoworker. Worked at the Rouge for years. Then one day, a press stamped his arm instead of the metal."

"Killed him?"

Bill shook his head. "Daddy was tough. Learned to use his other arm and worked at the Rouge for another five years. But he won a nice settlement that he passed on to me when he died. I bought this business with the money. Mom's an affluent old lady up in Saginaw nowadays. Living the good life. Didn't always have it so easy—cleaned people's houses until her knees had calluses. Or worse." He paused. "What about your daddy?"

I'd led him down this lane again. Now I had to answer for it. Come up with an abbreviated story.

"You know what they say about marrying musicians. They drift. And one look at me and he took off for good." I laughed as if it were a joke but it wasn't. "I've only seen him a few times since that day." I paused. "At first it was his choice but now it's kinda mutual. We don't seem to get on."

"Sorry." He patted my hand. "An only child?"

"Had a sister—she died."

He made the requisite face and started to ask the inevitable question. But then didn't. He was skilled at reading my face from the start. So I'd gotten past my recitation early—the wretched outline of my life. We could save the tale of how I was responsible for Daisy's death till later. Oh, there were lots of sad sagas left to tell.

We didn't talk much about our work or families after our first conversation. He came to me with the smells of death washed away. I came with the failures of my darkroom, my mundane jobs, left behind. There were other activities and most of them took place between those four walls. Sometimes we went out to restaurants or to a movie, a walk or a drive. But most often we had sex. And equally important to Bill was the afterwards. Bill lingered until I sent him home, returning to my own work with renewed energy.

It was nearly ten o'clock when the phone rang.

"This better not be a barroom drunk," I said.

"It's me, Vi. Bill. Sober as the dead guy on my table. Hey, can you drive down here?"

Bill lived and worked near the center of the city; I was ten miles away.

"Right now?"

I'd just knocked back two glasses of pinot noir, not planning on a late night drive. Was it safe to drive when the room jiggled like this? I flipped the switch on the coffeemaker, vaguely remembering it was "time" not coffee that made you sober. I didn't have time, but I had coffee so it would have to do. I looked down into the stainless steel of the appliance. Ugh! Now I had something else to think about: a double chin.

My mother's rule for women over thirty-five ran through my head: never look down at yourself, never look at your face from the side, look straight ahead and with your head tilted back a bit. Watch out for errant cameras that catch you unprepared. And this was back in the day when cell phones couldn't capture you at any moment.

Bunny had scant motherly advice to dispense, so what she offered up tended to roll around like loose ball bearings in my head. You'd have expected her to be a glamour girl—but she looked like any other mother of a thirty-nine year old.

"If you don't mind," Bill was saying on the phone as I pinched the loose skin, hoping it would snap back. "I could use your help."

It wasn't like Bill to be secretive or ask favors, so I threw water on my face, coffee in my travel mug, breath mints in my mouth, and ran for the door.

I was curious about Bill's living arrangements anyway, knowing only that he lived over his business. Over our months together, we'd gotten into the habit of hanging out at my apartment, Bill claiming he spent too much time at the funeral home anyway, and it was no place to take a lady. He'd never suggested I come before despite several pointed hints. The nasty mortuary processes, whatever they were, apparently happened in the basement; the middle floor was for the public. What I knew about the funeral business was based on watching *Six Feet Under*.

"There's often—stuff—going on there at night," he explained. "Don't want to walk in on more than you're up to. Might think you're tough but you'd be surprised."

Bill used two male assistants to help with the more skilled parts of the business, and another three or four employees worked in the office, in sales, assisted with driving, and various other jobs. His payroll was too large, he often complained.

"Hard to run a first-rate establishment without adequate help. I tried that routine the first two to three years—picking up the bodies myself, sitting down with the dozens of salesmen I deal with—you wouldn't believe how many—sending out the bills and collecting what was due if they didn't pay, consoling the bereaved, preparing the bodies, taking the cars to be serviced. Got by for a while with a cleaning woman with a cast-iron stomach for what she had to clean up, and my mother, of course. A few years and both of them bailed." He sighed. "Must have averaged four hours' sleep a night for the first five years." He sounded simultaneously resentful and nostalgic.

He was waiting at the door, tapping a foot, when I arrived. "Down in the prep room," he said, ushering me along the hallway and down the stairs without further comment. "Be easier to show you than tell you. Hope you don't shock too easily." He looked back at me for a sign.

I hadn't known what they called it, the prep room, and I looked around with interest. The stink—formaldehyde, I guessed—was overwhelming at first. Few tools were evident although surgical masks, scalpels, and incisors rested on a stand. It was as sterile as a surgical facility. I wondered what the machine looking like a blender was for. A second later I realized a table tipping into a sink was hooked up to it: embalming, of course.

"Over here," Bill said, walking toward a stainless steel table where a covered body rested.

Unadulterated curiosity propelled me across the room. "Wait a sec," I said suddenly. "It's not anyone I know, is it? That's not why you called me down here? Not to identify a body?"

"Identification's the coroner's job. I usually know who my customers are. They come with documentation, telephone calls, and anxious relatives at my door. Okay, now this is a young guy—an accident victim. Are you ready?"

Taking the corner of the sheet, he pulled it back, gradually exposing the body of a young black man dressed in a maroon-and-black-striped shirt with a pair of skimpy black shorts. His spiked shoes were well-worn, scruffy, and his knees were wrapped in bandages—the type athletes wore. He was handsome. Or had been until a day or two ago.

I blinked back tears. "Damn, he's so young, Bill. Why do so many young guys die in Detroit? Young black guys? Did someone kill him?"

I was remembering several other funerals he'd talked about since we met.

Bill made a small adjustment to the corpse's hands. "Seems to be mostly young black men, doesn't it? Detroit sure does come in near the top in the insurance tables for male deaths under age thirty-five. In other cities, it's usually car accidents, but we've got our own methods in Detroit. Though not our Rodney here. If you'll remember, I told you it was an accident. No, this wasn't a murder."

I peered at the body. Although it initially looked like Rodney was merely asleep, a longer look made it hard to believe there'd ever been a beating heart beneath his inert chest. His body looked irrelevant to any definition of life or death. He was a mannequin—a waxen image. Yet there was a stateliness about him despite the uniform. "What was it then?"

"Another player ran into him at a rugby match—an eighteen-wheeler of a halfback. Turned out Rodney had an aneurysm. Never knew what hit him."

Bill clapped his hands together to illustrate.

I shuddered. "Rugby in Detroit? Always seemed like an upper-class game. Like polo or fox hunting."

"Club's up in Rochester. They sent him to me because Rodney lived in Palmer Park. And 'cause he's black, of course." He laughed now, but there was no mirth in it. "No black people out in Rochester, Vi. You won't find a black face out that way till you hit Pontiac or Flint. Turn over a rusting car in Flint and find a cache of brothers. Otherwise it's all country clubs out in Oakland County." He shivered.

"Aren't you gonna put him in a nice suit—like the one Mr. Roland wore?" He deserved something better than this ugly outfit.

"This is what they requested," he said, gesturing.

"Oh, come on now. They actually want him laid out in those ridiculous shorts with wrapped knees? His family? Whoever?"

"It's his uniform," Bill said, his eyes still on the body. "And his teammates asked for it." He looked at me. "Okay, here's the thing, Vi. His parents—they're over in Manchester, England—they want a picture. They're not able to make it here for the funeral." He paused. "I think the father has Parkinson's. And they sounded like they'd never been farther west than Dublin."

"Isn't it a strange request? A photograph of him like this? In this dopey uniform, and dead?"

But the idea of taking a photograph of this fellow was making my fingers itch: the idea of taking a picture of a dead man. I'd never thought of it. Photographing a dying city, yes. But not its dying residents.

"Folks haven't seen Rodney in a few years. He came over to attend college or law school and stayed. I'm sending him home after the funeral, but in a closed coffin. So a photograph right now seems appropriate—so his family can see him a last time. It's not an unusual request, you know. People occasionally want a record. Or they need to show it to someone who can't make it to the funeral. A lot of black people like pictures at the services: a little program, a history of a life. The guy who usually takes photos for me is out of town or he'd give me a hand. But I have a camera you can use. Didn't think to ask you to bring one."

He went over to a cabinet and removed an inexpensive 35 millimeter job—a point-and-shoot from the nineties probably. I guess I looked at it as though it was an eight-track tape from 1975, turning it over in my hands, and Bill noticed my dismay.

"Anyway, this one's fine. Good enough, right?"

I shrugged, shaking my head.

Bill ignored my displeasure. "I'd do it myself but I don't have the eye and time's running out. Don't want to send his parents a lousy picture, do we? They'll never see him at the service so it needs to be a better photo than what I can do." Bill stood in front of me, the proverbial hat in hand.

"You should've told me to bring a camera. A photograph using this piece of garbage is going to be pretty hideous. It'll look like you shoved him into the photo machine at Walmart."

For the first time, I looked at the body like a professional. "The lighting's harsh—and those white, high-gloss walls. Ugh." I shaded my eyes. "It won't be much better than you could do yourself. The camera's more important than the photographer for a picture like this. The lighting, ugh. Couldn't we move him into another room? A room with flat paint and natural lighting? Why are the walls painted in high-gloss?"

"Why do you think?" he said. "Just take the picture, Violet. It's a *record*. No one's expecting a studio shot." He made a few minor adjustments to Rodney's shorts and stepped back. "With these silky shorts he's wearing, I don't want it to look like he has an erection." He sighed and leaned in again to examine him. "Hope he sent home a few recent pictures. Terrible to realize your son's changed over the years and you missed all of it."

He frowned, and I realized how much he cared about the details. I'd seen how it was with him during the funeral I attended but forgotten. I wanted the best photo I could take of Bill's rugby player. Try to match his professionalism—but what a rotten camera to do it with.

"People his age don't send their parents pictures unless they're in the army and think they might die."

I didn't know where my insight had come from, but it was probably true. Children at college, or older and without kids, never sent a snapshot home, but let them go to an army base overseas and a flood of photos found their way back. Or maybe that was changing too with cell phone cameras. But I doubted it. Friends yes, parents no.

"Boy, I hate to take a lousy…"

I interrupted myself; it was only going to be a parroting of what I'd already said. Bill would take the photograph himself rather than wait around if I continued to dally. Had to make myself do it and stop fussing.

"Never heard of a black English guy."

"His family's probably from one of those islands the Brits snatched. Didn't mess around much with Africans. Guess they preferred the lilt to the bass."

I was circling the table, looking for the best angle. "Do you have a stool or stepladder for me to stand on? I need a little height. Table's kind of high. I'd practically have to climb up on it to get a decent shot."

"If the tables were any lower, I'd have back trouble."

He walked over to a counter and pulled a wheeled stool out from beneath it. "Will this do?"

But it didn't. It kept moving and when Bill tried to hold it still, parts of him got in the way. Finally I settled on standing on an overturned wastepaper basket. Cheap camera or not, bad angle or not, poor lighting or not, I was going to take this picture, could already imagine pulling it out of the bath.

Together we stretched Rodney out on the table again, this time a dark sheet underneath, propping him slightly, trying to get him to look peaceful for his parents. Trying to make up for the fact he'd died tragically and with no warning. I shot away, taking pictures from various angles until the film was gone. I would've taken far fewer photos with one of my own cameras. But this toy might not produce a single good shot. I hadn't felt this panicky about a photograph in years.

When I finished, I stepped down and said, "I can't imagine these photos will help his family. My Deardorff would've been so much better, Bill. I'll bring it next time. It's perfect for formal shots."

I set Bill's camera down with disdain, already thinking that there'd be more photographs.

Bill shook his head. "You're taking this way too seriously, Violet. It's not like it's a wedding picture." He put the wastepaper basket away.

"My regular guy just takes a few shots. No sense fussing over it. They're not going to frame it and put it on the mantel. They'll look at it once and file it away—or toss it without looking at it at all if it's too painful."

So now the job was finished, it'd lost its urgency for Bill. He'd summoned me here late at night to perform a function he'd now devalued.

"Hey, I can tell you take *your* job seriously by how he looks on that table, Bill. You took a lot of time with him. This guy—Rodney—who's going back to Manchester in a closed box, looks like a prince. Don't you think I want to do my best work for the family too?"

Maybe it wasn't merely art. Not this photograph.

"He's the best-looking dead man I ever saw. Too bad his parents won't get a chance to appreciate it." I paused again for emphasis. "Except they will, Bill, because I took his picture. They'll see how fine he looked."

He shrugged. "Okay, okay. You can get down off the effing soapbox."

He pretended to whisk the imaginary piece of furniture away as he'd done with the wastepaper basket. I picked the camera up and removed the film, putting it into my purse.

"Hey, I can get them developed right down the street. Don't bother yourself."

"Like I'm gonna let a teenager with greasy hands and a funky bath fool around with my work." I handed him his camera. "Even when I took pictures back in college, I developed them myself. Before I knew what I was doing, I was better than a teenager earning beer money." I laughed a little, thinking about it. "I'd like to be at CVS to watch a sixteen-year-old pull these babies out of the tank."

Later, in the darkroom, I was amazed at how much I liked the photographs as the images rose up in the soup. The camera, inadequate though it'd been, invested the body with a patina of dignity. The photos were beautiful, eerie—though grotesque.

"Di?" I said, hearing his voice on the other end of the line for once. "You'll never guess what's staring up at me."

"Not X-rated, I hope."

He sounded like he'd been asleep. Well, of course he was. It was after one o'clock. He woke up a little after I told him.

CHAPTER 4

"I'm really just using the mirror to summon something I don't even know until I see it."

Cindy Sherman

A FEW DAYS LATER, I headed for Belle Isle again, telling myself I needed to check things out for an upcoming wedding I'd been hired to shoot. Some of the events I photographed took place in the Detroit Yacht Club. Though its membership had dwindled as its members moved west or north, many native Detroiters returned to the building and the island for various functions.

The slips were empty today, of course, the boats in storage for another month or two. There was always traffic circling the island though; sometimes it appeared aimless, but why shouldn't it? People weren't there to work. The few open venues had their visitors— although it was mostly senior citizens going to the Belle Isle Casino to play cards or do crafts. Earlier or later came the joggers and sports enthusiasts. Later still the patrons with less admirable pursuits arrived. Was I in that number? Not today.

Although I was familiar with the DYC building, I always liked to check out the lighting before an event, finding out if any obstacles might have popped up. Furniture got moved around, and surprises on the day of the event were never a good idea. Bare windows one year often gave way to heavy drapes the next, and you never knew when you'd find last year's rose-colored room painted green. The color of paint could have a regrettable impact on bridesmaids' dresses and flowers. If I knew the venue well, as I did the Yacht Club, I tried to steer the brides toward colors that would look good in the wedding photographs. Some women resented me for putting in my two cents; others were grateful. Some summer weddings took place under a white tent. It was almost impossible to get stunning pictures under the canvas, but tents seemed both picturesque and safe to the future bride.

The DYC continued to look like the enormous Mediterranean villa its twenties-era architect was going for. A little shabby now, it still hinted at its opulent past. In 1924, membership had reached three thousand. I wondered what the number was now. There weren't too many cars in the lot, but it was a Friday afternoon in March. At any rate, it looked a hell of a lot better than the Boat Club, which sat moldering down the road. No one could figure out which buildings to save or which to implode; this was true for the whole city.

"Only fools are willing to pay for what makes a building distinct on the outside nowadays. Their attention's on technological considerations and cash-generating amenities," Bill had said recently. He was a member of several Detroit development associations considering such matters. "Make the bar inviting, but forget about marble steps or fancy parapets."

I spent time at the Yacht Club as a kid—when my mother waitressed for a firm catering DYC affairs. Bunny couldn't always find a sitter, and I knew how to behave. The staff let me follow them around, showing me how to place napkins on the table, set glassware on the bar. I'd sketch the guests after that: women wearing ball gowns, furs, and brilliant jewels; men in tuxedoes with their shoes shined to a patina, musicians setting up, their glinting instruments blinding me; silver platters filled with food I couldn't name. It was intoxicating.

Once at a New Year's Eve party, when I was spying from a niche, a man in a beautifully tailored tuxedo asked, "Whose little girl are you?"

I paused a minute, thinking of Bunny sweating heavily in her polyester uniform, and then pointed at the most beautiful woman in the room, a woman sweeping across the flagstone terrace in a sapphire gown, her dark hair lustrous, held back with matching jeweled barrettes.

The man laughed heartily, a hand resting on his cummerbund, and said, "You're Lena Rossi's kid, huh?" I nodded, growing hesitant from his tone. "Then you must be my daughter. Funny but I don't remember your name."

Still chuckling, he moved away. I watched as he openly told his wife about it, both looking over at me bemused, wondering who I was, surely knowing from my clothing I wasn't the child of a club member.

"Where've you been?" Bunny asked me minutes later in the kitchen, grabbing my arm. "What've you been up to? You got a funny look on your face."

TODAY, I PARKED in the half-deserted lot and bounded up the steps to the ballroom, nodding to the porter, Stan Horsham.

"Got the Scribner nuptials, huh?" he asked. I nodded, and smiling approvingly, he stepped aside. The staff at the DYC was eager for events, ready to do what it took to keep their jobs a little longer, and also invested in the Club's success as a Detroit institution, one still hanging on. Employees were minimal during the week, but Stan was always around to lend a hand. He reminded me of the bartender in *The Shining* in his ancient uniform, his hair slicked back, a ready smile.

After scouting the ballroom, the bar, and several seating areas, I made a few notes and took off. On impulse, I decided to drive around the island once before heading home. The idea that I could find something memorable to shoot had been intensified by my recent work for Bill. I wasn't looking for corpses. At least I don't think I was. Detroit does that to you though—makes decay seem glamorous. You began to see denuded landscapes, windowless buildings, potholed streets as potential art.

It wasn't early morning, a time when Belle Isle looked rough and slightly out of control, but you never knew. Maybe I wouldn't be thwarted by bored cops this trip.

The circuit around the island was more than two miles with sensational views of the Detroit River and its tributary, Lake St. Clair. Of course, much of Belle Isle was in a state of absolute disarray. The contrast of natural beauty and the detritus of man was poignant.

On impulse, I stopped the car near a wooded area surprisingly free of debris, and began walking toward the river, cell phone in hand to be safe. Probably ninety-eight percent of Detroit's suburban population never set foot on Belle Isle, a big part of the reason it was languishing. It wasn't widely popular with most Detroiters either. It reminded them of what was lost. Maybe irretrievably.

I'd slipped a new battery and memory card into the digital camera I kept on hand, in case something out of the ordinary caught my eye. Even at midday, it was possible. I didn't mind using a digital for preliminary work.

Violent crimes on Belle Isle were actually few, especially this time of year, but it was the summer hangout of Detroit's teenage population and a place to sell drugs. Today it was nearly deserted, although trash and overgrown shrubbery was on the increase as I moved further from the road. Maybe it was the wind stirring the underbrush into something wild.

I stopped suddenly. A large, grayish bulky object lay not fifty yards in front of me. It appeared to be human. I looked around. No one in sight. Cautiously, I approached the…the body, for that's what it was, I was sure. My pulse raced. Shit. A body deserved more than a digital camera, though I certainly couldn't have set up a larger camera out here, no tripods in sight. Why was I thinking about art when what I should have been thinking about was calling the cops?

It couldn't be a body. Probably a homeless guy sleeping it off. A passerby or park guard would've spotted a body by now, wouldn't they? But who'd sleep out in the open? Wouldn't they find a more out-of-the-way spot? But the thought of photographing a body without Bill's touches—something raw and new—was thrilling, so I kept walking in its direction. Excitement and dread in equal portions rose in my throat.

No, it wasn't a body—it was nothing more than a large gray bag, probably filled with sand. Someone must've dragged it away from the river, perhaps to sit on the rise and look out over the water. There were no benches in this area, only a solitary picnic table eaten away by too many winters.

"It's a geobag," said a voice from behind me. "The gray thing you're wondering about. A geobag."

I turned around and found a young man standing with his hands on his hips. It was unclear whether he was homeless or merely dressed extremely casually. He wore a grandfatherly-looking blue jacket, a torn T-shirt from a nineties Rolling Stones concert, paint-stained khakis, and a pair of army boots, scuffed and without laces. I couldn't decide whether to be frightened or not. But his use of the term "geobag" was marginally reassuring.

"Parks Department uses geobags to prevent erosion," he continued. "There's dozens more down by the water." He seemed pleased to be able to offer this information.

"I guessed I'd about figured that out."

He ducked his head, embarrassed. "'Course you have. I dragged it up here to sit on. Bet you thought it was a body for a few secs though." He chuckled. "You wouldn't be the first. Week or two ago, a cop ran over here with his hand on his holster." He paused, adding, "About once or twice a week, it gets moved back to the shore—though the thing weighs a friggin' ton. Can't figure out why anyone would pay so much attention to a dumb bag with all the shit needs to be done here."

We both looked around. It was an untidy scene.

"They only pick the trash up on Arbor Day. Come in from the suburbs to help out, wearing rubber gloves, goggles, and protective clothes. Like there's ebola on the loose. Long time between Arbor Days though. They want to be getting after the phragmites before they crowd everything out."

What the hell were phragmites? It sounded like a rodent to me, but I let it go, saying, "And then brag all year about how they care about their city, how they do their part to maintain it."

"That's them, all right."

We exchanged wary smiles. "Do you sit here to look at the water?" I asked, mostly to be polite. It sounded like I was talking to a child, but he was probably bipolar. His fly was half-open, his jaw kinda slack.

"Sure, I watch the water—lots of cool boats go by. Industrial, pleasure craft. But mostly, I make sculptures from stuff I find on the island." He rubbed his hands up and down the sides of his jacket. "I sit there to ponder what my next piece of work might be."

"Have any pieces on hand?" I looked around as if a portable gallery might appear.

He shook his head. "I usually sit here to think. Oh, and to look for cool debris. Great spot for shit. Kind of inletty over there. I construct my pieces in a different spot. Closer to the water. Less trees." He gestured with his head and I was afraid he'd suggest we go over to see them. "I've been assigned a spot actually."

Assigned? I *was* curious. "Assigned? By whom?"

"City. Got tired of tearing 'em down, of me arguing with them. Gave me my own little gallery."

"Sell any?" What a kick in the head if this guy was more successful than I was.

"How would I do that?" He looked as if it were me who was a bit nutty. "They're part of the landscape—or they are until they wash away or fall apart. Or till someone knocks 'em down. Not all art is for sale."

"Why would anyone destroy—them?" I wasn't sure what "them" was.

"You'd be surprised. Naturalists don't like my pieces—not one little bit. Nor the boat people—I get in their way. I got my fans but not many."

Boat people? For a minute, I thought he meant the Vietnamese.

"Kids come down here, get a kick out of wrecking shit. Remember doing that? Back when you were a nipper." He laughed mirthlessly. "City said I can keep at it as long as I stay on that one shoreline and keep my work under a certain height and width. Pretty small area though. Limiting." He gestured with his hands. "I've been known to go overboard, but soon a suit or uniform comes along to remind me. I'm a big pain in the ass, but after Guyton—you know. They're not looking for trouble again.'"

Guyton's Heidelberg Project had been a blocks-long display of found objects, arranged artfully, which the City had mostly pulled down. Pieces of it were now in museums or in private collections. Other sections returned mysteriously to Heidelberg Street. Arsonists were also on hand. Nobody knew who they were. Any discussion of Detroit brought up Tyree Guyton sooner or later.

"And they'd *better* be careful." Crazy Guy sat down on the bag of sand with a big plunk. "One or two people who come down here regularly said to let 'em know if the City harasses me. Or if anyone does." He nodded, repeating, "I got my fans."

I nodded too, impressed despite myself. Crazy Guy had managed to garner respect despite his demeanor. Maybe his shit *was* outstanding.

"You know," he continued, "when you were heading over from your car and spotted the bag, you didn't look scared. People usually freak out for a second or two. You looked pretty damned excited, in fact—moved faster after you saw the bag." He chuckled with delight. "You into dead bodies maybe?"

Was I? I changed the subject. "How often do you drag that geobag up here?"

"All the time." He sighed. "But usually someone drags it back to the water in a week or so. Who knows why? City's full of crazies. Already told you, right? So I go get the bag again. This one or another. Hard to tell 'em apart."

Was he serious?

He stretched out on the bag now, his feet hanging over one end, his head the other. "I figure after a while, they'll give up. All the stuff that needs doin' and they bother with the damn bag."

"Well, I take pictures and am always on the lookout for interesting stuff. Maybe the kind of stuff you're into. Or what I think you're into."

He nodded and I decided on the spot to share my project with him; I needed another ear and maybe he really was an artist. "Right now I'm photographing dead people at a local funeral home." Suddenly, I knew this to be true: people, not just Rodney. I'd have to figure out a way to get Bill on board though.

He gave a long, low whistle. "Pretty gruesome. But anything you'd get here would be kinda further out?" He suddenly sat up. "Look, I can call you if something turns up. A body, a body part. What you're after today."

"Have you ever come across one?"

I tried to make my tone light and jokey, instead of macabre. I wasn't sure if this discussion was a sensible one if Crazy Guy was clinically bipolar. "Ever seen one—down here?"

He gave a start. "Nah, but I've found pretty cool stuff. Once an ear, nibbled a little, but you could tell what it was. Another time, a dog's head. A boxer. And last month I found a guy half-dead from a heart attack. Sooner or later." He shrugged. "Getting closer all the time. Odds are with me."

His hand was stroking something in his pocket and I tried not to stare. Maybe it was the ear.

"I can get my business card from the car if you can wait a sec," I said, deciding to go with it. It seemed foolish not to take him up on his offer. The objects he mentioned interested me. If he hung out on Belle Isle all the time, a body *was* bound to turn up. Or something I could photograph. It occurred to me that Bill's excessive handiwork on the departed actually camouflaged their real nature. Perhaps we were at cross-purposes in this endeavor. What might make a burial special might make a photograph souvenirish.

"I'll come with you," he said, rising. "Headed for my stuff now anyway. Found a pretty cool item I want to install." He reached into a large pocket in the front of his jacket and pulled out a piece of metal shaped like a rocket. "Hood ornament," he said. "Don't know what car model or year. When I go home I'll check it out on the Internet."

Then he did live somewhere.

He was struggling to keep up with me. "Got one going right now—a sculpture, I mean. This doodad will look awesome on it." He held the rocket out and flew it around like a child might. "Don't find stuff this good much. It may have drifted in from the river. Or maybe over from Canada."

This good. He had to be kidding? When I didn't put my hand out for it, he put it back in his pocket.

"I'll come over to see your work soon," I said, trying to pretend enthusiasm.

But after the hood ornament, I felt a bit deflated, and it was hard to take him seriously. "But right now I have an assignment—out in the 'burbs. A bar mitzvah," I said, unnecessarily. I didn't really have any immediate plans but was wondering by then if there actually was a sculpture site. It might only exist in his head. Not too different from my professed project though. Who was kidding who?

But if there was a chance he'd come up with an interesting find, well, it was worth a risk. We reached my car and I opened the door and took a card from the purse I'd left under the seat, remembering too late it was probably not a good idea to show him where I kept my purse. He could grab it and run. He could push me inside and rape me. Hell, he could grab the keys and steal the car.

But he didn't do any of those things, and I knew he wouldn't. He took the card, nodded, and drifted away, heading for a wooded area, quickly passing through a stand of oaks. Maybe the card would end up as part of his next project. He held it in his hand like a trophy. Shit!

After about twenty-five yards or so, he turned around. "Hey, Violet," he said, looking at the card again. "Name's Derek Olsen, case you need to know."

He yelled this information into the wind, and I had trouble hearing him.

"I'm down here most days. Mom—well, she likes me to get out of the house."

Derek had a way about him that set my teeth on edge—despite his friendliness and offers of help. I doubted he was dangerous, but he was strange. Old men with zippers at half-mast were one thing, men in their twenties another.

As I drove across the bridge a few minutes later, I caught sight of Derek Olsen on the shoreline. He was standing on top of a sculpture, mostly concrete from what I could see. It was pretty big. I wondered the exact limit the city had set. He was probably placing his hood ornament at the pinnacle now. From the distance, he looked like an explorer who'd discovered new land and was planting a flag. I could see similar objects lining the shore; each of them probably festooned with various found objects, much like children's sand castles at the beach. Wow, the Tyree Guyton debacle had made its mark. I couldn't believe the City put up with it.

CHAPTER 5

*"Your mind is like a live camera that is constantly taking pictures
of every single moment that comes onto you... So be a good
photographer!"*
David Acuna

"THE RUGBY PLAYER's teammates loved the picture," Bill told me a
few days later. "All of 'em asked for copies. Okay I gave it out?"

I shrugged. "Ask his parents. They paid for it."

My original elation had faded. Now I could see what a poor photo
it was; the angle bad, the high-gloss paint in the prep room giving it
the clinical look of a morgue shot. It was only Bill's highly skilled work
preparing the corpse and the eeriness of the subject matter that saved
it from looking like one of those photos tacked on a whiteboard in cop
shows. I'd thought about this guy more than I wanted to since taking
the picture. Dressing him in that rugby uniform emphasized his youth.
It was one of those freak accidents no one could have predicted, and
the thought of his parents pulling this photo out of an envelope was
tragic.

It reminded me of my sister, Daisy's death in its unexpectedness,
its assault on someone too young. One minute Daisy was bouncing up

the steps. The next, she'd tripped over my errant roller skate and was dead. Thirty years later, I could still hear her sharp scream, and I was standing at the rail, looking down as blood seeped over the worn gold carpet, the wheels on the skate slowly coming to a stop.

"True," Bill said, nodding. "But I thought it might be important to you. Who gets copies of your photo, I mean." He was lying in my bed, examining himself in the mirror above him. "Definitely have to give up that second scotch before dinner unless you can promise me this is a funhouse mirror."

"Or at least the bag of chips that goes with it."

"Now you've pissed me off." He reached out to grab me. "Have you ever, and I mean ever, seen me eat a bag of chips?"

I hadn't actually, but Bill *was* beefing up. He was propped like a fattened Thanksgiving turkey against the ornate headboard of my bed, a Victorian piece of furniture I'd hauled to Detroit from New York.

"You do take sex seriously," a guy once told me after jabbing his elbow on a sharp corner. "Ever discuss that with your shrink?"

"Or maybe I just buy a nice piece of furniture when I see one," I shot back at him.

I grew tired of insights about my sex life being flung at me by men who asked for seriously weird embellishments to theirs. Remain unattached after a certain age and you're labeled as promiscuous, witchy, or weird.

The bed *was* a beauty. The headboard was walnut and four feet high. Carved angels and nymphs chased each other across a forest of dour-looking trees and predatory flowers. The deep penetration of the carvings made for sharp edges. You could only lean against it cushioned by thick pillows. Head-banging sex was risky.

I tossed Bill the crossword puzzle, stymied by a six-letter word for

Pandora's Box. Risqué words came to mind, but this was the *New York Times.*

"Brooks," he said after a minute. "Louise Brooks played Pandora in the film." When I looked at him puzzled, he continued, "She was a 1920s-era actress—bangs, straight hair. You know."

"How old are you, buster?" I asked, grabbing the crossword. "Your familiarity with women from a hundred years ago is alarming."

He tossed me the pencil. "Don't you ever watch old movies? They show silent ones on *Turner Classics.* Sunday nights, I think."

"I don't like black-and-white movies much," I said, a bit embarrassed. "Except perhaps aesthetically. They seem more like an exercise than a story. Like playing scales on the piano." I paused, thinking. "I like to be swept away."

"Who says black-and-white films can't sweep you away?" He took a sip of his coffee. "Try *The Third Man.* Or *Casablanca.* Color would've ruined them. Where're the shadows in color? Rain on city streets? Can't believe I'm lecturing a photographer on the artistic merit of black-and-white photography, on the use of shadows."

"Anyway, I like black and white under this mirror," I said.

"So I've noticed."

It was true that I felt comfortable with black men. Or more comfortable at least. "Well, what about you and white women? Goes both ways."

"You're my first white woman—wait, let me rephrase that before you jump down my throat. You're the first white woman I've had a romantic relationship with. And if my mamma comes to hear about it, you'll probably be the last."

"Racism?"

"Black people can't be racists."

"Says you." I filled in another word on the puzzle and changed the subject. "Did his parents like the photos? The rugby player's?"

"Haven't heard a word. Body was delivered to their mortuary last week. They'll probably pay the bill and move on." He took the newspaper, looked at it, and scratched his head. "Let's do the Monday puzzle next time. I need the boost doing Monday's puzzle gives me."

"I never buy a newspaper unless you're coming."

He shook his head.

"I'd like to try it again, Bill."

The words somersaulted out of my mouth. Only through the greatest effort had I been able to delay my request this long—until it didn't seem like the primary reason for our date. My trip to Belle Isle had decided it.

It took him a few seconds before he understood I didn't mean sex or the crossword puzzle. I meant more photographs. Like the one of the rugby player.

He slowly shook his head.

"I told you, I use this guy who's perfectly adequate for my..."

"That's not what I mean," I added. "When I was finished with the photograph of Rodney, I realized it was art I was making—or trying to make—not just a record of a death. I wouldn't be taking a photograph for the family, Bill. It would be for me—for a project. A study."

My voice was shrill, pathetic; I struggled to control it. "I hate the photograph I took of him. I'm embarrassed I couldn't do better." I steepled my fingers intently. "I have lots of ideas about how to make the photos more striking. Make the lighting more dramatic. And I'd use my Deardorff. Also I'd like to try for a heightened color palette—so the photos don't look so waxy."

"My subjects *are* waxy. They're dead, remember?" Bill paused.

"So you're talking about art photography, aren't you?" I nodded. "A Deardorff? A camera, I take it?"

"Deardorffs are especially nice cameras for portraits." On my feet now, I headed for the closet. "Large format cameras give a subject more dignity and grandeur than most cameras can muster. It allows for depth of field and is really great for perspective. They capture a lot of information."

I brought the camera across the room and made him hold it. "Takes a long time to set it up though. It's not designed for a casual shot. But your clients—they aren't going any place, are they? At least not right away. That's what makes them perfect as subjects. They don't move, not ever. Deardorffs are made for that sort of shot."

"Looks like my granddaddy's old black box. Hide your head under a black curtain?" "Isn't photography digital now?"

"Not for this sort of thing—nor for a picture I'd take. I want a more formal shot than the one I took of Rodney. I wish Rodney wasn't back in England. I'd love to do him over. As it is now, the photo is practically unusable. If I ever have a show—I mean."

"You make him sound like a piece of meat. And trust me; you wouldn't want to be anywhere near Rodney now." Bill grimaced. "A show?" He pretended surprise but then smiled. "Don't you think I know what you're talking about?"

This was the right tactic to take—making Bill understand exactly how serious I was about this project. Surely, he understood dedication to craft.

Bill got out of the bed, grabbing his shirt from the chair. "You got off on it, huh? Lucky I called you over that night."

There it was again; he was trivializing or cheapening my intentions—conflating it with sexual desire, thinking there was an opportunistic element to it.

My voice was stiff as I put the camera back in its case. "It piqued my professional interest." I closed the closet door. "Don't you get satisfaction in making those bodies look good? In finding the right look?"

"It piqued something all right," he said, stepping into his navy slacks and ignoring the comparison.

Was he enjoying hassling me or was it something else? Maybe he wouldn't acknowledge me as an artist, but I wasn't about to let his attitude sabotage my work. I bit back the typical snarky response I usually tossed out when cornered—a retort to the effect that he made his living from the dead.

"Got anyone down there now?" I said instead, trying to keep my voice low and steady. "In the prep room, I mean."

He zipped and belted his slacks, ran a comb through his hair. "Now, where's my wallet?" He turned around, saw it on the dresser, and walked over. "Ninety-year-old woman who died of breast cancer is waiting on me now. Wanna take her picture?"

He looked at himself in the pocket mirror he carried and clawed his hair back again; it had the slack waviness of a white man's hair. "Only trouble is, you'll have to stuff her chest to make her look good. Maybe fill out her cheeks a little. Use a wig. Ready for those trimmings? You saw a healthy individual the other day. Dead, yes, but healthy hours before. Young. Remember that, please. There's an enormous difference. This gal is Granny Clampett, Vi, not Barry Sanders."

I had no idea who Barry Sanders was but figured it was a sports-related reference. It always paid to assume that with men.

He picked up a small bottle of cologne he kept on my bureau and dabbed a drop behind his ears. "It's better to have a consistent, manufactured smell," he'd told me once when I asked why he wore cologne. "In my business, that is," he'd continued. "Unpleasant odors tend to cling."

"I'll be sticking to younger people."

Taking pictures of either the elderly or children was—macabre. The project was sorting itself out as we talked, setting its parameters. "I want attractive dead people."

"That's pretty freaky, Violet." His face said even more.

It did sound odd and I started to amend it. "You know, vibrant ones. Or recently vibrant."

Hard for my words not to sound callous because they were. But there's no surprise in the death of the elderly and nothing but horror in the death of a child.

"And all of a particular sex, I expect." He made a face. "I'm gonna introduce you to a woman. I think it'd do you good to have a female friend. You two could knit scarves for the boys overseas. Take in a movie. Do some girl-talk."

I'd never learned how to make small talk, the friendly banter I saw in coffee shops and in a movie theater before the place went dark. No one gave me the instruction manual.

He looked at me carefully. "Taking these pictures is pretty important to you, I guess. I'm not sure why—don't know if you know either." He was heading for the door. "But I'll let you know if another— candidate—comes along." He nodded several times, massaging his chin a bit. "Not like it can hurt them, I guess."

"Photographing young dead men might make a statement. In Detroit, I mean."

He whipped around, chuckling. "A statement! Didn't know you made statements, Violetta. You're about the most apolitical person I've ever met. Do you even vote?" He paused. "Think quick, who's the vice president?"

Ignoring his question, I followed him to the door. "It's hard to understand why you're up here, Bill. You seem to find me so lacking… in everything."

"Baby, baby, baby," he said, turning to put an arm around me. "Sorry if it seems like it. You know I treasure your quirks. Mama always said I'd try to change the stripes on the flag to up and down if they'd let me."

"So you'll let me know when you have…someone?" I put a hand on his arm. "A suitable person?"

"Suitable for framing?" He started to laugh, but cut it off and nodded, still reluctant or unable to show much enthusiasm. "Remember, though, I can't let you shoot them without getting someone's permission. Things might not work out every time. You'd have to get to my place between arrival and interment." He put his hand on the doorknob. "Operations at a mortuary can move pretty quickly. It'd be strictly at my convenience. And with the families' blessings."

His feet were heavy on the steps as he added, "Never thought I'd find a girl who lusted after me for my dead bodies. Would've saved me a lot of sleepless nights." He flashed me a rueful smile. "Death, where is thy sting?"

I must have look puzzled because he added with a laugh, "And here I thought you liked me for my big, brown—eyes."

Laughing more, he took the steps in twos, then hurried toward the lobby and the light.

CHAPTER 6

Detroit Free Press: Two people were found stabbed to death Tuesday
morning at a sports bar owned by former Detroit Tiger infielder
Travis Slack. Slack's Shack, owned by the 1980s era infielder since
1998, is a popular downtown bar. The victims, a man and a woman,
both long-time employees of the establishment, were found by
the office manager shortly after 9:00 a.m., bound together with an
extension cord and locked in a refrigerator unit in the back of the
establishment. The victims were identified as Willis Dumphrey, 36, of
Detroit and Carla Roberts, 48, of Dearborn Heights. Dumphrey was
a bartender and Roberts, a short-order cook in the establishment.
Both victims were pronounced dead at the scene. The restaurant will
remain closed pending an investigation.

(April 2011)

THE CALL CAME the next week. I was waiting for it—hoping for it—
having read the news story a few days earlier. With no reason to
assume either the bartender's or the cook's family would go to Bill
for the funeral, I still hoped, waiting while the bodies were released
from the city morgue.

"How do they send them over?" I'd asked him a few days ago. "The bodies, I mean."

He'd showed me the pouch. "Nothing fancy," he said. "The letter counts, not the envelope."

It took me a second or two to get what he meant.

Bill's assistant, Ronnie, called me. "Someone's ready for his close-up downstairs," he said in a ghoulish whisper as soon as I answered. "Picked him up a few hours ago."

So Bill had filled Ronnie in on his grisly girlfriend. Just as well he knew about it if I was going to be running over there frequently.

"Be there in twenty," I said, consulting my watch and gauging the traffic on I-75.

Ronnie came to the door, and I crowded past him lugging my equipment, nearly knocking him over.

"Bartender at Slack's, right?" I asked, peering at the body on the table.

Bill, who'd come in, nodded. "Cook's over in Dearborn." He walked around the table, looking at the body from all angles.

I followed him, taking my own visual measurements. "I was so relieved to find out you had *him*. The guy. I was afraid the woman might be down here."

"Listen to yourself, woman," Bill said, his face stiff. "You're talking about two folks just murdered." He shrugged it off. "Woman's white. Nope, I don't get white ones much. Not unless they've gotten mixed up with the wrong crowd."

He was joking or being ironic, but either way I didn't know how to respond.

Bill had dressed the bartender in an expensive-looking tux. Subdued. His hair looked freshly barbered, his beard too.

I ran my fingers lightly along the fabric of the black jacket. "What a fabulous piece of clothing."

"His wife told me he liked to go out dancing when I asked about him. Ballroom variety. Thought he might be pleased about wearing a tux like this one for his final waltz."

"Don't they—the relatives—mind that kind of question? Hours after they died? Talking about something so trivial?" I must've snickered or made a face because Bill came right back at me.

"It may sound callous, but it isn't, Vi. Been saving this tux for a man who'd appreciate it. So I asked. He had the look of a dancer somehow. A mayor in the sixties wore this tux to his inaugural ball—or whatever they call the festivities when it's for a mayor."

"At the Manoogian Mansion?"

He nodded. "Jerry Cavanaugh, I think. This suit probably dates from the first year the mayor lived in the Mansion. Right after the Manoogians willed it to the City." He brushed off an invisible piece of lint on the deceased's sleeve.

Bill bought most of the clothing for his "loved ones" from high-end resale shops in the burbs—ones specializing in expensive garb. He'd paid a pretty good price for this suit, I'd wager. How did he decide who merited it? Being the right size would factor in, although Bill knew a woman skilled at alterations.

I shivered thinking about it—wearing a former mayor's suit to be buried? Why didn't they bury the mayor in it?

"I was at the Mansion once to shoot a luncheon the mayor gave for the City Council. Maybe it was Mayor Archer. Not as big a house as you'd expect." I looked at the body again. "Did they freeze to death? In the backroom, I mean." Bill looked at me blankly. "I'm talking about the dead bartender"—I gestured toward him—"and the woman."

"Nah. Both victims were stabbed—stabbed right through muscles, tendons. Newspaper did make it sound like they froze to death in that first story, didn't it? Second edition laid it out." He sighed. "Guess if you're gonna die, you might as well do it faster than you would with freezing."

"He would've had a strong arm." When Bill looked at me quizzically, I said, "You know—Travis Slack."

Bill hooted. "Doubt it was him behind it." He paused to think about it. "If it was his idea, he'd hire the job out. What makes you think he did it? Got some inside info?"

I shook my head. "Maybe they saw something they shouldn't have. Maybe it happened quick."

"Well, the cops'll look into it."

I stood on a stepladder to the right of his feet and looked into the viewfinder. Wrong again. I got down and shifted the ladder. "Robbery maybe?" We'd dragged a special 60s arc light Bill had in an office in as well as a portable studio light I'd brought along. The lighting was good. Now for the perfect angle.

"Who knows? Maybe the two of them were slinging drugs in the a.m. Before any regulars showed up."

He stepped out of the light when I motioned him away. "Something's off about it though. I don't think Travis Slack's exactly raking in the dough with this economy. Would he leave much money in that neighborhood overnight?" Having found the best angle, I wanted to get to work. But I tried to adopt an air of casualness and let Bill finish his thoughts.

"Not like the old days when Slack played in Tiger Stadium. We thought life in Detroit was bad back then—that the city was falling apart. Hooey! Good thing we didn't know what was coming down the pike."

"I remember him—Travis Slack. He was the resident heartthrob when Bunny and I first moved here. Gift shop at the stadium—heck, stores all over the place were full of stuff with his picture on it. Coffee mugs, key chains, T-shirts."

"Before the bobble-head phenomenon though. Slack could throw out people at first from shallow left field. Had to 'cause he liked to play a deep third base. Swung a good bat for a little guy."

"Little? I remember him as pretty big. Came into the restaurant where my mom worked. Joe Muir's. I saw him there once."

"Back in the day," Bill said. "I didn't know your mother was a waitress there. You never talk about her much, do you? Or your father. Do you have one?" He paused a minute. "Oh, yes, the sax player. I'd forgotten."

"Trumpet. And my mother's always been a waitress. Born with a uniform on." I started to elaborate, but his cell rang and he turned away to answer it.

A consoling tone came into his voice, and I knew he'd be a while. I could still remember Travis Slack coming out the front door at Joe Muir's years ago. I was doing homework in the car, waiting while Bunny ran inside and picked up her paycheck. Travis came out with a girl looking like an exotic dancer on his arm. Long legs in a pair of eighties patterned stockings, a feathery boa wound around her neck. Metallic blonde hair. She hung on Travis's arm like she couldn't walk without it. Perhaps she couldn't in her six-inch heels.

And Travis *was* big; Bill remembered him wrong. His shoulders seemed massive, even in the days before padding. Travis kept looking around, as if he were expecting a photographer to snap their picture. He said something to the girl that made her stop suddenly and plant a kiss on his cheek. But Travis was still looking around for fans or cameras or reporters and didn't react to it: either the girl or the kiss. She was there as eye candy, maybe before they called it that.

Oh, I remembered Travis Slack. Each incident of my childhood ran in my head like a film—should I choose to flip on the switch. I wasn't willing to flip it often. Just once in a while.

CHAPTER 7

Detroit News: Ramir Obabie, age 32, was found dead today in his home in southwest Detroit, the latest victim of an apparent opioid overdose. Death by opioid overdose, the third in recent weeks, highlights the devastating possibilities of a dangerous new illegal drug mixture: the combination of heroin with fentanyl, a powerful opioid painkiller used to treat cancer pain and in surgical anesthesia. Obabie was found by his girlfriend, Sheila Metzger, of Troy, who went to his house when phone calls and email went unanswered. It is believed Obabie had been dead for several days before Metzger's discovery. (April 2011)

BOTH BILL AND I were surprised when the first two bereaved families readily agreed to allow their loved ones' picture taken. He handled family discussions alone, not wanting it to look like the two of us were ambushing grieving parties for nefarious or commercial purposes. My photo of Rodney, and eventually the ones of Willis and Ramir Obabie, helped to assuage any worry it'd be something to be ashamed of. The most common reaction was that no further harm could come to their son, or lover, or brother, now that the worst had occurred. And perhaps I was offering a kind of lasting tribute with their loved one's inclusion: a reminder of a life taken too early. An acknowledgment that something wrong had occurred.

Bill became part of the project, albeit reluctantly. I wondered how long I could hold his feet to the fire. His interest in my work only went so far. He looked uneasy when I was setting my equipment up, finding the right angle, adjusting the light. I was conscious of his crossed leg, bouncing like a metronome as I snapped away, of his stifled yawns, of the slight whish of the hand fan he waved like an old lady at church. Getting it right was a longer process than Bill had the patience for. The "subjects" had better come along quickly if this was going to amount to much. Exactly what it would amount to was still up in the air. Would anyone find my portraits of the dead palatable—much less see them as art? Or would it fall into the queasy territory of photographing naked children, burning monks, or death camp survivors?

Bill's attorney drew up a contract, which the families signed, stating that I, Violet Hart, could exhibit the photographs of their loved one should the opportunity arise. I could also use the photos in a book or a film or in any way I chose with suitable notice and acknowledgment to the family. The photos would be the ones they saw and approved—I couldn't doctor or alter them. Bill offered each family a copy or two of the best photo and each one took it eagerly. I would've liked to have been there, but Bill flatly refused. I'd yet to witness any enthusiasm for my work—from anyone. And certainly not from Bill.

"So did they think I captured him? Did they seem pleased?"

"Pleased? I think it will take them a while to feel pleased." He reminded me I'd not been present for gallery sales of my past work either. I didn't bother correcting his mistaken notion there'd been many sales.

My suggestion that the family provide me with a photograph of the loved one before death had been scotched too.

Bill rolled his eyes. "Absolutely not. Look, you don't know what you're asking not being there for these discussions or watching their faces when they see the pictures. You never know how people are going to react to a photograph of a person they don't quite believe is dead."

Maybe the families were able to accept the photos because the men were still young and beautiful. Those first two deaths had been terrible shocks; neither man had died of disease or from any sort of lingering death. To my eye, each man had a slight look of surprise on his face. The photographs were remarkable—but in a macabre way. At night, I lay in bed imagining their deaths—how it'd been—how it'd happened—what their last thoughts had been. I followed the news, hoping the murderer of the bartender and woman at Travis Slack's bar had been caught. Nothing. Like it or not, I'd become invested in the outcome of those deaths. I began to hear news about the deaths of black men everywhere I turned. Had I been immune to it before or was it new? Some new phenomenon perhaps ushered in by recent events.

"You do know this has been going on since the ships brought us here," Bill said. "You just didn't have your antennae up until now."

I'd added more lighting to the work by this point and also moved from the basement to a much better room upstairs. The look of the morgue photo had disappeared. Three bowed windows filled the space with light. Only the first photographs—the ones of the rugby player— had been done in the prep room. There was no asset in making the lighting depressing, especially not with Bill's ornate wardrobe to show off. I wasn't sure whether I could exhibit Rodney. It had the air of student work. Still, an exhibit would be incomplete for me without the impetus for the project.

I used an unfortunate term aloud a minute later—referring to the cadaver as "the drug overdose"—and Bill grabbed my arm. "Don't ever call the departed by what killed them," he said, twisting my wrist in his fervor. "Don't call them 'the overdose,' or 'the gunshot wound' or 'the aneurysm' or 'the cancer.' Learn the deceased's proper name and use it if you want to work with me. These men might be dead now, but they were recently alive, with people who loved them. People they loved."

He dropped my arm. "Or I swear I'll call this whole arrangement off. You'd have been drummed right out of mortuary school with that callous attitude."

He stomped across the room, making me wonder again how long this enterprise could last. Not two months into it and I might be finished. Morticians dealt with the living too; I only spent time with the dead. I felt like an interloper or an opportunist, a woman without the proper respect. In order to live with this project, I had to distance myself from the subjects as living, breathing men. And why couldn't Bill see the pictures as a tribute to the men or to his skill in the prep room? Perhaps he saw me as getting a kinky pleasure from photographing black men.

Yes, perhaps my subjects were all African-American men, but nearly Bill's entire clientele *was* black. I hadn't initially planned on exclusively photographing young black men, but it seemed the right way to go. I was drawn to black men. It had always been there—this feeling of kinship. Perhaps because I'd always felt like an outsider too.

The guy today, *Ramir*, I made myself remember his name, was dressed in an electric blue suit with a pink tie. He also wore a fez.

"Does this costume have anything to do with his real life?" I asked Bill. It seemed almost pimpish.

"His real life was trying to get away from his real life, Violet."

Bill was sipping his usual Diet Pepsi on the sidelines, his legs stretched out on a wheeled stool, which he kept pushing back and forth. The squeak of the wheels was distracting, but I let it go. He was also eating a big chicken sandwich slathered with mayonnaise. His tongue darted out every few seconds to pick up stray smears from the side of his mouth. I tried not to watch. Tried not to look like I was trying not to look.

"This is an epidemic," he added.

"You mean thirty-three deaths from drug overdoses?" I asked, thinking piously of the apple I'd called lunch. Thirty-three overdoses didn't seem like an epidemic. "Over how long?"

"Not your ordinary drug overdose, dearie. *You're not listening.*" He shook his head.

Bill never understood the concentration necessary to get it right. Instead, he chose to see me as *not listening to him.*

"Look," Bill continued, "this guy died because someone mixed his heroin with fentanyl. Ramir Obabie didn't know it was in there until he couldn't breathe. It's a drug they use in surgery mostly. Poor suckers who get it mixed into their heroin stop breathing or suffer cardiac arrest. It's been in the newspaper for months."

Leaning against a sideboard now, he grabbed a huge peanut butter cookie from a china platter, glowering at me like it was my fault the guy died. He rarely left me alone with the bodies, but seldom offered a hand. I had to haul them into a suitable position without his help. And if I changed anything at all about their presentation, he gave a quick yelp.

"Hey, his family didn't pay for the slouch you created." Or, "Messed up his suit but good." Today my forearm smeared the cosmetics on his neck and Bill threw a fit. "You know how long it takes to get that applied correctly?"

He hauled out his cosmetics case, bigger than any woman's and housed in an even larger commercial tackle box, holding things up while he touched up Ramir's face. To me, it seemed unchanged.

Ramir's suit, much too big for the body of a decades-long drug addict, was pinned in the back, giving him the appearance of fine tailoring. Expertly tacked by a tailor, in fact. I shot away, taking more pictures of Ramir. Being a drug addict had taken a lot out of the guy, and I wanted to put some of it back for this final picture. He was handsome beneath the ravages of too little food, too many nights in the rough, and too many drugs. The bone structure was still there. I wasn't doing an exposé of heroin-cool cadavers. I'd save it for another time. An audience would notice the beauty in these men; cry out at their untimely deaths. I tried to forget my next piece of business would be photographing a dog show, followed the next day by a retirement party.

Buck up, Ramir, I told him silently. I'll make you a star. And maybe you'll make me one.

CHAPTER 8

*"She liked being afraid because there was
in it, the possibility of something great."*
Doon Arbus on her mother,
Diane

LATER, I HEADED for the gym. Spring was in sight and with it more revealing clothes. I liked to run at night and that night seemed especially fitting for a hard thirty minutes. I needed to shake off Bill and his growing animosity to my work, discard my own pessimism about this project. Or maybe it was the deep look of betrayal on the drug overdose's face making my shoulders kink with tension. Damn, I'd done it again, if only in my head.

"Sorry," I silently apologized to Ramir. "I didn't mean to call you that." How did Bill forget those faces?

The gym was open till eleven. Showing up late pared down the body count on the machines, giving me breathing space. Once in a while, the management threatened to roll back their hours and I'd write a letter saying if they shortened their hours, I'd move to one of the larger chains that stayed open till midnight. The owner always gave in.

Why were people who came into the gym at six a.m. seen as

virtuous, but night patrons seen as kooky? This was a maxim seeming
to hold true in any situation. No shame in going to bed at nine p.m.,
but try rising at nine a.m. A girl could spend the entire night in the
darkroom and still get treated to a superior tone from a client or
employer who phoned at eight and found me sounding sleepy.

"I couldn't allow myself such an indulgence," one suburban
matron, who'd never been employed outside her home, told me when
I let a yawn escape the morning after a wedding reception lasting till
one. "You artist types."

The people who ran the five-minute mile on the treadmill at the
gym were gone by nine p.m., and the folks who watched themselves
in the mirror were also scarce, probably getting the ten hours of sleep
their good looks required. This was the best time to enjoy a little peace.
Better yet, the TV monitors, turned to Fox News and the golf channel
earlier, were now blank. I could watch what I wanted or play my iPod.
Or better yet, I'd concentrate on the late-night trainer who usually shut
the place down: Levi.

Detroit Body Works was a nineteen-fifties sort of gym. No pool
or yoga classes, no state-of-the-art machinery. No healthy snack bar,
no massage room, no baby-and-me Pilates. The locker room smelled
vaguely of mold and I'm certain there were mice. But DBW was cheap at
thirty-five dollars a month and near my apartment. The only apparatus
that interested me was the treadmill. I'd twice become entangled in the
intricacies of the elliptical machine and spinning made my back ache.
Lifting weights seemed humorous, an activity for cartoon muscle men.
Thirty or forty minutes on the treadmill a few times a week cleared the
head. I could've gotten a cheap light model like the guy upstairs, but
space was a consideration—photography was a room hog. Plus I had to
consider my downstairs neighbor, an elderly woman who put up with

enough coming and going.

Most nights that I showed up, I closed the place down—me and whatever employee was working the late shift. If I was lucky, it was Levi Gardiner, "short for Leviticus," he told me once. He was effortlessly handsome and hiding his muscles under a big T-shirt and baggy shorts. I liked that about him though. Anyone could tell the kind of body he was packing despite the loose cotton he cloaked it in.

When the gym quieted, he stopped to talk as he wiped the equipment down, polished the mirrors, turned the machines off. We'd never had a real conversation, just niceties spiked with a mildly teasing air. Unlike the other trainers, he never examined himself in the wall-to-wall mirrors. Not an easy feat when mirrors encircled the room.

"So what are you—a phys-ed major at the university?" I asked him.

There was something going on with Bill now that made flirtation more palatable. Was it time for a more satisfying conversation with Levi? We'd been circling each other for two months. I knew he was older than the typical college guy. Perhaps early thirties? At least I hoped he was that old.

He shook his head. "Studying for a master's in library science. Classes are over by three so this job's a good fit." He made a face. "Being a trainer can only be entertaining for so long. No offense, but you're not a gym rat, are you?"

"You're kidding," I said, ignoring his last remarks. "You're gonna spend the rest of your days in the stacks."

I almost added, *hiding your magnificent body away*, but decided it was too early for such a blatant come-on. He intuited it though.

"I'm hoping to hide out there—if only in daylight," he said with a sly smile. He waved his hand around the room. "This is purely a temporary stint. Have to keep up a certain level of fitness to keep the paychecks coming in though. So far my natural metabolism's helping out. But I can't see myself around more than another year."

I turned off the treadmill and bent over to retie my shoe, giving him a glimpse of my best asset. "A librarian—like in the gray bunker on the corner?"

The tax-poor suburb I lived in boasted mostly bestsellers, dated encyclopedias, and children's books, with two old ladies guarding the inventory as if the library was the big one in New York—the one with the lions outside.

"I'd like to work at a place like the Reuther, a research library. Terrific collections."

"On the Wayne State campus, right?" He nodded. "I took a few classes awhile back."

"What were you studying?" He sat down on the bike across from me and pedaled slowly.

"Digital photography when it first came along."

"Hobby?"

Why did people assume that? Did I look more like a salesclerk or a waitress? Had the Bunny genes doomed me to the restaurant circuit? Wash my mouth out with soap, I thought to myself. Bunny's million miles of servitude supported me for eighteen years. Even if she'd never really been there for me, she was there with a checkbook. Unlike... well, you know.

"No, I take pictures for a living." I stepped off the treadmill, deciding twenty minutes was enough. If I began running again, he'd probably disappear in the back room. I picked up my microfiber towel and wiped off the treadmill. An overt show of consideration for my fellow members was bound to impress him.

"Weddings—that kind of stuff?" He glanced at the clock on the wall out of the corner of his eye, pedaling a little faster.

"Yeah," I said, suppressing my sigh of resignation. This was going nowhere. "But I exhibit occasionally. Projects of my own."

"Sounds great. You'll have to tell me the next time you have a show."

I could tell him about the current project—which was sure to scare him — but he was finished with me. Bored, ready to go home, get back to his books. Perhaps to his wife or to a male partner? No wedding band, but I didn't think he was gay. I had caught him looking at other women through that mirror, if not me.

"Okay," he said, switching the bike off and rising. "Guess I'd better see to the locker rooms. I'll do the men's first so you can—well, so you can do whatever you wanna do in there."

I'd have liked to think his words were meant to be provocative, but he walked inside the men's locker room without a backward glance. I walked into the women's and sank down on the floor. Before I knew it I was crying. Some kind of dam had ruptured. And crying loud enough to attract him apparently. But not in a good way.

"Hey," Levi said, walking in, the door slamming into the wall behind him. "What the hell!" He crouched down and put a hand on my back.

"It's the humidity," I told him, wiping my eyes. "You need to put in a dehumidifier. Ever hear of mold?"

"Yeah, I'll have to see to that," he said, helping me stand.

CHAPTER 9

"At our best and most fortunate we make pictures because of what stands before our camera, to honor what is greater and more interesting than we are."

Robert Adams

AFTER THE NIGHT'S interlude at the gym with its embarrassing finale, I scratched Levi's name off my list of future possibilities and drove home. I rarely cried, and when I did it was usually at a tearjerker movie rather than events in my own life. And tears never had the cleansing effect others claimed. But the work was getting to me. More and more my days were filled with googling my dead men and dead men across the country. Aside from my work commitments, I barely left my apartment. Di and my mother seemed busy with other things, making my isolation even more severe.

Should I bail? Bill seemed to think so. But if someone suggested to him that dressing the dead in preposterous costumes was insulting, would he stop? Or was that what made his practice interesting? Was that what made him an artist?

Putting on the stony face I'd used so often in the past and girding myself against psychological involvement with the men I was photographing was the only solution. But Bill found my feigned aloofness repulsive. It'd probably all come to an end topped off by another breakup. This time the reasons would be professional rather than personal—not because of a pop-up wife or the infamous "it's not you, it's me" speech. I'd given a few of them myself.

I was never confident about the commitment of any man— beginning with my father and ending with Bill. Men didn't seem to attach themselves to me in any discernable and uxorious way.

I was looking through my calendar, noticing again my lack of a social life and dreading the upcoming appointments and events—a sweet sixteen party, a portrait of a prize-winning dog, two retakes of photos a client hadn't liked—when I heard a scratching sound at the door. Not a knock but a minor disturbance in the hall. Like the noise a tree limb makes brushing against a window. My door did have a peephole and I looked through it. For a second, I was stymied. But that was quickly replaced by irritation.

It was that kid from Belle Isle. Derek Olsen. I hadn't thought about his ending up on my doorstep. I could tell he'd heard my feet cross the floor and knew I was examining him through the peephole. So there'd be no pretending I wasn't home.

"It's me, Ms. Hart," he shouted, grinning and moving closer to the hole.

I paused. I didn't want to let this Derek I'd dug or dreamed up into my apartment. He seemed harmless, but wow, he also seemed crazy. It looked like he hadn't changed his clothes since the first time we met. I didn't want to be the next body on Bill's table. Or the next addition to Derek's artwork on the island.

"Derek, do you see those steps going up to the next floor?"

"Yep," he said, swiveling around. "Geez, anybody ever sweep or mop in here? Or even paint?"

Wow. Who'd believe a guy who looked liked Derek noticed such things. I knew what he meant about the stairs. Filthy battered linoleum poorly cut and held down with metal strips, now coming loose. A loose railing next to them. A wall peppered with handprints. Okay, so I didn't rent in a classy building. But it was galling to hear him say it considering his attire and because he spent his days on Belle Isle—a place famous for being unkempt. He must come from a middle-class home—probably a mom who took a white gloved finger to her tabletops. Sadly attempts had been made, not so long ago, to tidy my floor up.

"Never mind that. Go sit on the steps while I throw something on."

"Just saying, it's good I'm wearing my work clothes." The thought of him in his Sunday best caught me up.

I waited another minute or two before opening my door as narrowly as possible, and slipping out, I walked over to the steps.

"Derek, when I gave you my card, I didn't mean for you to come up here. My street address isn't on that card for good reasons." I started to launch into those reasons when he interrupted me by standing up. A large paper bag sat on the steps.

"It's not hard to locate anyone now—not with the Internet," he said. "Took me about two minutes to track you down. You're in business, so there's that. And you have your phone numbers and email on that card. With Goggle Maps I could practically look in your window." He grinned, happy to be spooking me.

"Well, here I am," I said, cutting through a long conversation about proprieties, investigative abilities, and computer skills. He reached behind him and picked up the bag.

Instinctively, I stepped back. "Okay, what's in there?" I was getting the idea I wouldn't like it. A smell hung in the air. It wasn't overpowering, but it was there.

"You said you wanted to see weird shit, right? Things I found that were kinda dark? Edgy?" He paused. "I've been scouting the place ever since."

Ah, yes. I'd said it in a weak moment. But the possibility that what Derek found would be interesting was pretty remote, and I'd given him access to my life without thinking. Still, I was curious.

"All right, you'd better come inside."

I was taking a chance, but in a fist fight I could probably take him. He didn't run miles on a treadmill or cart heavy equipment around. I probably outweighed him.

"Good idea," he said and followed me in. He was clutching the paper bag—one from the long-defunct Farmer Jack's Grocery Store—as if the family jewels were inside. "You need to see this right away. I think it's already deteriorating."

Swell. I shrunk back a bit.

"What is it?" I repeated, not sure I wanted to know. The bottom of the bag was wet and threatening to disintegrate before our eyes. "Maybe you should take that into the kitchen." I gestured in the right direction with my head.

"Good idea."

I followed him into the kitchen, where he carefully placed his "jewels" in the sink, wiping his hands on his pants. "Okay, I think what I have here is an aborted fetus."

A little preparation for that statement might have been nice. "Jesus! A what?"

"An aborted fetus. Or embryo. I don't know the difference." He looked at what was probably my green face and said, "Well, you told me you wanted edgy things."

"You mean a human fetus? A baby?" I doubted I was ready for this and a wave of nausea swept over me. "How did this…fetus…come into your hands?" I was hoping he hadn't aided in an abortion to serve my weirdness. I could picture an ad offering his services in the city paper.

"I was scrambling around down there earlier today—on Belle Isle—and I heard a sort of yelping, like someone was in pain. By the time I got over there, it'd taken off and the only thing left was this." He opened the bag and we both peeked in. "It was lying on the grass."

It certainly looked like something once alive. A few inches long, it was pinkish white tissue with the beginnings of arms and legs—even hands and feet, a large head of sorts, a neck. I felt nauseated, yet sad to admit, interested. I couldn't photograph it, but this embryo or fetus was spectacular in its own right.

I'd never seen a fetus before—not even an ultrasound version of one—so I'd little experience in evaluating such a thing. There was mucus and blood. It was exceedingly wet. This probably hadn't been a painless expulsion of tissue.

I couldn't help imagining teenagers scrambling around desperately in the weeds and debris of Belle Isle. I'd never had to abort a child but it could've been me. Could've been a lot of women. How many women hadn't watched the calendar at one time or other, their hearts pounding? There were no happy stories to tell no matter what your feelings about such things. Pain, sadness, regret perhaps.

"Wait here," I told Derek and went to get one of my magnifying glasses. I also put on a pair of latex gloves. I'd be damned if I was going to touch this—this—small mass of tissue. I got a pair of the tongs I used in developing to handle it and returned to the bag's contents. Under the magnifying glass, I could make out more features. There were eyes and the beginnings of ears perhaps. I wasn't sure about that. Amazing that a few inches could reveal so much.

"So you heard people talking?" I repeated.

Derek gave a start. He'd been looking at my CD collection while I rounded up my instruments and still held a Jane Siberry CD in his hands.

"Well, I couldn't swear they were human voices, but I did hear a sort of screaming or shrieking and a lot of thrashing around."

I still hadn't put my hands on the tissue and felt little desire to do so. I poked it, gently turning it over two or three times.

"You know, I think it might be an animal embryo," I said. "It doesn't look human under this magnification. Maybe a possum or a rabbit. I'm not sure what animal life there is on Belle Isle. They haven't had a zoo there for ages, but parts of it are pretty wild. Do they have beavers? It could also be a deer, although the legs would be longer I think. They do keep deer there. Fallow deer. The four extremities would be of a uniform size though. These don't look like legs."

I pointed to the upper extremities with my tongs.

"There's enough water for a beaver with the river but no mud. Don't they need mud?"

I shrugged. "I took a class in anatomy and physiology in college, more to help us draw the human form than to edify, and I remember the professor saying most embryos of under two months' gestation look a lot alike. I think this embryo was probably only a couple months along—less if it's an animal. How long does a small mammal carry its child? A few months, right? The animal probably miscarried and that's what you heard." I paused. "I couldn't photograph this anyway, Derek. At best, it would look like a graphic for one of those charts in a textbook."

Derek looked disappointed. "I rushed up here at the speed of light too. Got a bunch of weird looks on the bus, I can tell you."

"You came here by bus?"

"You think I own a car?"

How did I get hooked up with this guy? Traveling by bus with an embryo on the seat next to him? There was a god-awful odor now that the bag was opened and the air was absorbing what was inside.

"I think we need to get rid of this quickly." I couldn't see making him take it back by bus. "My neighbor has a compost pile. Maybe we could add it to that."

Derek nodded and that's what we did next, my fingers crossed that my elderly neighbor was fast asleep. I followed Derek down the stairs and outside, to the backyard of the modest little bungalow next door. There was a shovel handy. I picked it up and covered the fetus, hoping an animal wouldn't dig it up and drag it around my neighbor's yard, scaring him to death.

I offered Derek a ride home, but he said he wasn't sure where he was going. We parted at the front door, he promising to communicate with me by phone should he find another object of interest. I brushed him off, convinced he was more than half-crazy and that what he found would be worthless at best, inappropriate or criminal at worst. I was pretty sure I'd made a mistake in interesting Derek in my work, but I still wasn't completely willing to dismiss him. Actually, I kind of liked him.

CHAPTER 10

Detroit Free Press: A 29-year-old man, a paraplegic since a motorcycle accident in 2003, was Detroit's second victim of West Nile virus this year, county health officials report. It is not believed the deceased, Barry Johnson of northwest Detroit, came into contact with the city's first victim, Lisa Swaggerty, of Plymouth. The manager of Environmental Health Services stated that the two had apparently never met; nor did they frequent the same stores or restaurants. Both victims were probably bitten by affected mosquitoes several weeks earlier.

(May 2011)

"KEY-RIST, IT TAKES you a hell of a long time to take your precious pictures," Bill said from the maroon velvet chair across the room. "You're the Edward Hopper of the photography world."

"Did he work slowly?"

I was miffed with Bill. After Derek left, I'd dialed Bill's number, needing to touch base with a sane person, and got his voice mail. Bill was straying, I was sure of it. Viewings were over long before eleven-thirty. Were we in the death throes of our affair? Had my new venture—a project that would appear to bring us together—pushed us apart?

But now I was with him again, and I focused on the man in front of me, wishing I could take each photograph at the same time of day. No way that was gonna happen. I adjusted the light head for a third time after a quick look at the meter. My back was aching, head pounding. Sometimes the right shot simply eluded me. Couldn't get the focus or angle or lighting or…well, I didn't always know what. No magic today.

"Hopper only finished one or two paintings a year at points in his career." Bill stretched his arms and yawned. "Then there's de Kooning. Spent an entire year on one canvas, painting it over and over because he didn't think he'd got it right."

"I know *that* feeling. Hey, when did you become such an expert on art?" I asked, still looking at my subject critically. "Anyway, de Kooning was an asshole." I thought for a minute. "Is an asshole?"

"Was an asshole. I'm studying you is what I'm doing. Trying to understand what you see in the little window and why such a particularly constricted view constitutes your whole world." He stretched out his legs and yawned again. "Didn't you study any art history at school in Chicago?"

"Didn't stick. If I didn't need information to take a good photograph, I let it go. Very Zen. Keeps my head clear."

Bill laughed. "Clear or empty, Violet?"

Despite the barrage of insults, I was still trying to compose the shot. Damn. I didn't care for Bill's choice of clothing for Barry Johnson: the guy was dressed like a participant in a NASCAR race.

"Why this costume?" I asked. "Didn't you say he was paralyzed? It's macabre dressing him like this."

And why did you choose a canary yellow shirt for him, I felt like asking but didn't. See, I could keep criticism to myself. Black people didn't look good in yellow—at least not in my viewfinder. And this yellow was too loud; the color slid off the garment and shone on his face like a dandelion. Almost no one looked good wearing yellow in my opinion. Okay, maybe Tweety, but that was about it.

"Did you read the bio I emailed you?" Bill sighed. "I laid it out there."

I couldn't please him today. Truth was, the less I knew about my subject the better. It was different from Bill's relationship with the deceased. He needed to bond with his client to a certain degree to relate well to the family and friends. To choose the right clothes perhaps. But for me, it just made my job more difficult. I could get lost in their story, lost in their face.

"He must have been bitten by the first mosquito to make a foray around southeastern Michigan. It's hardly May."

"Back to the choice of yellow. The fellow drove in motorcycle races, then he got into a bad accident a few years back," Bill continued. "Parents brought over these duds when I asked if there was anything significant in his closet. You'd think this outfit would be the last way they'd want to see him dressed, but I'm guessing since he died of something else entirely, they were okay with it. Maybe racing was his finest moment. His dream."

"West Nile, huh? I'm surprised he got out of the house often enough to get bit." I cleaned the lens and looked through it once more.

"Parents tell me he spent most of the day outside when he could. Although with Detroit weather, it was limited."

I got the shot I wanted and was about to leave when Bill grabbed my arm. "Shall I come over tonight?" His breath on my neck was warm enough to make the hairs stand up. His lips ran across it. Bill wasn't usually this direct. I was taken aback. It'd been nearly two weeks since

Bill and I made love.

I'd always found it difficult to keep men interested over the long run. Once it was clear we weren't going to marry, weren't going to meet each other's parents, no children were going to come along—once the major sexual games had been played to varying degrees of success, things began to fall apart. Slowly but irrevocably. Once my tricks were out of the bag, one of us took off. Usually me. Before it looked like *he* might leave—whoever the current *he* was. It wasn't like there were truckloads of men in my past. A van's worth perhaps.

Bill came over. He stayed until morning; it felt like a final rite.

CHAPTER 11

"I was on the scene—sometimes drawn there by a power I can't explain..."
Weegee

I'D RELUCTANTLY AGREED to meet Bunny, and before I was fully seated at the restaurant was treated to a string of complaints about her current job waitressing at an Ethiopian restaurant in Ferndale.

"Why'd you take a job there?" I asked her. "Don't they haul the food around in big serving dishes and eat family style? Do they even serve alcohol? Muslims, right?"

Bunny had rarely taken jobs in restaurants that didn't serve alcohol, claiming the tips were less than half.

My mother's waitressing odyssey dominated my childhood. Deadbeat dads were permitted to remain on the financial lam in the eighties, so my childhood memories were of packed bags sitting in the foyer, on a bed, on the curb, in the cargo hold of a Greyhound. Of reading road maps in a vintage Buick seeming to require a new muffler twice a year and new brakes even more often. Of being the new kid in school, on the street, at the church, in the Brownie troop. If there was a man involved in any of this travel, I never heard mention. And the reason for finally landing in Detroit when I was eleven had never been satisfactorily explained. Bunny may have run out of steam. Some waitresses spend their life in one spot, but Bunny must have had a travel bug. One thing was certain, she wanted out of Massachusetts.

My father's complete disregard of my birth and subsequent life did little to increase sympathy for my mother with her family there. When my sister, Daisy, was still alive, she'd brought out the best in neighbors, in relatives. But I evoked tidings of death and destruction once Daisy died. People kept their distance—we were tragic, bad luck, nasty.

Bunny survived this treatment by appearing strong, and I both held this against her and depended on it. Hal Hart's weaknesses passed for strength to my immature mind. He ditched the things holding him back—a good lesson for me, I thought. Put the art first. Family on idle; career got the gas.

The fickle ones, the irresponsible ones, always attract young women and daughters, and I was no exception. I knew this but was helpless to alter it. Over the years, I had analyzed the hell out of my family to no avail.

Bunny shook her head across the table now. "No booze and lousy tips. After the last place—a little cubbyhole making crepes—went belly-up, I jumped on this one. A local institution with a Muslim population nearby—it sounded like a great gig. Little did I know the number of Middle Eastern restaurants would mushroom. Imagine living paycheck to paycheck at my age, scrounging for the extra quarter's fall to the sticky floor."

But as was Bunny's style, she quickly assembled a second list of the job's positive aspects. "Look, I like being able to walk to work. It saves a lot of money. And the owner's pretty nice. Paid for a pair of shoes with orthopedic support when he saw how crippled I was by the end of the night."

We both looked down at Bunny's feet, now clad in a pair of duck-yellow Crocs. "I only wear the orthos to work in," Bunny explained. "They're ugly as sin."

"Do you mean the orthopedic shoes or what you're wearing now?"

Bunny made a face and added, "I get a lot of the Ethiopian holidays off. Plus the American ones. Two Christmases probably." She squinted. "At least, I think I do. It hasn't come 'round yet."

"There are a million restaurants across Nine Mile Road and up Woodward Avenue, Mom. You could walk to any of them from your apartment."

She didn't hear me. "I hate wearing the African clothes. Sure, they look cool on a twenty-year-old—all those swirling pieces of cloth, bright colors. But I look like the fortune teller at a seedy carnival. I get vegetable alecha on me and have to run a load of wash at midnight. If I forget to push the delicate cycle on the 1950s washer they have in the laundry room in my building, I'm screwed. The fabric is real fragile. Like papyrus. Can you believe it? Using that kind of material for a waitress's uniform?"

And as I was thinking her list of pros and cons would go on forever, she stood up. "Gotta have a cig, chickie." She looked for the pack in her purse. "Another tricky issue, the damned fabric goes up in flames if you don't watch it. You could solder it to your skin."

I watched as she briskly walked outside and lit a Marlboro, immediately sucking the smoke back with a well-practiced cough, standing against the brick building, one foot propped on the wall behind her, looking like an employee of a factory. Or possibly like the world's oldest hooker.

The people sitting near the window turned to watch, noticing in an inchoate way that Bunny was spoiling their view: Bunny, who picked imaginary pieces of tobacco off her tongue though she'd smoked filtered cigarettes for the last forty years, was an eyesore. Her stomach pushed at the spandex of the pink pants she wore like an overfilled balloon at the helium pump.

"Vodka on the rocks," I said to a passing waiter.

Two stiff drinks before one-thirty wasn't a good idea, but it'd get me through the lunch and possibly assuage my continuing worry about Bill and my project. And the image of that fetus—no matter what kind it was—was burned on my retina. The waiter, not mine, threw me an irritated look, nodded, and after a few minutes, my own waitress returned with the drink. Bunny had lit a second cigarette and was talking to the valet, laughing in the raucous way she had. Though I knew it was impossible, I imagined I could hear her through the plate glass. It was likely the opening and closing door let in Bunny's laugh like an unwanted gust of hot air. Why was I so hard on her?

I remembered one Thanksgiving, soon after our arrival in Detroit. Bunny'd brought me along to her current place of employment when the sitter hadn't shown up. I passed the next six hours reading *Archie* comic books and sketching at a small table at the back of the dining room, watching family after family celebrate the holiday. Bunny ran back and forth with a smile on her face all evening, carrying heavy platters, her last table at nine o'clock getting the same careful attention as the first one at four.

"The only thing standing between us and the poor house is good legs and a big smile," Bunny often said.

But rather than admiring her for her fortitude, I blamed her for settling for this life. Why hadn't Bunny gone to night school like the mothers on television and become a secretary or a teacher?

When I complained about the injustice of our Thanksgiving later that night, Bunny told me I should feel sorry for those families at the restaurant.

"The ones to envy," Bunny said, slicing up the small turkey breast she'd brought home for us, "ate Thanksgiving dinner at home with their families." Putting a piece in her mouth, she added, "Like we're doing if only a little late."

I found it hard to believe after seeing the soft lighting, the gleaming silver, the crisp white linen, the festive centerpieces, the gay conversations heightened by gales of laughter, the well-dressed patrons, the sumptuous food. It seemed like the ultimate in holiday celebrations. How could any dinner at home compete with that?

Dinner at home was at a battered kitchen table with mismatched chairs, or on sticky TV trays, sitting propped against a wall until mealtime.

I couldn't imagine the typical family celebration well enough to envy it until years later, when I'd actually experienced one—or at least partook of one as a guest. All my childhood notions of families came from the shows Bunny and I watched when she had the night off: *The Waltons, Family Ties, Who's the Boss?*

Each of us sat with one of those plastic TV trays, watching television characters live a life that seemed more real than ours. There was always one more thing for me to miss out on—nice clothes, a vacation, a holiday dinner, a dead sister, a missing father. A missing father. I hadn't seen Hal Hart for years. Did he know his first child was dead?

I began my search for him the summer after seventh grade, haunting libraries in the Detroit area, which all seemed to have a room with out-of-state telephone directories in those days. Hal Hart wasn't an unusual name, but it was a vague one. Was Hal his real name? Or was it Howard or Harold? Over the years of searching, I called more than a hundred Hal Harts.

"Hal Hart?" This call was to a man in Boston, Massachusetts, the year I was thirteen.

"Yes."

His voice was high—not the way I remembered my father's voice if I actually did remember it. Perhaps it was Pa Ingalls and not Hal Hart's voice that flitted in my head.

"Hi, Mr. Hart. Are you by chance a musician?"

Laughter. "Only if you count the kazoo."

I didn't.

"Hal Hart?" This Hal Hart was in Gainesville, Florida.

"Yes." This voice was deep, raspy. He sounded too old.

"Are you a musician?" I don't know why I didn't ask the obvious question: *Do you have a daughter named Violet?*

"I play a little."

"Trumpet?"

"Why do you want to know?" He seemed amused.

I soldiered on. "I'm looking for my father."

"You sound like a white girl, honey." He laughed a little more.

"Yes, I'm white." I couldn't imagine why he was asking this. Of course, I was white.

"Well, you got the wrong branch of the Hart family, sweetie. The Florida Harts are all black."

The occasional Saturday sleuthing lasted until at fifteen or so I gave up.

A year later, Hal Hart appeared with nary an apology for his long absence, never once mentioning Daisy's death. It was as if his first daughter never existed. After that visit, I never looked for him again, didn't ask him where he lived, what he'd been up to all those years. I took his infrequent visits over the next twenty years for what they were. Not much and not worth thinking about often.

I LOOKED UP from my empty glass in time to see the valet escaping from my mother, probably thankful for a customer wanting his car. Bunny looked around, smiling at passersby. Maybe Bunny was no more eager to return to the table than I was to have her there—both of us wishing we were having lunch with someone else, somewhere else.

Bill, or was it another guy, once told me I was missing the "pleasing gene," the magical trait many women seemed to possess.

"Except in bed, of course," Bill had said, concluding his observation. "There you're the best. Aces."

Well, I certainly worked hard at it. Sex and photography. I needed a viewfinder to get through the day and a mirror over my bed at night. Apparently watching the world through glass was my safety net.

"And isn't that important in the scheme of things?"

"For you, no doubt," he said, covering his smile with the back of his hand.

I hated the superior tone creeping into his voice and lashed out.

"I don't see you climbing out of my bed any too quickly. Something must hold you here. Once the sex is over."

That was true; he was always slow to leave.

We were headed for the conversation where I asked Bill why he was still with me given his list of complaints. But given my current project, any discussion of strengths and weaknesses was better left unvoiced. I had left my exact ambitions regarding the photographs somewhat vague with him and wasn't sure why.

Bunny made her way back into the restaurant. We finished our lunch, driven to a familiar and almost comforting silence. We only needed *Charles in Charge* playing on the screen behind us—rather than the start of a Lions game—to feel completely at home.

I DROVE BUNNY home fifteen minutes later and then made my way to the nearest post office to buy stamps and mail additional prints to a new client living in Michigan's thumb. The guy had entered the annual Port Huron to Mackinaw sailboat race last summer and I'd been there to capture it: a bunch of rich guys in their forties, wearing Dockers and loud Bermuda shorts, hoisting beers. The boat was named *The Merry Widow*. I made sure to capture that piece of information. If the beer drinking went on too long, the prophetic name might have helped me to place the photograph on the front page of the *Freep*.

Coincidentally, Ted, the freckled Ferndale gallery owner with the fox-like fur on his back, stood in front of me in line at the post office, several packages under his arm. I hadn't seen or heard from him in weeks, not that he hadn't been on my mind. The value points I'd amassed were still on my scorecard.

"Hey, how are you doing, Miss Violet? Fancy meeting you here." He looked down at his packages ruefully. "Didn't sell a single piece of this guy's work. I thought it would fly off the walls. Ah, Detroit, I hardly know ya." He shrugged, an arm shooting out to capture a tube beginning to slide from under his other arm. "Don't want any of these babies getting swept up with the day's trash. The artist will accuse me of holding out on him if they don't arrive in Saugatuck safe and sound. Seemed pretty dubious when I told him I didn't sell a single canvas—

especially after we slashed his prices."

I remembered feeling that same way in March and wondered if it ever occurred to Ted his gallery might be at fault. Or him? Maybe his unctuousness kept buyers away. Everyone has a shop they avoid because the proprietor turns their stomach.

Ted moved up to the counter, dispensed with his packages, and turned around. "Still snapping pictures of hotels on their way to the wrecking ball?" His foot was tapping a beat on the floor.

Shaking off his caustic tone, I said, "Speaking of my work, Ted, I wonder if you have time to look at what I've been up to lately." I hadn't planned on showing the photos to anyone this soon, but chance seemed to have intervened.

"Sure, bring a sample over to the shop. I can usually make room for something new. It *is* new, right? You're not still working the disappearing buildings act?" He propped an elbow on the counter, waiting while I bought my stamps.

Counting to three, I said, "No, I told you. It's new." On sudden impulse, I added, "Doing anything now?" I shoved on my sunglasses, hoping to hide any desperation in my eyes. "Only take a few minutes to run over there."

He looked at his arm, realized he wasn't wearing a watch, and shrugged. A man without a watch or a cell in his hand couldn't be in a hurry. "Actually, now's fine. I could use a little pick-me-up after breaking the guy's heart." He nodded toward the front counter where the six cardboard tubes sat forlornly. "Hey, it's not only a roll in the hay you're after, is it? You can level with me." He grinned in a way almost certainly meant to be seductive.

"Give me a—" I said, starting to get angry. I was about to tell him the last time had only been a mercy fuck on my part, when I stopped and smiled. "What kind of stuff did he do?" I motioned toward the counter, hoping the tubes weren't filled with photographs of dead bodies in fancy suits. "The guy from Saugatuck?"

"Sadly, it's a series of crayon drawings. Yes, you heard me right," he continued. "John used a lot of action figures in his pictures. Superman, Spidey. The occasional interspersing of rather alarmingly graphic violence with the superhero dolls makes for a dramatic canvas. Or so I thought." He sighed heavily. "Hard to persuade many adults in an economy as depressed as Detroit's they couldn't walk into their kid's room and rip similar stuff off the walls. Well, it seemed like a good idea last fall when I was over in Saugatuck for a vacation."

He continued to stand there, his foot still tapping the same tune. Was it "Yankee Doodle Dandy"?

"So *now* is good?" What the hell! Any work following a series of crayoned pictures of Aquaman would probably appear saleable. "You can follow me home."

"I know the way." There was no mistaking the glee in his voice.

I rolled my eyes, but he couldn't see them.

In my apartment, Ted stood looking silently at the photographs until I thought my head might explode. "Shit," he said at last. "This stuff's gonna make you. It'll make *me* for being the first to hang it. No one else's seen it, right?" He whistled lightly. "Talk about edgy. This stuff's on the outer ledge of edge." He put the fourth photograph down, picking one up again a second later. "You could probably get a show in a bigger and better venue. Chicago. Maybe even Manhattan." He put his fingers to his lips. "Sh! Forget I said it. I'm your man."

"Better than ghostly apartment buildings on Cass Corridor, huh?" I was dissing myself here, but the censor was on a break.

"Baby, these are in a different universe." He looked around. "Got any more?"

I shook my head. "It's been a little slow."

He laughed sharply. "Wow, you *have* grown jaded. Next you'll be taking matters into your own hands and hunting men down."

Little did he know about my treks to Belle Isle. He looked at the picture of Obabie again. "Who turned you on to these guys?" Suddenly a new thought occurred to him, and I watched it cloud his face. "They *are* dead, right? It's not a gimmick?"

"No gimmick. I've got a friend who's a mortician. In a pinch, he asked me to photograph that first guy to send back to his family overseas." I motioned to the rugby player. "I liked how it turned out— at least the subject if not the actual photo—and asked him if I could do a couple more. I did the first one under poor conditions—that's why it isn't as good. Fell in love with the subject matter from the outset though."

"Who wouldn't? Does he always dress them up like this? Your mortician friend?"

"Unless they want something more subdued. Most of them like it. Their families, I mean. It makes their last appearance special. Like they weren't totally vanquished by death."

"Too true. Most dead people look like they died from boredom. Not this bunch though."

He sat down at the work table and looked at the pictures again. "Never knew morticians had shticks, but this one's a killer. Pardon my words. Played right into your hands, didn't he?" His eyes had a knowing look. "Did you know about it before you started screwing him? His manner of burying the dead, I mean?"

"Hey," I objected. "Not that it's any of your business, but I'm not that conniving. Bill and I had a personal relationship long before we had a business one."

"I remember how that one goes." Now Ted rolled his eyes. "Look, if you're serious about this, I'll gladly show them."

He reached into his back pocket for his calendar. It was a cheap one from Hallmark with a puppy on the white plastic cover. No fancy technology for Ted. This cast more doubt I'd picked the right guy. But I couldn't bear to swap the quick deal now for a better deal later. The bird-in-the-hand philosophy ruled my life. Disastrously.

"I'm serious." I could feel the beat of my heart in my ankles.

He was flipping through the pages. Frugality had led him to buy a two-year calendar and he struggled to find the right year. I sighed inwardly, wondering again if I was setting my sights too low.

"You'll need at least a dozen photos," he said. "We'll want to fill a wall. Less, we'd have to place them too far apart." He shook his head. "And we don't want to do that 'cause we want it to look like a rush. A rush of death." He paused. "Like what happens in Detroit. Did you hear Rush Limbaugh said being a soldier in Iraq wasn't much different than being a black man in Detroit?"

Like I listened to Rush Limbaugh!

"I could probably get twelve over the next few months." Could I? Could I keep Bill onboard till then?

"I guess if the prints were bigger, we could make do with fewer," Ted continued, "but I don't know—eighteen by twenty-four inch seems right. Bigger might be repulsive or unseemly, taking it out of the realm of art and pushing it somewhere else. Smaller and they'd look like morgue shots and a guy already thought of it."

"I think you mean mug shots." Idiot.

"Well anyway, this is the right size."

"That's what I thought too—after a few experiments," I said, sitting down on the stool next to him and picking the photo of Willis Dumphrey up. "Size is important. Scale is why Paris will always be more beautiful than Vienna. This was the guy who got shot in Travis Slack's restaurant a few weeks back." Blank face. "You know, the one where the cook and bartender both died."

"No shit!" Ted said, looking at it carefully. "They're not all celebrities, are they? I don't know about doing celebrity deaths. Turns art into a freak show."

"He was a bartender at Slack's restaurant. Nobody famous."

"Sure, I remember the news story now. Did they ever nab anyone for it?"

But before I could answer, Ted had whipped out his pocket calendar again. "You know, I have a nice hole in my schedule in late November. What's it now? June? Think you could come up with the twelve in five months?" He shook his head. "Probably impossible, right? Impossible if you're gonna limit yourself to black men. Young black men. Too bad—though I think it's the way to go. Nobody wants to look at the elderly, dead or alive."

Although Ted was saying aloud the things I thought, he was a first-class prick.

"And women would be—I don't know—more problematic," he continued. "I guess if you got stuck, you could do men up to age fifty or so."

"I'll get enough young ones. Don't worry."

"But no kids, right."

"Absolutely not. And don't worry. I'll have enough in time for a show in November."

He laughed. "Sounds again like you're planning to take them out yourself. Like some goddamned vampire. Or a serial killer." He wiped his sweaty forehead.

"With the camera, Ted. Don't get excited."

I sounded calm, in control, or at least thought I did. Actually, I was icy with fear and excitement. "Put me on the schedule." My heart was pounding at each pressure point. Surely he must hear it. "Bill's got friends in the business. If I need more men, I could go to them."

This was the first time I'd thought of this solution. Of course, no one else suited them up the way Bill did. No one had his panache. I could hardly mix in the typical blue-suited, church-going corpse with Bill's Mardi Gras boys. Or could I? Maybe one or two as a contrast?

Ted stood up, his stool scratching the floor as he pushed it back. "Well, let's see what happens over the next couple of weeks. Have to put you on the schedule by the end of August or so. Ads need to go to the printer. I have to publicize it. And in this case, I'd be doing us both a favor by advertising widely. Maybe even radio ads. Let's give it till Labor Day or so and see what develops." He smirked at his pun.

"Won't be a problem." Or would it? Was I overly optimistic about death in Detroit?

"Now how can you know that? What if the bodies dry up?" He saw it too.

"In Detroit? I don't think we need to worry."

"You're full of confidence."

"I have to be."

As he walked down the stairs, I saw a bit of hair poking out of his collar. Good, that part of the deal was over. I knew what fur was like on a hot day. In fact, Allure Furs had given me the first taste of what my eventual passion would be.

CHAPTER 12

*"Look at the subject, think about it before
photographing, look until it becomes alive
and looks back into you."*
Edward Steichen

M R. POLIFAX HIRED me to work the counter at Allure Furs in the fall
of my junior year in high school. I didn't like the looks of Arvin
Polifax from the moment I walked into his foul little shop. He was
the most hairless man I'd ever seen and walked with his midsection
thrust out, the rest following behind in a slithery crawl.

But I was tired of being poor. Working after school was widespread
in the eighties and early nineties; parents, suddenly pressed for cash
to buy little Carrie or Jason designer clothes and electronic gadgets,
found reasons to endorse the employment of children. Businesses
were discovering teens could sell shoes, tote heavy trays, and check
out videos practically as handily as adults. Plus, bottom line, you could
pay them a lot less. You didn't have to think about medical plans or
vacations either. Newspapers ran articles on how working part-time
taught teens skills that would be invaluable as adults. It was the Reagan-
Bush-Clinton years, after all. Preachers told their congregations God
wanted them and their offspring to be rich. It was in his Plan for them.

We were sick of Carter's self-sacrificing, frugal philosophy from a decade earlier. Even the high schools began to back it with work/study programs that allowed early dismissals.

Few would've guessed a shop selling furs could look so down on its heels and still succeed, but Allure Furs managed it, squashed between a movie theater with a torn marquee showing second-run films and a donut shop with a missing "u" in its sign, dating from the nineteen thirties. Dont, as the sign spelled out in electric green letters, seemed to warn off potential customers. And the warning stuck. The trio of businesses attracted little interest except for an early-morning donut rush and the Saturday evening midnight showing of *Rocky Horror Picture Show*. With no incentive for entry, Allure Furs managed to avoid customers for days at a time, and I learned quickly how to sleep on my feet or read a paperback under the counter.

The noise from the theater and the sugary, yeasty smell from the donut shop turned out to be two of the many negative aspects of working at Allure Furs. Hours after I left each night, the incessant hum of the movie soundtracks still played in my head. My clothes carried the combined scents of popcorn and yeast. Animals, ignoring significant discouragement, followed me home.

"Sure you can be here by two on weekdays and ten a.m. on Saturdays?" Mr. Polifax asked at the interview, brushing the nonexistent hair from his face for the tenth time. "Last girl didn't turn up till three most days. Then she used the time to read romance novels under the counter." He made a face and sneezed wetly. "You a reader?"

"I hardly ever read," I assured him, stepping incrementally back.

Twice now he'd put a hand on my arm, the last time several inches above the elbow. But worse than his strangely smooth touch was his breath. Perhaps he'd hung around his pelts too much.

"No talking on the phone either," he said suddenly, remembering another errant clerk I guessed. "Don't have any boyfriends across town, I hope? Birmingham, Ann Arbor?"

"No boyfriends." I waited for another question, but Mr. Polifax had run out of queries and hired me on the spot. It seemed like a better deal than hawking pizzas or shelving library books.

Initially my duties included manning the front counter, answering the phone, ringing up sales. The sales came mostly from storage fees and the occasional purchase of accessories. Never for a purchase as consequential as a coat. Three months passed. After the first week I brought a paperback along, but I never made a phone call, and I showed up on time each day. It was god-awful boring but hardly demanding work. Often the time passed without a single customer coming into the shop. The storage fees must carry the business, I decided, or perhaps sales took place on the frequent trips Mr. Polifax made. Invoices for new furs sold in the shop were rare. I'd expected autumn to be the prime season for buying a coat, but not at Allure Furs.

"Violet."

It was Mr. Polifax, rushing out of the backroom. I hadn't known he was back there. Often he didn't come into the showroom at all, letting Myrtle, his bookkeeper, run things.

"Lisa's down with the flu. I wondered if you might step in for her tomorrow." Lisa, the regular model at Allure Furs, was a skinny blonde, who wore too much makeup, staggeringly high heels, and fancied herself the next Elle Macpherson. She seldom deigned to talk to me, preferring the petting she received at the hands of Mr. Polifax and Myrtle. Lisa was a year younger than me, but the world-weary look of a middle-aged woman was already in place.

"A customer's coming in around two on Saturday, and he'll want to see the furs on a model." Mr. Polifax looked at me critically. "Can you do something with your hair, Violet? Maybe put it up? No, it's probably too short for that," he said, running a hand across the nape of my neck. I managed not to shiver. "I've never understood why young girls cut off their hair."

He sighed as if it were one of the tragedies of life. "Well anyway, ask Myrtle for advice." He motioned with his head toward the backroom, a hand on his hip. "Try to look like Audrey Hepburn in *Breakfast at Tiffany's*. Do you know who she is?"

I nodded. Did he think I was the biggest dope in the world?

"Good," he said. "That's the kind of look we strive for here. Classy."

It was hard to reconcile Lisa's choice of makeup and hair style with Audrey Hepburn's. Maybe he'd shown Lisa pictures of Lana Turner instead. "Go see what Myrtle can do with you."

Though Myrtle's wildly permed hair and penchant for wearing jewelry made from shells, bird feathers, and fish skeletons were hardly selling points for credible beauty advice, I dutifully walked to the backroom where Myrtle spent her days performing the miraculous bookkeeping tricks that kept Allure Furs afloat. She seemed harried, suspicious, and ruthless all at once.

"A wig would probably be the best way to go," Myrtle said finally, spinning around in the desk chair when I told her about the task at hand. "Can't do much with the pixie cut you favor. Need more volume. Selling furs is easier if they're modeled by a glamour girl. What can we do with you?"

It was hard to take a critique on hair styles seriously when it came from a woman like Myrtle, but I tried to smile brightly. Maybe there'd be more money in modeling. Lisa certainly seemed well-clad.

Reaching over with a frown, Myrtle yanked open a drawer, pulled out a ratty-looking auburn wig, and tossed it to me. In the split second before I caught it, it seemed like a ferret was headed my way.

"Of course, you'll have to play with it, tease it, and plump it up. Give it a little flair. Why don't you take it home with you? Practice."

I looked hard at the scabby wig in my hands. Acquiring flair would constitute a miracle wearing this mop. "You might throw it in Woolite. Let it soak for an hour or so. Woolite can do wonders." Unconsciously, Myrtle's right hand went to her own head, making me wonder if she applied it to her hair directly. "I've been known to pull a wig on in a pinch. I may have worn that one once or twice."

It took all of my wherewithal not to drop it because it bore the faint scent of Myrtle's favorite perfume. Or perhaps it was the back office itself, pickled in *Charlie* after all of Myrtle's years at Allure Furs. Mr. Polifax wisely kept her as far from the furs as possible.

I showed up on Saturday, wig in place, makeup on, the highest heels Payless sold jammed on my feet.

"Well, that's more like it," Mr. Polifax said, coming out of the back room. "I wouldn't have believed you'd clean up this good. We might sell a coat today after all." He circled me. "The added height is terrific. You must top six feet in those shoes."

He was flush with approval, and when the customer bought a $4,500 mink an hour later, Mr. Polifax was even happier. Happy didn't cover it; he was ecstatic.

Soon Lisa and I were sharing the modeling duties. "You know when to shut your trap, Violet," Mr. Polifax said, in a rare attempt at a compliment. "Lisa likes to chat up the customers. Sometimes it works, but…."

Several weeks later he asked me to come in on a Friday night. "This customer can only make it after eight," he said, running a nervous hand through his nonexistent hair. "Could mean a big sale for us. I hate to turn it over to big-mouthed Lisa. This guy's the silent type." He shook his head. Lisa had definitely lost her luster after a few big sales on my watch.

He squinted as he licked his thumb, flipping through his Rolodex. "Your mother works Friday nights, right?" He was looking at the card with my name on it. "Well, I can give you a ride home," he said. "It's practically on my way."

I'd no idea if this were true or not since he'd never confided his address. But so far he'd seemed harmless enough, so I agreed.

Friday night, I tried on a lynx and a karakul lamb coat for a tiny man who never said a word. After the lynx, Mr. Polifax came hurrying into the back room and suggested I model the next coat—a Persian lamb—with nothing underneath it.

"Look, Violet—just the coat, never mind the rest." He looked me up and down as if I'd already stripped. "Leave your clothing back here. You know."

But I didn't know. I wasn't sure he'd actually said what I thought I'd heard. He'd swallowed half the words.

"What would be the point of that?" I said, watching him in the mirror. It wasn't like my skimpy dress was making the coat fall unevenly.

Mr. Polifax turned a bright pink. "This client—well, he's a little odd—but he'll probably make a purchase or at least worth our while if he gets a peek."

I stood frozen.

"Look, Lisa does it all the time. Well, not all the time, but on occasion. Some men—well, you know." He was stuttering and turned a deeper red. "Look, there'll be extra money in your paycheck next week. Be a good girl and show him the goods."

The goods?

"What if he still doesn't buy anything?" My hand was on his shoulder as he attempted to open the door. "I'll still get the extra pay?" I wasn't the fool he took me for. "I'll get it even if he doesn't buy a thing? Right?" I repeated more firmly. A good girl wouldn't be considering this stunt, so I might as well put any thoughts of that aside.

Mr. Polifax paused and then nodded.

"And no touching, right? He has to keep his hands to himself!" I was hardly going to allow that nasty man to put his hands on me.

Polifax shook his head. "No touching. I'll be right there. But if you exhibit such a prissy, superior attitude along with the fur, he won't make a purchase and our little arrangement will quickly end. Lisa's been trying to get me to give her more hours." He straightened his back, annoyed with my ability to get the upper hand with him for once, and pushed open the door.

The little man was standing in the same spot when I walked out of the back room wearing a hugely expensive sable. He gave no indication that either it or I was anything special, remaining mostly mute and using his hands to indicate certain moves he wanted me to make. It looked like he was conducting an invisible orchestra. I followed his instructions—never fully disrobing, but certainly modeling more than the coat.

The show went on for about fifteen minutes, and it wasn't an entirely dissatisfying experience. I enjoyed watching in the full-length mirrors circling the room. The thought of photographing it flew into my head, though I had nothing more in those days than a point-and-shoot camera. Maybe I'd buy a better camera with my increased wages. It wasn't me I wanted to photograph, but his face watching me. The way his features seem to slide off his face, turning to liquid. I was already planning what the photo would look like, how I would pose him.

The small man seemed unchanged by my performance; I might never have disrobed at all from the placid look on his face. But Polifax was visibly panting, seemingly ill-equipped to show the customer to the door.

When the door closed behind the customer, Mr. Polifax sank into the nearest chair and fanned himself. "You did good, Violet. You're a born model."

My little ballet netted an extra twenty-five bucks in my next check. I finally understood how Allure Furs stayed in business despite its poor sales.

The day, six months later, that a bear of a man put his hairy paws around my neck and a knee the size of a battering ram between my legs was my last one. I quit the job, having made more than enough money for a high school girl's needs.

It was only a month or two later when the trio of stores burned to the ground. The fire marshal couldn't decide whether it was the faulty projector at the theater or the ovens at the donut shop that caused the blaze. Although the fire was at night, Mr. Polifax and a client were on the premises and perished in what was called an extremely rapid-moving blaze. Myrtle called to give me the news. No woman was in the shop. I wondered if Mr. Polifax modeled furs himself in a pinch. That would be the last time my body was under such a gaze. I'd find ways to support myself I could live with.

CHAPTER 13

Detroit News: Rapper Cajuan Grace, age 27, was shot and killed at approximately 3:30 a.m. last night outside of Daddy Majestyk's, an upscale club and poolroom on 8 Mile Road in Detroit. Grace was recently nominated for a Grammy Award for his second CD, *Nobody Gonna Tell Me Nothin'*. At the time of his death, all four members of his group, R'RSTD, were standing within twenty feet of the rapper. The shooter was said to be a bodyguard of longtime rival rapper, Nikl Defenz, who was not on the premises at the time of the shooting. The fight started inside the club, moving outside when longtime Detroit businesswoman and club owner, Florence Arpelle, threatened to call the police. Grace was declared dead at Henry Ford Hospital at 4:05 a.m. Grace was remembered by fellow rappers as "funny, smart, and talented but a bit of a hothead."

(June 2011)

"YOU AREN'T GONNA do Cajuan Grace," Bill told me when I showed up a few hours after the body was released. "No way, no how. So get that idea out of your head. Family's made other arrangements." Bill rubbed his face with a handkerchief and refolded it.

I hadn't said a word yet and the use of the word *do* stopped me in my tracks for a minute. I wondered if this was how Bill saw my work—as bordering on something sexual. Did he imagine I got off on taking these pictures? Or off in the usual way?

"Grace was shot in the face. You wouldn't want him hanging in that gallery with your pretty boys. Got a hole the size of a baseball over his eyes. Well," he amended when he saw my incredulity, "the size of a golf ball anyway."

"I bet the hole will hardly be noticeable after your handiwork," I said in a wheedling tone. "Couldn't I take one or two shots? I wouldn't show it publicly without the family's consent." I put my hands on my hips in what felt like a provocative pose. "Oh, come on, Bill. It's the first celebrity you've had in here. Let me take a quick shot or two."

He shook his head. "I could lose my license. I asked them point-blank if you could photograph him—his mother and one of his sisters—and they said no. Flat-out refused."

"Did you tell them about the series of portraits? Tell them I'm a serious—"

"Sure, sure. They know about it. Not impressed."

He walked over and put a consoling hand on my shoulder. "Look, Vi, not all black folks are cool about letting a white lady nobody ever heard of take pictures of their famous son. They don't know what you're up to. Probably thinking you're going to exploit them somehow. I hear they've got a photographer-to-the-stars from New York coming in to do the job. Gonna have a bound book ready for the funeral. They have agents and managers and people up the wazoo taking care of business. They'll sell the prints later and make a mint. This kid—well, he was big-time. He's only here because one of 'em read a story about me in the *News*."

His tone altered between consoling and confrontational. He

finished speaking and ran the back of his hand across his upper lip. Then he pulled out his handkerchief and mopped his face again. "I gotta lose some weight, baby. I'm sweating all the time now."

I was a bit surprised by Bill's dismissive tone, having assumed that though Bill might be troubled by certain aspects of this venture, he had confidence in my talent and my motives. I certainly talked about my ambitions for this project enough.

Now it seemed, once again, that my whiteness was part of his problem. Did being white make me seem more exploitative? Was it always to be about race?

"The photographer's shooting in an hour or so for the tribute book. He's not going exhibit the work himself. His people—Cajuan Grace's people, that is—are putting it together. Black people often put together a book like this—though usually not on this scale. Look, his mother and the sisters were real nice ladies. They're not trying to screw up your plans, you know. You don't enter into things. You're irrelevant."

He said it softly but it still stung. Swell—irrelevant.

"I get it! But what would be the harm in taking a few shots first? I promise I'll never exhibit them without your say-so. Not ever. You may not understand it—I don't exactly get it myself — but I feel like things would be incomplete without Cajuan." Drawing a deep breath, I finished my thought. "It's part of what happened. Part of what I saw."

He sighed. "You promise?"

I drew a cross on my chest.

"Okay, but just a few quick shots. Guy's coming anytime." He looked at me hard. "And if you break your promise, I'll tear the other contracts up. I will. I swear it," he said again, wiping his face for a third time. "Sue your ass myself if need be."

"You need to get your blood pressure checked," I said on the way out of the room. "It's perfectly comfortable in here and I'm starting to worry about you."

Cajuan was dressed in what I assumed were the clothes he performed in. Bill hadn't needed to go to his special closets for this one. He wore what looked like a black and gold basketball jersey nearly long enough to touch his knees, and partially obscured by a gold leather jacket. His pants were baggy and elasticized at the ankle. Unlaced black high-tops, a scarf (gold and black checked) and a baseball cap from some team I couldn't name finished the outfit. Oh, and numerous gold chains, woven bracelets, studs, and tattoos.

There was little left of Cajuan's head under that cap. And the hole was only partially obscured by his headwear when you got in close. He was a skinny little guy, pumped up by his wardrobe. Didn't even have much of a beard. The dizzying colors and accoutrements made shooting a decent photograph difficult. But the more I messed with his outfit, the more pathetic it became. This was at last the death I'd envisioned shooting, and I was sick at having done it. Maybe I wouldn't use this one. But probably, if I could pull it off, I would.

CHAPTER 14

"Twelve significant photographs in any one year is a good crop."
Ansel Adams

IOGENES CORTES HAD been my friend since our days at the Center for Creative Studies in Detroit in the late eighties. We'd first met in a sculpture class, an art form we'd both mistakenly signed up for. It turned out to be therapeutic but little else.

Di was already in his mid-twenties; I was seventeen. We both produced piece after piece meant to be representational but turning out abstract. Our work would go into the kiln looking like one thing and come out fired, looking like another. No one could figure it out. My group of sunning seals and his sleeping woman were practically interchangeable. It was Algebra II all over again, and we were the two kids snickering at the back of the classroom because we didn't get it. We listened when the instructor quoted Michelangelo's famous words— that when he took away what was extraneous to the piece of clay or stone, he was left with David.

The end of the term came and neither of us found David nor

anything remotely like him taking shape, and soon I turned to oils and finally to photography, and Di switched to a culinary program at Schoolcraft College. For the last twenty years, we'd met for dinner, a movie now and then, a drink at a local bar, or on the occasions I needed to buy drugs. Well, if you think of pot as a drug. We also spoke via telephone or email several times a week. He was the closest thing I had to a friend, the only one who knew most of my secrets; the only one whose secrets I knew. Unfortunately he also had Alberto. Alberto and I got along as well as two cats tossed into a burlap bag. Snarling and scratching most of the time.

When I lived in New York, Di camped out on my floor for three months, thinking he might want to live there too. But he soon realized the skills placing him on the top rung of his profession in Detroit were commonplace in the infinite talent pool of New York.

I thought otherwise, thought he was wasted in Detroit, but couldn't convince him to stay the course. It was about then he met the love of his life at a jazz club in Ann Arbor and settled happily back into Michigan life. Alberto played keyboard and was prettier than me. Prettier than most girls.

I gave New York another year to woo me, but it was too easy to turn any corner and find a gallery filled with photographs more compelling than mine. What exhilarated me at twenty-two, exhausted me three years later. I'd never be bigger than Detroit; I knew it.

DI WAS GAY, Filipino, and had been selling drugs without incident since his teens. He only sold the soft stuff, and only to his friends, and only to friends not too badly hooked. It was a small clientele. A desperate call to Chez Diogenes in the middle of the night brought an end to the buyer-seller relationship. He was cool; you had to be too.

He was the head chef at a popular downtown Detroit restaurant, but he'd never given up his sideline. In Detroit, restaurants came and went, but a dependable drug dealer was gold. I was not a habitual user, but on occasion, I indulged. Di never let me down. If he wasn't rock solid on the quality, he didn't sell it. Everyone thinks this about their source, but in my case, it was true.

We met at the Belle Isle Turkey Grill during the winter months or on a rainy day when crowds were scarce. Di found other spots for other customers, so I was never too concerned about being watched. He steadfastly refused to bring drugs to my apartment or to have me come to his house or the restaurant.

"Do you want cops watching your house? I sure don't."

We hadn't met for a drug purchase in months, and it'd nearly stopped raining by the time I arrived. He handed over a small bag of grass tucked into the brown Ace Hardware bag he always used. "I thought maybe you were done with this."

"So did I. Life's been tough lately." I opened my mouth to begin my spiel, but closed it. I didn't want to lose the one friend I had with my endless rants.

Diogenes relaxed and leaned against the deserted picnic table. It was raining but only a fine mist. Each of the perhaps five guys hanging out on the island today was wearing a Tigers cap, but Diogenes sported a yellow rain hat, which flapped in the breeze like the Morton Salt Girl's. He was a thin guy with the best haircut you've ever seen. Over forty now, he looked ten years younger. The benefits of taking skin care seriously, he pointed out when I mentioned it, and a little judicious knife work. He also never drank more than one glass of wine, had never smoked, and never took drugs himself. His physical perfection was an occasional source of anxiety for me. I'd photographed him from time to time, but he never looked real in the shots. His almost stone-like perfection looked better in the flesh where the mobility of his face and the melodiousness of his voice softened it.

"Love your hat," I said now, stifling a grin. "Surprised you want to stand out. A cop could spot that banana yellow from Indian Village."

"Okay, so I borrowed it from a waitress. Couldn't wear my chef's hat out here, and it was raining hard when I left." He looked around. "Baseball caps put a dent in my do." He looked me over. "You know how I feel about my hair, sweetie. You don't pay a hundred dollars for a haircut in Detroit and let it get rained on. Hey, so why were you in such a hurry for the gold today? Not like you to get all panicky. Made me a little anxious."

"I'm not all panicky. And if I am, it's not about grass."

"You seem pretty damned jumpy. I almost detect a line of sweat on your brow. Or is it your personal glow?" He smiled, his teeth as white as a laser polish delivered. "Let's take a walk. Come on."

"It's raining." I looked at my feet. "And I don't have the right shoes."

He held up his left foot, shod in a gray suede number probably costing three hundred dollars. "I don't even own the right shoes. We'll stick to the concrete."

"Oh, all right."

What I wanted to do was go back home and roll a joint. I *was* panicky. These altercations with Bill were starting to wear on me and any excitement about the possibility of a show had turned to tension and dread. I was completely dependent on Bill for this project. Dependent on a *man*: something I'd vowed never to be and yet increasingly was. What were the chances I could find another mortician who'd provide me with bodies should Bill pull out? Black bodies. Young, black bodies dressed for a night on the town. The chances were zero. Zip. I was screwed if I couldn't keep him on Team Violet. And no new ideas were coming down the pike. I was like car-happy Detroit: an entity with but one idea.

Plus I hated the thought of a breakup; I'd been with Bill two years. Familiarity had become attractive. Maybe I was getting old, soft. Coming home at night to a friendly face seemed like a good idea. Had I ever come home to a friendly face before? Bunny'd always been at work. Was an urge for domesticity seeping into my soul? Would a kitten be my next passion? Buck up, I told myself. It'll never happen. Who would stick with me forever after?

"I want to walk through the conservatory while we're here," Diogenes was saying. "I'd like to see what plants they're exhibiting. Need a few new ideas for the teensy garden on the side of my house. The shade is killing the miniature lilac…"

"The conservatory? Isn't that like a greenhouse? Is that where we're headed?"

I stopped in my tracks—and they were tracks. Despite the concrete, my feet were leaving a trail of mud. "Christ, Di, I don't have time for trip through a greenhouse. I got film to process…"

"It'll wait." He grabbed my hand and tugged. "We're practically there. Come on." He looked at me sadly. "Have you ever had your own garden, kiddo? No, I guess not, living in apartments like you do. My poor little Vi. I'm gonna buy you a houseplant."

"Had one once and it didn't make it through the night."

Di smiled, and I admired his teeth again.

"Jeez, those teeth are white. You gotta be careful, Di or they'll make your skin look sallow."

"It couldn't have been *your* fault if it died overnight. It was probably a bum plant with no root system to sustain it. You should've taken it back. Bet you bought it at Home Depot."

"It was before the days of Home Depot. Kresge's I think. I lived in a row house for a while when I was a kid. But no garden. Bunny never had time to plant flowers. Barely had grass."

I wondered if I could identify more than five or six kinds of flowers. It was embarrassing. The only ones I knew were used at weddings. "Go over and stand by the—roses?" I'd suggest to the bridesmaids.

The bride's mother usually set me straight. "Carnations, dear."

"Kind of sad for a woman named after a flower," Diogenes noted as we arrived at the conservatory, the best-maintained building on the island.

Funny no bride had ever asked to be photographed in here. Probably not enough room for pictures anyway with all the flowers. Too many flowers shouted funeral. Or had before the charitable donations in lieu of flowers trend took over. And the lighting was iffy in the greenhouse.

"My father's idea," I explained, "naming both of us for flowers. His last expression of interest in the coming birth."

Di slapped his forehead. "Right, a father. I always imagine you coming barreling out of Bunny fully formed and fuming. Cal Hart, right?"

"Hal."

I couldn't believe I'd mentioned my father. Maybe it was the proximity to flowers making me go soft. We walked through the main door where an African-American woman wearing a bright pink slicker and hat sat solemnly at a Formica table. A trickle of water from the leaking glass panel above dripped on her head, but she seemed unconcerned.

"Can I ask you two to put your names and zips down here," the woman said, smiling up at us and pushing a clipboard forward.

Diogenes quickly grabbed the pen and added his name to the list. I scribbled an illegible name and a fictitious zip below his—always sure I was being tracked. Funny it was the drug dealer who was unconcerned.

Di'd already passed through the door and slipped into a cacti display.

"I bet the plants occasionally swallow a visitor and they need the information for identification," I joked, half-believing it as I looked around.

"Never mind the jokes. Sit down right there and breathe it all in," he said, pointing to a bench.

"Smells exactly like it did outside. Whole island's crazy with the green stuff. I can hardly breathe."

It was quiet except for the sound of dripping water. I looked down at my shoes and slid the bottoms across the floor, trying to remove the mud. It made a rude noise and a man on the other side of a large tree peeked around and shot me a disapproving look.

"True," Di responded, taking in his surroundings with a Zen sort of pose. "In winter, it's more startling than now."

"Startling?" I looked around. Plants, rocks, water, and little else. What you'd expect to see in a greenhouse. Or whatever he'd called it. A conservatory. I'd thought a conservatory was a place you learned to play a piano.

"So what's going on with you, Vi?"

"Nothing."

He sat down and squeezed my hand.

"Okay, okay." I pulled my hand away. "Well, I'm still working on that project I told you about."

"The dead bodies?"

I nodded and found myself telling him more about the project despite my pledge to keep it secret. If I failed at this…

"This is starting to remind me of your shopping cart debacle," he said with a shudder. "That one got a little dangerous, didn't it?"

I nodded, having known he'd bring it up.

When I first returned to Detroit after a year in Chicago and two or so in New York, I came up with the idea of photographing shopping carts of the homeless. More than one of the shopping cart owners had come after me too, thinking I was trying to steal their stuff or expose them to—to what—ridicule? Most of the homeless people believed their cart was like a house, identifiable to the onlooker. Distinctive. Personal.

After I finished developing the first half-dozen photographs, I realized the carts were completely indistinguishable from each other—in a photograph, at least. Each photo showed a cart piled high with clothing, blankets, spare dishes, the stuff of dumpsters; you quickly lost any sense of individual items, individual people. It looked like I was making a sort of cruel, crude, and artless comment. Once again, the social commentary I fled from. And what it taught me—which I should've known—was the means to their survival rested inside those carts. Or, on another level, their home. So the only message was political—not artistic.

I fooled around with the idea of creating my own shopping carts for a while, tried it once or twice, but even those carts—more creatively assembled than the real thing—looked dull on film. And the lack of authenticity bugged me. Although many photographers stage their work, this seemed particularly tasteless. Pose the rich if you're going to orchestrate it.

Any attempt to persuade the cart owners to stand next to their carts was completely out of the question. I'd begun to have nightmares about being surrounded by faceless people with shopping carts. It was like a scene out of a zombie movie. So the whole idea was a bust, and I never sold a single picture. I didn't try very hard, not liking any enough to take along to an art fair or a Christmas bazaar. Actually I was afraid those photos would turn people off to my work altogether. I swore I wouldn't go near a project that used people in that way again. Were dead people any less vulnerable, less open to being used, than homeless ones?

The spare closet was going to need to be a lot bigger if success didn't come soon. It was more than a little depressing to see the sea of envelopes waving to me when I opened that door.

The most distinctive thing about the carts had been the streets they sat on, often the most dilapidated blocks of Detroit. Even then, in the early 2000s, the streets in Detroit were apocalyptic. Now—well, what's the next stage? Post-apocalyptic implies bodies, disease, fire. I guess we'd arrived.

But that's when I first got the idea of photographing the demise of apartment houses. Apartment houses from the twenties and thirties were architecturally interesting—or what was left of them. There was a period when middle-class people were sometimes apartment dwellers. Even in Detroit, traditionally a city of home owners. Maybe it was the Depression that made home ownership iffy. And the idea of all those abandoned apartment houses—little ones mostly with four to eight flats, places once desirable—was poignant.

Or so I'd thought. Funny how I seemed to move in circles leading nowhere. Or how I stumbled onto signifiers of a society gone bust and tried to make it art without making an overt political or sociological statement. Good ideas turned to smoke in my hands. Di was probably talking about the problem of exploiting people again, the possibility of getting myself into a dangerous situation, being open to lawsuits or physical harm.

"I've got waivers from all of them. Their families, I mean. Bill's attorney drew up an airtight contract. Actually the families seem to get a degree of consolation from the pictures. Or sort of."

"And what if a lover or a neighbor or a friend—a person you didn't ask to sign a form, someone else—sees the photo and objects?"

"Well, a photographer runs that risk, doesn't she?" I hadn't thought of that. The idea an objection could come from another quarter: an old lover, a friend, the guy down the street.

"Look, you'd be surprised by how much people like the pictures," I repeated. "The families, that is. They've all asked for copies." Di shivered noticeably. "I think you've got the wrong idea about it. They're respectful. Not nasty-looking, like you seem to think. Come up and see them."

"You scare me, girl. What you're willing to do. The places you go. Roaming around here at six in the morning? Having run-ins with cops?" He stood up and stretched. "I'm breathing better already. A little chlorophyll can do wonders."

I sighed, rising too. "So what's new with you anyway? Still seeing Alberto?"

He shook his head. "We've been *seeing each other* for years, Six." The nickname "Six" dated from our days at the Center for Creative Studies. VI was, of course, the Roman numeral for six. On occasion, I called him Five-Oh-One for Di although that sounded like those eighties jeans. Pretty Star Trekian and the names were definitely part of our nineties days, but we'd been geeks. Geeks who thought we were cool, of course. Cool art, cool music, books, clothes. It was the two of us against the world...for a while. But after a point, it became dysfunctional. Only the Millennials, the generation that came after X, might remain children forever.

"Why do you insist on thinking of me as promiscuous? You're the one who drifts from relationship to relationship. So does any of this do anything for you?" He motioned to the plants as we prepared to leave. "Does it change your outlook, soothe your soul?"

"I guess not a lot. Urban girl with feet of concrete."

"Any number of photographers take pictures of flowers."

"Unless you're O'Keeffe, it's damned hard to make something interesting out of a flower. Hard to make it more than pretty. The two-dimensionalness of it on paper, I think. And O'Keeffe, if that's who you mean, *painted* them. It gave her a lot more freedom; there's a more tactile feel to paint. She invented those flowers." I paused. "I never dug what's his name, for instance. Ansel Adams. Calendar art. Static."

He held the door open and I passed through. It was raining harder now and we both ran for our cars. Ahead, Diogenes seemed to run a bit above the ground. He should've been a dancer, but his cooking was pretty fine too. I slipped and nearly fell; he turned around to grin at me as I suddenly shrieked.

"You almost sounded like a girl for a minute, Violet."

The water streamed from either side of his rain hat, but he still looked impeccable. Whereas I was smeared with mud, moss, dirt from top to bottom.

"Probably from being around you too much." I threw him what I hoped looked like a playful smile. "Hey, why don't you come up and see them, Di?" He looked at me quizzically. "The photographs, I mean."

"Another day, chica. Gotta get back to work." He climbed into his two-toned Mini Cooper. "Be careful, will you?"

"Of what?" I said, trying to get my keyless lock to work. Humidity seemed to confound it.

"It's Detroit, remember."

I went home and rolled a joint—more out of habit than need. I wondered if the greenhouse *had* done the trick. Maybe I *should* buy a plant. Maybe take pictures of plants. There'd been a grotesque feel to the greenhouse: the plants growing so thickly you couldn't see past them. Sucking all the light from the sky, casting huge shadows, men hiding behind gargantuan leaves, women in pink rubber asking for your zip code without saying why.

My mind slowly returned to the carts of the homeless. You didn't see the towering carts as much anymore in Detroit. Had times gotten so bad the homeless had nothing left to push around? Were both the people and their carts in the Detroit River, the way New Yorkers claimed their homeless had been tossed in the East River. Maybe Bill would know.

CHAPTER 15

Detroit Free Press: Albert Flowers, age 38, died last night after a struggle with Southwestern Mall guard Pedro Juarez. The fatal scuffle took place after the security guard accused Flowers' stepdaughter of stealing makeup from a Target department store in the mall. Flowers died from suffocation, which occurred when Juarez held him in a headlock while the stepdaughter was being restrained by another guard. Local officials are considering whether manslaughter charges should be filed. The Flowers family is considering filing a lawsuit against the guard.

(July 2011)

"I DON'T GIVE A shit whether his wife signed the form, Violet. I'm reluctant to get mixed up with these people. They've already shown themselves to be a litigious bunch." Bill sighed heavily. "Guy's not in his grave and they're talking about filing lawsuits. The *Free Press* hinted the video's going to back up the store's claim she was stealing cosmetics."

It was Bill on the phone about an hour after he called to tell me he'd be picking up the body, and I could come down later to photograph him.

"Little idiot had a boatload of cheap beauty products in her bag. You gonna steal cosmetics, go to a tonier store. I use far better products than that on a corpse."

Having once been a teenager who stole more cheap beauty products than I liked to remember, I held my tongue. Girls like her, or the one I was once, would never make it past the front door of a store that carried high-end stuff. But there was one fact kids didn't understand. Low-end stores were more skilled in ferreting out theft and much more likely to prosecute. Tony stores didn't want the publicity.

"If it were up to you, William, I wouldn't have any photos except the one of the rugby player. That's 'cause you needed me to take it."

"I can feel you sticking out your tongue, girl. Life doesn't always work out. I keep tellin' you that."

"Let me take a few pictures. I'll be in and out in a flash. You can't be second-guessing what's going to happen years down the road. And what would my stuff have to do with a lawsuit anyway? My photos wouldn't be used as evidence. The police photographer's work goes to court. So too, the coroner's records. By the time, I come on the scene, the body's been corrupted. Wouldn't make either side's case in any lawsuit. The body's tainted by you too, as a matter of fact. You corrupt bodies pretty good."

This long harangue won me a half-hearted laugh, and after a lot more cajoling, and quite frankly begging, Bill agreed, and I broke my record for getting to his place.

The deceased was dressed in a marine uniform. "So he no sooner came home from Iraq and this happened?"

"No, no, the uniform's at least fifteen years old. Served in the Gulf War," Bill said, sitting on the sofa and flipping through one of his burgundy books. When he looked up and saw my blank look, he sighed. "Desert Storm? Daddy Bush's war. To keep Saddam out of Kuwait. Any of this history ringing a bell?"

"Right," I said, taking the first shot. "I forgot. I was like a kid. So were you."

Bill shook his head in despair. "You have no idea what's going on, sugar, do you? Ever heard of Kuwait? How about the term 'weapons of mass destruction'? Or 'the war on terrorism'?" He threw this out and rubbed his eyes. "How about Nine/Eleven?"

I wasn't listening anymore; I was thinking the uniform would make a nice change from the hoopla of peacock-blue shirts and velvet jackets. "Bill, has anyone ever sent a body back to you from the Middle East? A soldier, I mean."

"Not yet." He continued to page through his binder. "And I hope the day doesn't come." He looked up. "The military takes care of its own mostly."

I wasn't sure if he'd let me know about the death of a soldier or not. It was the possibility of bodies I'd never laid eyes on—ones where Bill knew the family too well, or didn't want to tackle the contract issue—that gnawed at me. Deaths seeming inappropriate, unseemly, inconvenient to photograph to Bill. This hadn't occurred to me before now. Was he holding out?

I took enough photographs of Albert Flowers to be sure I'd have the perfect one and stowed my gear. I took fewer pictures now, knowing better what was needed. I hung around a little longer, hoping for an invitation or even a conversation. But Bill got a phone call, and after that his accountant wanted him to look at some figures, so I gave up and left without Bill ever mentioning seeing me that night or any other night. Once again, we hadn't had sex in weeks. Hadn't done more than squabble over my damned project.

At home, there was a message on the machine. I pushed "Play," expecting a client's voice.

"It's me," a slightly familiar voice said. "Derek Olsen."

A long pause followed—as though Derek believed I might not remember the name and needed time to summon up his face. Before that fetus, possibly. Since that night, no.

"Guy on Belle Isle, right. One who brought a fetus over your house. Look, I think I have something. Down here on the island." I felt him pause as he probably looked at the time. "It's about six o'clock now and you probably won't get this message until late." He chuckled again. "I don't know why but I always picture you out on the streets turning over trashcans or rocks, looking for the nasty." He cleared his throat. "Anyway, why don't you come down early tomorrow? Dawn maybe. Bring a little light along too." He paused. "I mean enough light to shoot with. Not a flashlight."

"I guess," I said, forgetting he was on the tape because it was oddly conversational for a phone message. I didn't want to go to Belle Isle at five in the morning. But I'd set this scheme into motion, so I supposed I'd have to drive down. It'd probably be something akin to the hood ornament or fetus but still…

He'd left his number, "In case you misplaced it."

Was this a cell or his mother's landline? He couldn't spend all his time on the island. What happened when it rained?

In the hours before our rendezvous, I tried to summon up enthusiasm. But the attraction Derek Olsen held for me several weeks earlier was gone. I was well into this new project now, and the stuff Derek might come up with would be a diversion at best. The project was too well defined. Ted Ernst was in on it now. Perhaps even Bill had mustered up some respect for my project if not for me.

And I'd forgotten how creepy Derek was. That fetus in the kitchen sink. Our midnight burial in my neighbor's compost pile. What ghoulish find did he want to show me tomorrow? What did he have secreted away in his little hidey-hole? The problem was—it was probably nothing. I'd show up and be treated to a closer look at his work. His new stuff would be like my old stuff. Mundane, amateurish, mawkish. But still—it wasn't like I was pressed for time. I might as well go down. Bill wasn't going to call.

THE SKY WAS olive pewter when I crossed the bridge. The island smelled cleaner, if a little sulfuric, in the aftermath of an early morning thunderstorm. Perhaps the goose dung, littering surfaces lavishly and indiscriminately, had been neutralized by the rain. The birds were shadowy specters along the shoreline. As I drove along the southeast tip of the island, I saw a line of parked cars and looked around for a predawn event that had brought out the crowd. A race? A religious service? A fraternity rite? Silence reigned. My car lights picked up people inside several cars as I made my way north: a few in pairs, others seemingly alone—most appearing to be asleep under covers probably dank from humidity; I caught a few in an embrace and looked away. It was so damned quiet; that was the scariest part.

In two or three of the cars, I could make out single men sitting upright at the wheel, looking on guard, wary. Drugs? Hookers? Male partners? A man, youngish and underdressed for temperatures in the fifties, walked along the sidewalk, head down. Headlights flashed at him from several cars, but he didn't look up. Whatever mission he was on, it wasn't here or wasn't this. Was it sex the men in the cars wanted? Drugs or companionship? A muted beep, a foghorn on the river, a birdcall, and the young man disappeared into a fissure, a passage through the dense green.

Now it was my slow cruise drawing their interest. Catcalls and invitations erupted from several vehicles when I slowed at a stop sign.

"Hey, baby," one man called, throwing open his door. "Got something fine to share with you." He laughed raucously. "Bet you thought I meant my dick. But it's NZ Green! Ever hear of it?"

When another car door started to open, I picked up speed. It was getting late and I realized it only when two joggers in reflective vests with flashlights ran by, nearly blinding me. I wondered if there was a way to capture this scene, this early morning procession of parked cars, warm desire, fluid bodies, desperation, loneliness: each car telling a different story. Or maybe the same one.

Derek waited in the spot I'd parked in before; I could barely make him out though he held up a lantern flashlight that bounced light off both our faces.

"Come on," he said, motioning with the light. "It'd be better to get this over with before it's too light."

I didn't like the sound of that, but I followed him anyway, still mesmerized by my voyage along the river.

"Hey, you don't seem so anxious to see sick stuff today. Thought you were the gutsy one who wanted to take pictures of fresh bodies." He stopped for a minute, putting the lantern down and his hands on his knees, wheezing a bit. "Sorry, the night air makes my asthma kick up." He reached into his pocket for an inhaler and stuck it in his mouth. After a few puffs, he added, "Not usually on the island at this hour. Bad air for asthma. Humidity from the storm…"

"I could've come later. You set the time. Right?" Derek seemed a tad nuttier than last time. "Don't you usually sleep here?"

"No, I told you before. I sleep at my mother's."

He put the inhaler away and looked at me as if my failure to remember his words was a surprise. "She doesn't kick me out till morning." He saw my look and clarified his comment. "Okay, she doesn't *actually* kick me out. Not like the homeless shelters do anyway. She likes me to do stuff in the daytime—get out of the house, keep busy. Right now she thinks I'm on my way to deliver flyers in Livonia."

"Deliver flyers? Do you get paid more than a pittance for that?"

He shook his head. "Nah, but Mom likes to think I'm trying to make my way in the world. Trouble is, you have to get yourself to the spot where they pick you up too damned early." He looked at his watch, a surprisingly expensive-looking one. "If you get chosen—if you look fairly clean and sober—they dump you along with the flyers miles away. You're not sure where you are. No one drops flyers in Detroit. Only ones I've ever tossed here were for gambling, addiction, and cancer of the mouth. Do black people get that a lot? Probably from that damned city incinerator." Before I could answer, he shook his head and continued, "Occasionally, they pick you up afterward but not always. Certain drivers think it's funny to leave you hanging."

He'd recovered his breath and we started walking. "Once they sent me downriver, and neither the other guy nor me had any idea how to get back to the city from—where was it?—Wyandotte, Lincoln Park? One of those downriver 'burbs. Guy with me was hardcore and in need of a fix by the end. Shakin' and sweatin' and swearin' his head off. I managed to hitch a ride at a truck stop, but the trucker wouldn't take him."

"So you left him alone there?"

"Lucky I did. For him anyway."

"Why?" There had to be a punch line in this.

Derek stopped again, but this time to shake his index finger. "You don't wanna be doing that too often, Violet. Hitching rides from those guys. Truckers get lonely and horny and want you to blow them while they drive. Fellate them, I heard a guy call it on a cop show. The polite word for somethin' that ain't too polite. Does fellate sound any better than blow to you?"

"So did you?"

Derek grinned noncommittally and continued toward his space. I followed, leaving a bit of distance between us, not exactly happy with the direction his conversation was taking. Talk of sex usually led to an attempt to procure it, and I was not having sex with Derek no matter what he showed me today. He was a kid—and a half-addled one. Gallery guy was one thing, barmy boy another.

"Those truckers—they're *flying* from doing speed in those rigs, and they like to drive with your head in their lap at eighty miles an hour," he said, his back to me.

So he *had* done it. He turned around, making a face when he saw mine.

"Most of 'em don't wash down there too often either," he added, pointing. "Got crotch sweat from their bellies hanging over their balls all day long in those rigs. A real bad smell when you get up—or down—close."

So he'd done it more than once. Cripes! "Enough," I said, holding my hands over my ears.

He stopped, suddenly looking serious, professorial almost. "Now, what you're gonna see today is probably the start of something big goin' down. A vendetta maybe." He looked around. "That's why I called you down here before daybreak. Before other people got turned on to it."

"Like a crime?" I'd almost forgotten our mission, lost sight of it in picturing the scene in the truck.

He nodded. "This kind of thing—what you're gonna see in a second—couldn't have happened without help, that's for sure." He reached for my arm. "Are you ready or have you gotten more jumpy since you first told me you wanted to see a dead body?" He looked at me quizzically. "I don't want to freak you out. Was that embryo more than you could take? 'Cause this is a helluva lot worse."

"I'm ready."

The words were out of my mouth before I could stop them. What the hell was going on? Had he gone out and killed someone? Upped the tension level to get my attention? He seemed too gentle. His hand on mine was negligible.

"Is that what it is, Derek—a dead body?" My voice was shrill in the morning's quiet.

He shook his head, putting a finger to his lips. As the light sharpened and I began to see better, he led me to his sculpture—or whatever the hell it was—the one farthest from the pathway. Up close, his sculptures were not so different from the shopping carts I'd photographed all those years ago. Hundreds of found objects were attached to each base; it was kind of like Stonehenge with clutter.

"I got another flashlight around," he said, hunting through a pile of objects left on the shore. He came up with one and tossed it. "Now, position the light there," he said, pointing toward one side of the piece.

I pointed the light toward the spot he'd indicated and for a minute I only saw a doll's head. Its curly blonde hair and staring blue eyes gave me a start though.

"Oh man, if a doll's head freaks you out, you'd better go home," Derek said, looking at the beam of light and dancing in glee. "You talk a good game, but you're a girl at heart."

"I was startled."

Not wanting to be called a girl, I braced myself and looked again. Below the doll's head were several indescribable objects. Teeth? I'd started to speak when he grabbed my arm again, moving it to the right. The light shone on two hands and two feet, all four fastened to the structure with huge iron nails. I gasped.

"What the fuck, Derek—is this for real?"

Of course, they couldn't be genuine. This had to be a bad joke. Derek had found a life-sized doll or mannequin and amputated the hands and feet. It had to be that.

But he was nodding. "And it shouldn't be any time at all before the head washes in." Derek was partly proud but partly something else. Maybe terrified. "I found all four of 'em on the beach night before last. They were scattered around but easy enough to find. Took me another half-day to get the nails and mount them. I never hung pieces like this before. Had to go out to Home Depot in Harper Woods and get these special nails."

I shivered at Derek's practicality—going to Home Depot to finish his grisly task. Probably by bus. Oh, he couldn't be right in the head to be this casual about it. But still my questions came.

"What about the torso?" I started to walk closer.

"Might want to stand back, Violet. Awful smell. I may have to throw bleach or vinegar on 'em if it doesn't go away."

I backed up, noticing it then myself.

"Rest will wash up too, I bet. Probably take a little longer. Heavier body parts." He paused a minute. "Although you never can tell—a freighter might push the torso or head upstream. They could've gotten caught on a rock or a tree limb too. It's unpredictable. Neighbor of ours, out walking alone, fell in a couple years ago up in the Pointes and they never found his body. Shaped like a saucer up there—once it turns into a lake. Easy to slip in. Impossible to climb out."

"I didn't know bad shit ever happened in the Pointes."

He smiled appreciatively. Nobody ever minded a dig at the Grosse Pointes.

"How did they know that's what happened to your neighbor? Maybe he got into his car and drove north. Escaping from his wife perhaps." *Like my father had.*

I continued to talk, but my eyes were glued to the crucified feet. They were big feet with nails needing trimming, and it looked like a corn on one toe. Feet were damned ugly; why would anyone become a podiatrist or want to give pedicures? Nature didn't put feet so far away from the eyes, nose, and mouth by accident.

Despite what was sitting in front of us, Derek continued with his story. "Nah—he wouldn't have left his dog behind. The dog was still sitting there when the cops went to the lake to look for him. Damned dog ran back to the same place whenever the door opened after that. Learned how to jump the fence in their yard after a few weeks. Eventually they put him down. His grief was awesome." Derek smiled slightly. "Guy's wife though, she married a man down the street the next year. Makes you wonder." He laughed again. "So do you want to take pictures—when the sun comes up?"

"You don't think this is the end of it, do you? That you can keep these—appendages for yourself? You have to report this, Derek. Or have you already?"

The hands were better cared for than the feet, I noticed next. Each nail was cut squarely—like the guy had trimmed his nails moments before. Or someone gave him a manicure. Of course, people see your hands all the time and are more likely to be able to identify them. This guy cared about his hands—or the murderer had cared about what they gave away about the victim and hacked them off. Or maybe he'd been stuffed in a small place before he was dumped. A space so small, he'd have to have been dismembered to fit. I'd never realized my mind could work this way—putting together a possible story. Maybe I was not just about pictures.

"I know, I know. I gotta call the cops, but I thought you might want a picture first. I promised you a nasty find, right? If I have to give 'em up, at least I'll have a picture of it. Maybe just another day or two." He seemed tranquil in his decision—like he'd kept a bargain. "Wasn't this what you had in mind?"

Was it? I stood silent for a minute, considering the situation, slowly pulling out my camera and taking a look. "I'd like to wait a bit. Got a few minutes?" It was all too ludicrous—the two of us standing in front of this installation. Both of us with a cell phone and not using it to call the cops. Both of us selfish the way artists are selfish.

"I'm in no hurry." He sat down on a camp chair and pulled out a crumpled pack of Salems, holding it out. "It's up to you if you want to risk being around here when the sun's up. Soon as someone catches sight of this, there's gonna be bedlam here."

I waved away his offer of nicotine. "Is smoking good for your asthma?"

Damn, when did I start lecturing people on their health?

"Only smoke one or two a day."

"You'd better call the cops this morning. What you're doing here has got to be some kind of crime. Withholding evidence, at the very least." I looked up at the hands and feet again. "And tampering with it, Derek. You probably destroyed some valuable forensic material hanging those body parts up like that."

The nails or whatever it was he'd pounded through the hands and feet must be the biggest Home Depot carried. Jesus nails.

"They'll take them down soon as I call, Vi. The cops will. How would you like them to mess with your work?" He lighted the cigarette. "I think of them as mine. Had to swim fifty feet out into that pisspot of a river to grab the second foot. It was about to float out of reach when I grabbed it. And if the smell seems bad now, well, it was much worse back then."

"Well, sure they'll take them away," I said, fanning the smoke. "It'll help them to identify the victim. They can probably match up a weapon with the cut marks on the limbs. Must be a lot of other evidence."

I'd learned all of this from television, of course. And maybe a bit of it from Bill. I wondered if semi-knowledgeable citizens made the job of the police easier or more difficult.

"I'll have to call them if you don't."

"Go ahead," he said. "But if you're gonna tattle, don't take a picture."

"Why? Taking a picture won't hurt your work. You said you wanted one yourself."

"Why should you get to do your art if I can't do mine? Why should you get to use my hard work, my find? You wouldn't know about any of this if I hadn't called you." He stubbed his cigarette out. "They'll find the rest of him soon enough. Then they'll ID him. If not, I'll call in a few days."

"You don't know that. The rest of him might've been dragged out into the Great Lakes." I thought about it for a minute. "I bet he's decapitated too. If hands and feet are used to identify a body, heads would be considerably more important with teeth and recognizable features."

I walked over to the sculpture again. No rings: nothing special on the hands and feet. Or at least not from what I could see in the half-light. Though feet were never pretty, remove them from a body and they became grotesque.

There was a considerable amount of dried blood on the ankles; it looked like the job had been inexpert. Or maybe the tool used hadn't been heavy-duty enough. At some point, the murderer began to hack and saw away at them. The skin color was impossible to assign. Greenish-grayish; he could be white, black, Asian, Hispanic. Who could tell? No telling what the river water would do to skin color.

"Probably there's not a person in the world I could identify by their feet. Maybe a few by hands though." I said this more to myself, almost forgetting Derek behind me.

"I think I'd know my mom's feet," Derek said, stubbing out his cigarette. "She hardly ever wears shoes inside." He walked around his piece, admiring it again. "Her toes kind of point up—like some kind of leprechaun." There was an affection in his voice I envied.

I wondered if I'd know Bunny's hands or feet. Not unless they were clad in orthopedic shoes.

"Well, you can't take a picture if you're going to call the police today," he repeated.

I started to raise the camera, and he made a lunge, nearly knocking it out of my hands. "Are you going to call?"

I shook my head. "Hey, let me use a couple of those lanterns, will you?"

I angled them to provide some oblique illumination, wanting those iron nails to show up, wanting them highlighted. Once again, I wished I'd brought a better camera along. I gave some thought to setting up a sort of tripod; Derek probably had something I could use. But I certainly couldn't set up the Deardorff or any larger camera.

There was no time and it'd bring too quick a response if someone saw me trooping through the park with it.

I started snapping pictures from far enough away to get the whole sculpture in, closing in on it slowly. The close-ups were amazing. Maybe I had a future as a crime-scene photographer.

CHAPTER 16

"Be daring, be different, be impractical, be anything that will assert integrity of purpose and imaginative vision against the play-it-safers, the creatures of the commonplace, the slaves of the ordinary."

Sir Cecil Beaton

"VIOLET, IT'S ME. Got something to show you."

It was Diogenes—later that morning. "First promise me it's not a dead body. Or any part of one."

The image of those hands and feet with the huge iron nails piercing the flesh was more unsettling by the hour. Apparently, I had limits after all. And excised body parts might be it. Maybe the memory would be less chilling once I was done developing the film. Surely, it would make them seem more ordinary. I could file the pictures away and forget about it, because let's face it, what could I do with them? But I was going to finish what I'd started—like it or not. These photos would be a test of my skills, of whether I had any.

"Now that you mention it…" Di laughed heartily, and I yanked the phone away from my ear, grimacing. "I do have one or two."

"Are you serious?"

"The bodies in question have been dead a long time. Besides, I thought dead bodies were your new interest. I expected kisses all around." He made the appropriate sounds.

"Kiss, kiss, yourself. Is it bones? A skeleton?"

He wouldn't say.

"Sure, I'll take a look," I finally agreed. "Do you want me to drive to your place?"

I wanted to get to work on the extremities photos, and Di lived out near Ann Arbor. Driving out there would eat up the whole day.

"Nah, I'll come over later if you're gonna be around. Maybe you can cook me a meal. We'll call it a dinner date."

"Like you'd want to eat anything I could cook. Don't you have to work today? Oh, right, it's Sunday." The B team took over in Di's kitchen on Sundays. "Will Alberto be joining us?"

"He makes his weekly trek to his mother's kitchen for empanadas on Sundays. Apparently, I don't have her touch."

We agreed on a time and I hung up, starting for the darkroom. The phone rang again. It was Derek Olsen.

"The guy's head washed onto the beach about ten o'clock last night. I ran down as soon as I saw the lights and heard the ruckus. But it was too late. Someone had already called the cops. Three squad cars pulled up a few minute after I arrived. Not a scene I'd want to see again."

"I'd have thought you'd be ready to put it right up with the hands."

The thought of it was repulsive, like those heads on pikes in old gladiator movies. There was no beauty in mutilated bodies; the extremities on Derek's sculpture settled it. Bodies had to be intact and cared for. Bill made them art. Or my camera did.

"I'm not talking about the head being sickening," Derek said, chuckling. "I'm talking about the crowds. People were barfin' right and left. That's what I meant."

"The head washed onto the shore?" I pictured it coming in like a bowling ball, but could that be right?

"Nah. Got caught on a floating tree limb. Guy had long hair and it'd tangled around the limb—knotted tight. Wish I'd gotten to the scene first." Derek's teeth were chattering like little maracas. "It was certainly el stinko along that piece of shoreline. Between the one thing and the other."

I kept picturing the head nailed to Derek's sculpture and swallowed hard. "What did he look like—other than the long hair?"

"Looked kind of Asian, but maybe it was bloat. Youngish, maybe late twenties, full-faced but clean-shaven. Weird greenish-gray color—like the feet. Couldn't get close enough after the first minute or two to see good. It was dark. No stars nor moon."

"Did you tell the cops about the hands and feet?" It would've been the perfect time.

"I thought about telling 'em. Went back to my usual spot, sat on a rock, and gave it some thought. Guess I'll probably have to tell them soon. Some dude will see the fuckers hangin' there and call it in." He sounded morose. "I could take them down, save it for later. Rehang it all when the hullabaloo dies down."

Hullabaloo? "I think you'd better get to the cops first. The longer you wait, the worse it'll look."

This guy seemed to have no idea he was going to be suspect #1.

I could picture the cops thinking he'd killed the guy so he could hang the hands and feet. Like Jesus. Or like Ed Gein, who'd killed women in Wisconsin to make costumes from their skins, masks from their faces.

And my tenuous involvement with Derek and his shenanigans might look like more than it was. This kid was trouble—I'd ignored the signs. And now he was starting to get to me emotionally. What if the cops thought he'd killed for his art? Or mine? I remembered my last encounter with the Detroit police—they immediately saw me as a threat. A marginal person who might do something just like this. And how the hell would they see him? Derek in jail was a thought that made my stomach hurt.

Derek sighed heavily. "Maybe I will. I'm home for lunch today, but when I get back down there I'll go over to the harbormaster's office."

"Right in the middle of this…hullabaloo…you went home for lunch?" He was completely nuts.

"Promised my mom. She made shrimp salad. And the big shrimp, not the bitty bay kind. With walnuts." He hung up after saying, "But I'll call it in or find a cop on the island before the day's out."

Shrimp salad. I hung up too, doubting he'd call anyone or go anywhere. Once again, I headed for the darkroom. The phone rang again. It was Ted Ernst, the gallery owner.

"Look, a new issue occurred to me last night." He paused. "Well, that's not exactly true. I was having dinner with my attorney, and she raised a question we hadn't considered."

"About the exhibit?"

I was on pins and needles now. Would these alarming calls never stop? I shuffled through the kitchen drawer to see if I had any grass. Zero.

"Right. She told me we need to get your undertaker friend to agree in writing he won't make any financial demands. You'll have to get him to sign a contract spelling it out." He paused. "If you want to go forward with this show, that is."

"You don't know Bill…" I started to say. "He'd never…"

"No, I don't know Bill. Which is why I have to protect myself." Ted cleared his throat. "And you too. We both need protection."

I took a deep breath. "Are you certain you can sell these pictures, Ted? I mean I hate to bring this up with him if it's not going to even be an issue." I moved the phone to my other ear. "I'm sure he's never once thought about making money from my photos. He's not like—"

"Nobody's 'like that' until the chance to be 'like that' comes up. Look, I can't take risks if I'm gonna to spend money on advertising and go for a classy opening." Not for the first time, it occurred to me that people who used the word "classy" seldom were. "And yes, I do think money will change hands," Ted went on. "A guy in New York's interested already. A little gallery in Hell's Kitchen—but an up-and-coming one. And my attorney brought up the possibility of a book deal. She has connections with Random House. Had you thought about a book?"

Shit. I hadn't thought about a book. Well, maybe a catalog like the ones the better galleries put out, but a book? I'd have to ask Bill to sign the contract, but maybe not yet. Maybe I could take a few more photographs first.

"I'm on thin ice with him already, Ted. If I bring this contract up, it might be the end of—of his involvement."

And Bill's involvement was the only way to get the photos. It wasn't like a million morticians were ready to let people photograph their work. And certainly none of them prepared bodies the way Bill did. It came back to his special touch. I was so close now, so close to a degree of success. Was it wrong to value it so highly? My hands balled up at the thought of it.

"How many finished pieces do you have?"

"Just five. And one of them is pretty dicey. I wasn't supposed to take the picture and the family certainly didn't sign off on it." I didn't tell Ted it was the famous rap star that was iffy.

"Five, huh? Still time, I guess. But you'll have to have him sign the papers eventually. I'll have them drawn up and you can wait for the right minute. Maybe after a particularly good..."

"Don't even say it."

Don't say it because that part of our relationship had pretty much come to a halt. I wondered if married couples who worked together suffered a fall-off of interest in the bedroom. I mean how much time can you spend together without growing bored? Except, I wasn't bored at all. Why wasn't I? Usually I was long gone by now. And, in my heart, I knew it wasn't because of the access to Bill's loved ones.

I couldn't get my mind off Derek Olsen either, wondering if he'd kept his promise and called the cops. I picked up the phone two or three times but was unable to decide whether to call Derek or the police. Eventually I returned to the darkroom and finished the morning's shoot.

When I saw my work, I had to sit down. The hands and feet in the early morning gray had a medieval look, which was almost elegant. They looked less waxy than I'd expected: more real. Derek's crazy-ass concrete hulk made an effective background, looking like stone as it did. Like a cool arty graveyard near the water. Like a Greek or Roman cemetery.

Di arrived a few minutes early, his arms full of food and what looked like a library book. "Let me get dinner started and then we can talk," he said, heading for the kitchen.

I watched mutely as he prepared an elaborate marinade and dumped a piece of fish into it.

"Damn, got any shallots?" he asked, hunting in his netted bag.

"Maybe—what are they?" I began to hunt through the jars.

He shook his head and went forward without them. "Won't be the same though."

"I'll never know the difference."

"Sadly, that's probably true."

Looking for soap and finding none, he used dish detergent to wash his hands. Holding the plastic bottle up to the light, he said, "This looks like it's been here since the W administration. Look at the price! Ever wash dishes? You stand at the sink and eat food out of a carton, don't you?" I shrugged. "Okay, enough with the insults. Let's take a look at the book now. I picked it up at the DPL." I must have looked blankly at him because he continued, "Detroit Public Library. That big building across from the Institute of Art? On Woodward. Santa Parade starts there?"

"I know, I know. You ran the letters together and threw me off. DPL. Right."

I sat down next to him on the sofa and he opened the book. I looked at the title: *The Wisconsin Death Trip.*

"I remembered it yesterday afternoon. Hadn't thought of the book in years." He flipped over a few pages. "See, it was published way back in seventy-three. I was like twelve when I came across it and immediately got off on it. Intrigued might be a better word."

He continued turning pages, and suddenly my interest rose when I saw a photograph of a horse with a ghostly mane nearly enveloping its head. A few pages later a series of photographs of dead infants caught my attention.

"Jeez. Are you going to explain what this is?" I asked, staring at a picture of twin babies in matching caskets.

More ghostly babies turned up on the following pages, and groups of people with faces circled or enlarged above the group shot. Along with the photos, hundreds of newspaper items about inexplicable activities in that area filled the book. Stories about houses burning down, incest, rapes, suicides, cross-dressing, acts of violence against strangers and friends, obscene letters, insanity hearings, and deaths: so many deaths.

"I'll leave the book with you, but the story is the people who lived in this part of Wisconsin went crazy in the late eighteen hundreds. These pictures were almost all taken by the town photographer." Diogenes smiled. "So you're not the first one to take pictures of the dead."

"But what started this? This death trip?"

"The theory is that an outbreak of financial failures, along with the deaths of dozens of children from influenza and typhoid, sparked mass hysteria. Lesy, the author, hypothesizes that when large numbers of children die before their parents, a sort of insanity can take hold. Very Freudian, our Michael Lesy." He turned a few pages. "Look at these faces. Don't most of them look distressed or insane?"

He'd turned to a photograph of a woman wearing a large hat draped in snakes. On the next page, a girl tossed a bouquet into a lake.

"Try reading a newspaper with stories like this all the time," he said, pointing to article after article of financial failure, death, fires, and violence. "And because the deaths came so quickly, these small Wisconsin towns became places of perpetual mourning. Death rituals became their life." He paused. "The sense of doom must've been overwhelming."

"Kind of like now in Detroit, right? Or even in the world as a whole-especially in black communities. How did he do it? I can't imagine taking pictures of dead children day after day. Or the families mourning them." I paused. "Hey, you're not equating me with this, I hope?" Despite myself I kept turning the pages. "I'd never photograph dead children for a profit—or for art. Is that how you see me?"

"What if Bill had first asked you to take a photograph of a child instead of the soccer player?"

"Rugby." I shook my head, almost positive I'd have refused. "I may have taken a picture for his family, but never would have imagined making it a project." I hoped this was true. "I couldn't do it. Not without going mad."

"Of course not. I remembered the book and thought you might get a kick out of finding yourself in good company. There's a documentary about it too."

"One guy took all of these photos?"

"Charles Van Schaick, the town photographer. Took thousands of pictures between the years 1890 and 1910. He got paid to take pictures so he did. Like the newspaper writer got paid for his articles. I wonder if both men went nuts before it was over."

"The photographs don't seem particularly artistic, but they're certainly competent—given the time especially." I looked at another photo—four men standing in front of four deer heads. "Clearly he wasn't planning on mounting a show."

Di chuckled obligingly. "Maybe he knew his limits."

"So what am I to take away from this, Di? What lesson should I learn?"

"I'm concerned you're too invested in death. Like the good people of Wisconsin, you're becoming obsessed. On a death trip of your own."

"Like Charles Van Schaick?"

"No. Van Schaick was recording events like any town photographer—it was his job. The goings-on in his town happened to be about death over those years. I doubt he sought it out."

"I'm doing it as an artist. I know that sounds snotty or arrogant, but..."

"Okay. That's my sermon for the day." Di got up and went into the kitchen. "Got a grill pan?"

"What do you think?" In a few minutes, I smelled fish and limes and heard the sound of chopping, but I was lost in the book.

CHAPTER 17

Detroit News: Detroit firefighter Peter Oberon died last night from injuries received while he was on duty at a hotel fire six weeks ago. Oberon, age 34, was a thirteen-year veteran of Ladder 14 and had been twice commended for valor in his years of service to the City. Oberon was a second-generation firefighter. Memorial donations can be made to the Detroit Children's Hospital Burn Center.

(August 2011)

"**M**ISS HART?"

I nodded, looking warily into my hallway at a man wearing a black linen jacket, an expensive-looking striped tie, and a crisp white shirt despite the summer heat. He didn't look like the sort of guy who'd be up to no good but you never knew.

"Joe Saad."

I took his hand.

"I'm an inspector with the Detroit Police Department." He flashed a badge in my face.

I smiled, trying for one engaging enough to win him over. Unfortunately, Inspector Saad continued to look grim, immune to smiles.

"Yes?" Was I supposed to know why he was here? Of course, I did. There was one chance in a thousand it was something other than those body parts that brought him here. Had I paid my delinquent parking fines? When had I last contributed to the Police Athletic League? Did cops still have Policemen's Balls?

"We're investigating a crime that took place on Belle Isle," he said, dashing any hope.

From his tone, I got the impression he already knew exactly what I had to say, knew the color of my underwear, in fact. Derek had apparently found it necessary to involve me in his stunt. I might already be a "person of interest" or "a woman helping the police with their investigation"—two of the euphemisms used in the newspaper when the police were looking at the person as a serious suspect.

I wondered what Derek had told them—what kind of crazed explanation he'd come up with—because I didn't see how I could rightly enter into a discussion of what actually took place. I hadn't been around when Derek made his discovery, when he carted the hands and feet off to his site, when he hung them, when he drove out to Home Depot, when he hammered those nails into the sodden flesh. Had Derek called the cops or had he'd been found out—perhaps by a shocked passerby? The island had probably overflowed with cops all night. Once the head rolled onto the beach, an intensive search would've been mounted at once. It was possible the cops saw me as an agitator, maybe the one initiating Derek's actions. Taking advantage of a lonely and disturbed guy.

"Yes?" I repeated. The only safe response. Better to wait him out, hoping his interest in me was minimal, that I might only be needed to verify dates and times.

Silence. So he was playing the same game?

Then, "I'm waiting for Inspector Bates to arrive before we go any further." He looked toward the door. "Not much parking available on your street today. She's circling the block."

"There's an open house today for realtors. Usually you can pull right up."

The row of "For Sale" signs on my block *was* dispiriting. It was a popular neighborhood for laid-off auto workers; life had never gone well for the residents of this suburb. There was never a nineties boom, which was why I could afford to rent here.

"Well, it's a losing cause," he observed. "I've had my house on the market for eighteen months. In the last two months, only one fellow stopped by and it turned out he had the wrong address."

Was this chitchat meant to throw me off? I was almost relieved to hear footsteps on the stairs. Saad opened the door himself, apparently taking over hosting duties for the time being.

"This is Inspector Bates, Miss Hart."

A tall, athletic-looking African-American woman wearing a beige pants suit with a green and brown silk scarf stepped into the room, smiled briefly, and pulled out a notebook. So I'd be at the mercy of Inspector Saad. The setup seemed pretty sexist. Had they ever considered I might have greater rapport with a woman? That I might more easily confide in a representative of my own sex? I wouldn't, of course, but how could they know it?

I waved them over to the sofa, sitting down in the chair across from them. Inspector Bates was ready for work, pen in hand, but Joe Saad roamed the room. He'd walked through my gallery of masks with barely a glance, but various items in my living room seemed to hold his interest: a Diane Arbus photography book on the coffee table, the current issue of *EW*, an old White Stripes CD, a quarter he found on the rug and pocketed. I was grateful *Wisconsin Death Trip* was stowed under my bedside table. Detective Saad liked the CD well enough to walk over to the shelf and examine my collection. He stooped down and pulled out a Detroit Cobras CD. And another from Guitar Slim.

"Pretty eclectic tastes." He blew off the dust without comment and set them down.

I shook my head, ready to disabuse him of this idea. "Clients give me CDs. I photograph recording artists for local record labels from time to time. They always throw a handful of demos at me when I leave. Most I've never played." Actually, I had a bad tendency to play the same music over and over again. I'd made no changes on my iPod in years.

Saad nodded, seemingly bored with the subject he'd raised. "We're hoping you can help us with our investigation, Miss Hart."

He said it like *I'd* been the one doing the dallying, chatting about superfluous topics, and I found his mannerisms and his interrogation method annoying. But I nodded and he resumed his pacing.

"You're a professional photographer, right? That's what you told me. Been doing it since?"

"Since college."

"Local school?"

"I went to school at the Art Institute of Chicago after a year or two here at CCS. College for Creative Studies. Or Center back then," I clarified when he looked puzzled. "The Art Institute in Chicago has an art school associated with it."

He nodded. "And how long ago are we talking about?"

"I'm thirty-nine if that's what you're asking."

"Family live in the area?" He gestured outside.

"There's my mother. She lives in Pleasant Ridge. A waitress."

"Father dead?"

"Dead to me." When I saw the look on his face, I amended it.

"I offended him as an infant and he never got past it. Hal Hart: deadbeat dad," I said, anticipating his next question. "An itinerant trumpet player, last I heard—a long time ago now."

He nodded like he'd heard it all before. "Ever been in trouble, Miss Hart? With the law, I mean."

I shook my head. Didn't cops run names in Detroit?

"How long have you lived at this address?"

"Around six years."

Was six years right? Well, what did it matter anyway? But he was looking around again. I hoped a tour of the premises was not on his calendar. The mirror over my bed might lead him to a wrong conclusion.

"All right," Inspector Saad said, settling into his real agenda. "Derek Olsen called the station yesterday and told the desk sergeant about the hands and feet he had hanging up on a crucifix on Belle Isle. Olsen's a friend of yours, right?"

"More like an acquaintance. And it's not a crucifix; he's an artist. It's installation art."

"So he told the sergeant," Saad said, nodding. "We went over to his 'sculpture garden' lickety-split as you might expect. And it turned out to be one of those things you hadda see to believe. Almost worse than the head found earlier that day." He sank onto the sofa. "It takes quite a bit to get the full attention of Detroit cops, but Derek's artwork did the trick."

He looked over at the female inspector, and she nodded her agreement.

"Didn't you think the smell was particularly loathsome? I mean the head was bad enough, but those hands and feet…" He stopped and shook his head, remembering.

Could've been talking to either of us so I didn't say a word. No telling what might raise red flags.

He continued. "Submerged bodies tend to stink. Those extremities weren't the only objects of interest on Olsen's sculptures." He looked over to Officer Bates again and smiled. "I think Jimmy Hoffa might've been part of the first piece. Did you recognize those teeth?"

Officer Bates laughed obligingly, but I maintained a stony pose, shooting the female a sharp look. What kind of routine did they have going? Did they always work together and use this strategy or did Bates get to be first chair on a rotating basis?

"No, seriously," Saad continued, "Olsen had objects hanging there that looked like they came from any number of crime scenes." He paused. "Did you see the dog's jaw, for Pete's sake?" He waited for a response and when it didn't come, continued. "Someone forgot to tell Derek art doesn't take precedence over the integrity of a crime scene. We could charge him with a felony for a stunt like this one. Even a nitwit knows floating body parts have to be of interest to law enforcement." He shook his head. "Or is he nuts? Let me in on it. Bipolar?"

"I'm no expert in the field of mental illness, Detective. Artists tend to be a bit unusual."

"You unusual too?"

I shrugged. Would he ever get to it?

And he did. "Miss Hart, Mr. Olsen told us he summoned you down to Belle Isle when he first found the body parts. Is that correct?"

"Not exactly. He called and asked me to come down after he'd already hung them." Stop now, I commanded myself. Don't add a single detail.

"And why would he call you?" Saad cleared his throat. "Why would he call *you*, in particular, after finding body parts if you're just an acquaintance? Have a reputation around town for liking such things? You Derek's number one fan? Or did you hire him?" Saad had a slight smirk on his face. "Give him a mission to dig around? Or worse."

"We met a few weeks ago on Belle Isle. I told him I was a photographer and always looking for a good subject." I was watching the female officer out of the corner of my eye; she seemed satisfied with this explanation, her face smooth and untroubled.

Saad, on the other hand, rose and began pacing again. "Now why would he think hands and feet made a good subject? Why would he call *you* about that?"

How many times had he asked me that question now?

"I told him I was looking for an edgy subject." Was this so unusual for an artist?

"Edgy, huh? Asked him to call you if and when he found it— something edgy?"

I nodded.

"Did you tell him point-blank you were looking for a body?" He looked over at his colleague. "You know, I've always hated the word— edgy. Makes me think I'm not in on it, and I don't much like the feeling."

"I don't remember spelling out anything specific," I said, getting back to the question. My voice sounded shaky to my ears. I was getting worried Saad knew about the fetus, might even think we'd had a hand in illegal activity.

"I certainly didn't suggest he should come up with a body if that's what you mean." Or had I? It was growing murkier by the minute.

"So how did he first get the idea? That you were interested in dead bodies?"

"He saw me mistaking a geobag for a body on Belle Isle. Look," I said, standing up, "I'm a photographer and photographers tend to look for interesting material to take pictures of."

"Like what, for instance?"

Shit! Why had I gone down this road?

Before I could answer, he continued. "I'd like to see your recent photographs, Miss Hart. The ones you'd categorize as 'interesting' or better yet, 'edgy.' Maybe I'll be in on it then. Get what you're talking about."

I looked at him for a few seconds and then walked over to the file cabinet and took out my photos of a recent wedding, a Detroit Red Wing goalie in action, a sweet sixteen at Henry Ford Village.

"Now, you know we're not talking about this stuff," he said, tossing the photos aside. "Let's get down to the edgy photographs."

So I took out my photos of imploding buildings, thinking ironically that at last my building photos were going to be looked at. No dead bodies here.

He flipped through them, pausing once or twice. "I remember that apartment house from my childhood," he said, holding one up for Inspector Bates. "Oh, and this one disappeared in the last year or two. I investigated a suspicious death in the basement after a fire—the Halloween before last, I think." He handed them back. "Nice work. But this stuff's pretty tame—nothing I would categorize as edgy. Got any more? Maybe a few pictures of bodies?"

I doubted I'd ever use the word edgy again.

There was no way around it. I told him about Bill's business, about the rugby player, about the photos I'd taken since, only leaving out the part about the possible gallery show in Ferndale. The show made it look like I might be desperate, overly anxious to succeed at any cost. I took the finished shots from the file, and he looked at them, eyes wide.

"Well, if there's any power or glory in death, you two have found it. The way he dresses them…." He whistled and handed them to his partner. "I may need copies later. I don't see why I would, but you never know." I nodded, waiting for the woman to be done with them.

"So do you think Derek Olsen might've taken matters into his own hands and murdered a homeless guy lying on some park bench?" he said, after the prints were safely stowed. "Wanted to impress you, so he found what he thought you were looking for?" His eyes narrowed. "Maybe he was hoping to score?"

"I don't know Derek well, but he seems too gentle to kill anyone. Especially to impress someone. And me, I'm fifteen years older than him. Look, he's not interested in me sexually." I paused, adding, "I can sense stuff like that. Really, I can."

"Can you?"

I waited patiently for him to challenge this, but he returned to the main subject.

"So how did you find out about his *objets d'art*? That's the term, right?" He was looking over at Inspector Bates, who shrugged. Probably not an art major either.

"He called me down to the island the night after he found them."

"And you photographed his sculpture? The hands and feet hanging like a—I don't know what."

I sighed and walked over to the cabinet again and removed a contact sheet. I hadn't gotten to the final prints.

"Now I will definitely want copies of this group of pictures," he said, walking over to Inspector Bates. She rose and looked at them. A low whistle; I wasn't sure whose.

"Why mine? Don't you have a police photographer who took

pictures of the site?" Certainly there'd be one. The Detroit Police Department couldn't be that underfinanced.

"Your photographs were taken a day earlier if I understand you and Derek Olsen correctly?"

I nodded reluctantly. I saw his point.

"Knowing as much as you do about both corpses and photographs, you should be aware of how much could've changed in one day out in the elements. Might be all kinds of information on your photos that could help us. The rate of decay, for instance."

"Of course." I was resigned to it now. "You can have the sheet."

He nodded and Inspector Bates slipped them into an attaché.

"Anything else relevant to the case hiding in your cabinet?" He motioned to it. I shook my head. "And I think I should mention you had a duty to call the crime in yourself. It's against the law to not report a crime. Especially knowing what Derek Olsen is like. Knowing he was sitting on this stuff."

"I did tell him…"

He shook his head impatiently. "Not good enough. I'm sure this won't be our final interview, Miss Hart, but I have another meeting across town."

Inspector Bates got up and they headed for the door. "We'll have a statement for you to sign in a few days and Inspector Bates will scribble you a receipt for the photos." He opened the door and was down the steps in seconds.

Inspector Bates wrote a receipt, a rather casual acknowledgment of the confiscation of my work, and followed him out the door.

CHAPTER 18

News: The body of a 20-year-old Jackson youth, was discovered
Friday night near the Motown Casino by a man exiting the
premises. Wylie Edwards had been reported missing a day earlier
after authorities found his abandoned Ford truck at a truck stop on
I-94 near Belleville. It is believed that Edwards was killed and his
truck stolen as he drove home from his job at an auto body shop in
Dearborn the day before. The authorities are uncertain how or why
his body turned up in Detroit.

(August 2011)

TOO SHAKEN TO return to work, I called Derek's number several
times, but began to feel like a pedophile when his mother told me
he wasn't home for the third time.

"I'm sorry you're having trouble getting hold of him, Miss Hart.
He's usually down on the island about now." She paused and added,
"I'm sure Derek wouldn't mind me telling you that. He's talked about
you nonstop for the last few weeks. An artist, right? You're working
together on a project?"

There was enough hope in Mrs. Olsen's voice to make me droop.
The woman probably believed her son had found a friend, a partner,

and a female one at that.

I'd already decided not to go anywhere near Derek's sculpture or Belle Isle but assured Mrs. Olsen I knew its location. It was probably a bad idea to be calling him at all with the ease in which phone records were made available to the police. It might seem like I was a little too eager to get in touch with Derek should Inspector Saad look into it, which he was likely to do.

The phone rang and it was Bill. I must've sounded angry or surprised because he began throwing excuses out, the most compelling one being, "I've been up in Saginaw with my mother three times in the last week. She's been diagnosed with diabetes and they're having trouble getting her insulin straightened out."

"God, I'm sorry, Bill." I'd never met Mrs. Fontenel, who lived two hours north of Detroit. That I hadn't met her made me question his commitment to any future in our relationship. "That's terrible. What can I do? I could run a few errands for her. Or help you out here."

He didn't bother to respond, which was also pretty insulting. He probably thought me uncaring, too incompetent, too white. None of these sat well with me, especially after my interrogation.

"I've got someone here for you."

For a moment, I didn't get his meaning. "It should be tonight. Violet, are you listening?"

"Be right there."

Bill didn't sound as fidgety as he had lately, more like the more placid Bill of several months earlier. Maybe his mother's problems had worn him out.

I was surprised there was another body already. It'd only been three days since I took photos of the fireman. That one—the guy'd died a few weeks after being badly burned—had been a rough job for Bill.

Although the burns hadn't affected my photos since he was dressed, I could see the ruined flesh on his neck, arms, and hands.

Bill asked about it. "How did the Pete Oberon photos turn out?"

"Haven't gotten to them yet."

I didn't want to go into my current issues with Bill. It'd make me seem more deranged. He'd certainly find my relationship with a bipolar guy at the park incomprehensible, and be angrier still if he knew I was down there photographing body parts. And the visit from the cops—I certainly couldn't mention it. That'd probably be the end of both our business *and* personal relationships. He already thought me ghoulish, perhaps crass; this would push things over the line. These two ideas preoccupied me once again. Was it too late to rekindle our romance? We seemed to be drifting further and further apart. If Bill couldn't understand what I was trying to do, our relationship—hated the word but used it repeatedly—was doomed. Unless, that is, I put my project aside and returned to weddings, forgetting funerals.

"Wow. You rocked my world," Bill said. "I always picture you rushing home and developing the photos with the film still hot in your hands."

I was jolted back to the present. "That's what I prefer, but other jobs intervene. Like a bar mitzvah." I used the area's Jewish population shamelessly in my lies.

"Hey, a guy told me recently Jews are spending six figures on bar mitzvahs out in Bloomfield Hills," Bill said suddenly. "He said the host gave all the teenage guests iPads at one recently."

There was a bit of hypocrisy in Bill's comments. It was okay to spend a fortune on a funeral, but the rest of life's ceremonies were priced too high. I didn't say any of this, of course.

"This bar mitzvah wasn't about spending a lot of money."

I decided to foster good will with my invented description of a fictitious event. "It was an extremely religious family and the celebration after the ceremony was dignified. The cantor trained in Israel," I added, inspired. "Had an operatic voice. A distinguished rabbi flew in from a temple on Park Avenue to assist."

It sounded like a grand event even to me. I wished I'd been there instead of the places I'd been.

"Must've been hard to get many good shots at such a stuffy affair."

Why was he so interested? Was he playing me? Did he know?

"The family was only concerned with a record of the day—a commemoration of a religious occasion." Enough! Back to the important issue. "Should I come over right now?"

"Sooner rather than later."

"Anything I should know?" By know I meant, were there wounds or other issues that might affect my work? Over time, I'd learned to show up well-prepared if at all possible. Taking photographs in the same room had resolved a few of the lighting issues, but other problems occasionally flared up.

"Nah, he's pretty clean. Took a knife to the chest. Nothing the camera will pick up. You probably saw the item in the newspaper. A hijacking in Belleville? Just a kid."

"And they killed him over some car?"

"I guess there could have been extenuating circumstances." Bill sighed. "But I doubt it."

"And he's just a kid. Some poor kid in the wrong place."

"Nothing new in that, Violet. Aren't you getting used to it by now?"

"Do you, Bill? Do you get used to it?" Silence. "Okay, what are the clothes like? What you've dressed him in?"

I was hoping no uniform was involved. The fireman had been

buried in his dress uniform. But too many men in uniform would be dull—not that there was any way I could influence the burial dress. I'd already had one guy in military dress. A policeman might turn up eventually and I could hardly refuse his uniform. I hoped this guy hadn't been an Eagle Scout. It was disheartening—seeing young dead faces week after week. Have I said that enough? That it made me sick. That I had bad dreams about it. That I'd lost ten pounds since the project started. That the taste of bile was now a familiar one. That the feel, smell, and sight of dead bodies were familiar too. That my belief in the project was ebbing. And a twenty-year old. But babies in their cribs were being killed as gunshots went off mark. Block parties were turning into shootouts.

Was it like this in other cities? Did the body count rise daily? I hadn't wanted to be a photojournalist, but how could these pictures not make more of a statement than any article in a newspaper? Who was I kidding? And my original desire to have a variety of costumes was nauseating. Especially since I personally wanted to be wrapped naked in a biodegradable blanket and planted like a tulip bulb.

"He's looking pretty subdued. Parents wanted it." He paused. "Looks nice though. Handsome boy." His voice rose again. "Killed him to steal his damned Ford truck," he repeated.

"So how did he get downtown? Did they figure it out yet?"

"No idea. Maybe they dumped him into the back of his own truck and took him along for a night of gambling and drinking. I wonder if the casinos have cameras?"

"Next they took the truck back out to Belleville and ditched it? Seems like they were doing a tour of I-94." All of the cities Wylie Edwards had been to—dead or alive—were along the Interstate.

"I don't know. Guess the police will have to figure it out. You could have been down here by now. All this talking we're doing. See you when you get here. Hey, let's have dinner afterward," he said suddenly—as if he had just thought of it. Had he? "I'll make reservations at The Rattlesnake Club."

"Okay," I said, going dead in the feet. Bill never sprang for such an expensive meal. He wasn't cheap, but this was a $200 evening. Minimum. "I'll have to get gussied up, I guess."

"They'll be glad to have money coming from any kind of pocket on a Tuesday night in Detroit. Wear what you like."

The Rattlesnake Club? What did I have that was clean? I owned one or two outfits to wear to dressy or work-related affairs—almost uniforms. On a photographer, they looked innocuous, on a dinner companion, dull—unimaginative. I hated to shop and got most of the few clothes I bought online nowadays. More often than not, I wore clothing five to ten years old. Broken in.

As a kid, the few clothes I owned often arrived in cartons from distant relatives, so I learned not to care about clothes. The stuff in those boxes looked like they'd been worn by missionaries. Once I pulled a bright red dress with a full skirt out of a box—only to find the white collar irrevocably stained.

Bunny shook her head when she saw it, muttering, "Bitch." When she saw the look on my face, she added, "Never mind. We can take the collar off." But it didn't look right without the collar and I never wore it. Not once.

Nowadays, once in a while I took a peek in a resale shop a few miles away—one Bill had recommended. Perhaps I was perversely drawn to clothes with wear in them. The shop kept a rack of nicer dresses in the back—items rich people from Birmingham or Bloomfield Hills wore once or twice and passed on. Occasionally I found outfits with the tags still on them. I always wondered if the owner had died or was too lazy or too rich to bother returning it.

It was precisely such an outfit, purchased a year or so ago at Yesterday's Gone for a client's sixtieth birthday fete, that I pulled out of the closet: a silky black pants suit that fit nicely. Or had when I was a bit heftier. Four months of this venture and I was wasting away. The outfit begged for a first-rate necklace, but none of mine would work— all of them were funky or damaged. I rummaged through a drawer and came up with a rose made of ivory-like material, given to me as a parting gift at a wedding last year. I fastened it on a piece of lacy black ribbon left over from Christmas and tied it around my neck. Damn. I needed to buy new clothes, but I hadn't earned enough lately to afford a shopping spree. Lowering the stratum of resale shops I shopped in was in my near future.

Something told me I should look good tonight. Or at least look like I'd tried. I pulled my hair up and tied it with more of the ribbon, glanced in the mirror, and yanked it down. Who was I trying to impress? I nearly pulled the rose from my neck too, but eventually left it alone. I'd change after work.

Occasionally when I looked into a mirror, I'd see Bunny's mug or my grandmother's stern, near-sighted peer. If my father's face had looked back at me, I doubted I'd know it. When was the last time I had really looked at myself? Examined my face for flaws that might be remedied: dry skin, dark circles, a need for revision in my makeup's color palette. No wonder Bill was drifting away.

I shrugged, got my equipment together, and left.

WYLIE EDWARDS, "THE Jackson youth," as the newspaper described him, looked about sixteen. "His parents signed off on this?" I asked Bill before setting up. We stood side by side over the body for a minute or two, paralyzed by the look on his face. "God, he looks like he expected to die. He looks resigned." A shiver worked it way down my spine as I peered into his face. My throat closed. This damned assignment grew harder by the body.

Bill nodded. "Most black kids expect it down deep. In this town anyway." He shook his head. "Let's not talk about it now. Anyway, his folks asked to use a photograph in the service day after tomorrow if you can finish it in time." Looking a bit embarrassed, he added, "Well, actually that's part of the deal—you have to finish it in time. Hope it's okay I said you could do it."

"Actually it helps a little." I stepped back. "Boy, this is the hardest one yet."

We looked at each other. Would an even worse death turn up in his prep room before this was over? Bill was used to it, but my work raised his anxiety level too.

Bill sighed. "Both his folks work at the prison in Jackson so they're not the squeamish type. I have a printer standing by with a program."

"No problem. How come they're having the funeral in Detroit? Jackson's like two hours away."

"Mt. Elliot Cemetery's right down the road. They bought a plot there years ago. Never dreamt their kid'd be the one to use it first, I bet."

"Christ!"

"Exactly. Guess they moved to Jackson a few years ago to take jobs at the prison." He slid his arm under the boy and adjusted his jacket to lie flatter. I took my pictures.

"Imagine the dinner table discussions at the Edwards' house with a prison guard and a prison nurse holding forth," Bill said, an hour or so later when I was finished.

"Cherry Ames, Prison Nurse," I said, but of course, Bill didn't get it. Once in a while a girlfriend comes in handy for references, I guess. "The family business, you mean? Well, what do we talk about at dinner?" Was there ever a time when we'd talked about the usual topics—like movies, books, music?

"Let's find out. We can use a stiff drink or two."

I quickly changed and earned a nice smile for my efforts. Our hands were trembling as we walked hand in hand to the car. I could feel his; he could feel mine.

THE RATTLESNAKE CLUB sat on River Place, off the Detroit River. A hotel was a few hundred feet away and both were bordered by a few blocks of new luxury lofts and apartments, but you could spot trouble by the potholed roads snaking around it. There were one or two other retail concerns, but the area hadn't managed to shake off its recent past of empty warehouses and questionable river and street traffic. A river walk was slowly making its way up the river, but it hadn't reached here yet. It remained a tiny pocket of affluence.

The Rattlesnake Club put on its happy face though. The boldness of its location was matched by its insistence on serving expensive food and wine in a sophisticated setting. Our table was by a window. We hadn't said much on the short drive over and I was still feeling subdued.

"This is all original artwork," Bill whispered, breaking the silence. "A Jasper Johns, I think."

Yes, and what are we doing here, I thought—after where we'd been. Our last dinner out had been at Pegasus in Greektown, with the total bill well under $60. Neither of us were devoted foodies despite Bill's new portliness. Expensive restaurants made me nervous, perhaps because of my mother's profession. She'd worked at a few fancy places and disaster had always ensued. She could only pull off the demeanor required for so long.

We ordered drinks and watched the river traffic for a few minutes. "Maybe we should have sat on the terrace," Bill wondered aloud. "Nice night." We looked outside at a group of largely empty tables.

Well, it was a Tuesday in Detroit, for God's sake, and well after eight o'clock. Not a prime time for dining. "Nice? It's humid and we'd get eaten alive by mosquitoes within an hour."

Bill laughed, perking up. "You know, I can't think of a time we've ever spent together outdoors. Not a single instance. Can you?"

I thought for a minute. "We went to the Thanksgiving Parade last year. Remember sitting on the bleachers on Woodward Avenue?" I almost shivered at the memory. It had been about twenty degrees and snowing.

"We sat for about ten minutes before you spotted an open Coney Island and took off. Never did see Santa. Hey, and we were only there so you could take pictures. It was no outing. No fair counting it."

"There was no reason to shoot the whole parade. Santa's too generic to be interesting, and it was damned cold for November." I thought a minute. "I could have used footage from the past ten years and got away with it."

"Nope. Some of those floats were pretty year specific."

Here we were again, sparring and sticking our metaphorical tongues out.

We gave our orders to the waiter and sipped our drinks. I'd thought about mentioning Ted's ultimatum. I needed Bill to sign off on the fact the photographs were solely mine—or mine and Ted's. But it seemed like a bad time to bring the pictures up. Especially after spending the last hour with poor Wylie. Despite our mutual depression, this seemed to be a special night although I didn't know why. His birthday was in January. Mine, December.

When was the last time death hadn't propelled our conversation? We defaulted to it as a subject for endless discussion, but it was also driving us apart. I decided to put it on hold a little longer. This was an evening for finding less contentious subjects.

Bill brought it up anyway. "So how many photographs do you have by now? I lost track. Eight, nine?"

"Eight. Well, nine if I could see my way clear to using the one of Cajuan Grace, that rapper. Any chance of that happening?" It was my best photo—both in the final product and in its potential for generating public interest.

Bill shook his head. "Mentioned it again to his sister, Athena, a few days ago, told her you'd actually got one by me, but she said Mrs. Grace was adamant about exclusivity. It'd screw up their copyright for the book." He paused, adding, "We've gotten to know each other a little since his funeral. I remembered she was a nurse for an endocrinologist so I called her when my mother was diagnosed."

I fidgeted with my napkin. I hated to talk about illness. "Is diabetes that serious nowadays? I mean, don't most diabetics control the disease now without using a needle?"

I'd heard this somewhere, although coming out of my mouth now it sounded crass—like I wanted to downplay his mother's illness. A woman he'd never thought it necessary to introduce me to. There it was again.

"Sometimes it works out that way," Bill said, patient for once. "But the disease is still serious—a leading cause of death. It has implications for feet, eyes, the heart. A lot of organs can be affected by it." He took a bite of his salmon. "Sorry. I'm becoming a bit of an expert out of necessity, I'm afraid."

I looked at his plate. Salmon and steamed vegetables. "Bill, is it only your mother who's been sick?"

His eyelids fluttered and he shook his head. "Pre-diabetic. That's what the tests showed. All the sweating, weight gain, and drinking water had to have a cause. I was putting off finding out what." He dropped his napkin on the table. "When Mom was diagnosed, it fell into place. Sad to say, it took her sixty-two years to contract it. I have indications at thirty-eight."

"God, I'm sorry." I put my fork down, looking with no appetite at the bloody red steak on the plate.

"Hey, it's not a death sentence and it certainly doesn't mean *you* have to change what you eat. You're a fine, healthy specimen. All the running probably."

I must have still looked grim because he went on. "Athena, that's Cajuan Grace's sister, tells me if I'm careful I may never get it. My cholesterol count wasn't exactly great, nor the triglycerides. But this new regime will help. I was in a sorry state." He looked at me, his voice soft. "And you tried to tell me. I remember that, baby."

I couldn't believe he was finally giving me positive credit.

"Well it won't hurt me to make changes either. I've been more lucky than smart."

After our discussion, there was no way I could ask him to sign a paper promising to never demand money for his part in the project. I also got the feeling he wanted to say more but didn't. So we were quiet; the evening ended early. If he wasn't going to suggest sex, neither was I. Maybe sex didn't fall into the good for you column.

CHAPTER 19

"A creator needs only one enthusiast to justify him."

Man Ray

A DAY LATER, I was taking photographs of the new chef at a restaurant in Rochester. I had to carry on with these prosaic assignments if I wanted to eat, although I cut them down as much as I could. I mean how many ways can you photograph a chef? I was bringing no enthusiasm to the meat of my employment. Photographers did such work, and I'd probably never join the elite group who didn't have to. But my head wasn't in it, especially after Bill's news. How long had he waited before telling me? And why? Did he know I was scared to death of any sort of illness or did he think I wouldn't care? Or—did he not think about me at all?

Years of experience let me work on automatic mode at times, and this day was one of them. The cell rang as I was adjusting the lighting. Only a few people had my number. Well, a lot of people had been given the number over time, but I assumed it was none of them. Did people enter cell phone numbers they were given casually into their phonebook or contact list?

I picked up the phone, glanced at the number, saw it was Bill, but didn't pick up. Clients didn't take well to being made to wait while I answered my phone; it always affected the photograph. They got sulky, irritable, impatient. The guy today was already ill at ease, sitting stiffly on a stool in his restaurant's kitchen, looking like he'd never worn a chef's hat before. I smiled encouragingly and shot away.

He brightened noticeably when I mentioned Diogenes, trying to get him to relax.

"Sure, I know Di," he said. "Terrific chef. Don't know why he sticks it out in Detroit when any restaurant in four counties would have him." He looked around. "This one, for instance. They'd give me the boot for Diogenes Cortes any time."

His statement, dismissing Detroit as a destination for a great chef, didn't endear him to me. I was used to Detroit getting kicked in the butt, but it still made me angry and, on the spot, decided against using a shot showing this guy to his best advantage. His jutting forehead, peeking out from under his hat, would take center stage. I always expected creative types to be less prejudiced than normal folks and when they weren't it made me especially angry.

I finished half an hour later, after taking a few shots of the dining room and several of his signature dishes. Was anyone else getting tired of food being arranged like miniature Eiffel Towers and drizzled with a green cilantro/basil sauce? Was any meal served without garlic "smashed" potatoes? My steak at the Rattlesnake Club had come imbued with these touches—charging extra for the sauce, in fact. What ever happened to sauce-less food? Was food spread out across a plate considered vulgar now? Did it have to have height to matter or did piling it up hide the scant amount?

The image of a spread-legged woman lying prone on a plate came into my head. Could I use this idea? Would such a photograph be more than amusing or kitschy?

The magazine running this particular story was more interested in photos than words, and I was lucky to have this assignment. *Hum* had guaranteed the use of at least three shots in the word-starved story. It'd be a nice credit to add to my resume and would probably spawn similar assignments. I hated *Hum* though. Years ago it'd been called *Detroit's Hum*, but when the U.S. car industry began to embarrass people with its rust, its dullness, its flagging sales, the magazine altered its name. *Hum* was only interested in the one-percent. It discussed, illustrated, and advertised what appealed to that group—its subscribers fantasizing they lived in Aspen or Beverly Hills or Palm Beach rather than outside Detroit.

I called Bill a few minutes after I finished. "Took long enough," he said.

I could hardly hear him over the traffic on Telegraph Road. "What?"

"Never mind. Do you know who was here?" He sounded out of breath. "Well, an hour ago now."

My heart sank. What was the title of that book by Kate Atkinson? *When Will There Be Good News?* "Who?"

"Inspector Saad." The name came out of his mouth like a hiss. "Violet, why didn't you tell me what was going on at dinner last night? You sat in the restaurant like all was good in Violet-land, and there you were smack in the middle of a murder investigation. Sometimes you plain scare me."

Hadn't someone else said those words to me recently?

"I'm only a character witness, I think. It's nothing to do with me." The traffic on Telegraph Road made telling a lie easier because I couldn't hear my own voice. "Not really."

"It didn't sound like Saad thought so. Flat out asked me if you'd ever suggested anything of a criminal nature—to procure, his words, not mine—these photos. He made me feel like one of those ghouls who dug up bodies for medical students in the Middle Ages. Had to show him the paperwork on the bodies you'd shot." He laughed humorlessly. "Shot with a camera, that is."

"Did he suggest I asked you to do something illegal?"

I was pacing back and forth in front of the restaurant. Me—a person of interest apparently. Several patrons exited, looking at me worriedly. I walked over to my car and got in, leaving the door open for air.

"Not specifically," Bill continued, "but the suggestion was there. Bodies besides the ones coming to me in the usual way. He'd read the police files on all the photos you'd taken and asked a lot of questions about the homicides."

Homicides? Which ones were homicides? I quickly flipped through my files. There'd be three: the boy dumped at the casino, the rapper, and the bartender at Slack's Shack. Cajuan Grace, the rapper, had been murdered in plain sight so he wouldn't count. Or was there another murder I was forgetting? Certainly they couldn't be counting the guy at the mall—Albert Flowers, was it? They'd arrested someone on the spot. Did they think I was using my wiles to get Bill or Derek, or the guy who killed Cajuan Grace, to murder men so I could photograph them? The other three deaths: the guy from England, the fireman, and the paraplegic who died from West Nile, weren't murders at all.

In Saad's mind, the body parts on Belle Isle might count as a fourth murder. Well, of course they did. And in this case, I was linked to the body or its parts before it was safely ensconced in a mortician's house.

It might look like my appetite for corpses was rapacious. Like I might go after men with a machete or chainsaw. "Did he seem satisfied with what you told him?"

"Who knows? He managed to twist it around whenever I opened my mouth." Bill sighed. "I don't think he *actually* believes you had anything to do with these deaths. But he does think you're strange. A kook. I could tell from his questions he thinks you're a magnet for trouble—someone who might ignite Derek Olsen." He paused. "You might want to back off taking photos of dead men till they close the book on the body parts. They sent divers in the river two days in a row to look for a torso but came up empty-handed."

Didn't anyone understand I couldn't "back off" this project—that it was now or never? I was closing in on September now with the show just a few months away. Of course, Bill didn't know about the show.

"He probably thinks Derek has the torso secreted away." Or did Saad think I had it? Or that I knew where it was? Why did the hands and feet turn up together? Had I ever asked Derek? Yes, he'd said he swam out to get the second foot. But it seemed unlikely the hands and foot were lying on the beach on Belle Isle in a heap—or spread in a row—unless someone wanted them found like that. Arranged them.

"How long do you think they'll stick with it? The investigation?"

Bill closed his eyes to think. "From my limited experience of handling the bodies of murder victims and from my years of watching endless TV crime dramas, I think they'll poke around for a few more days, maybe a week, and the case will go cold until new information turns up. Or new evidence. The Detroit Police Department has suffered huge cuts and it's not a high profile case despite its visceral appeal. If no one comes forward to identify the body parts, if no one puts in a missing person's report, it'll disappear from the front page." He paused. "For all the cops know someone could've dumped the parts off a freighter passing through Detroit. They could have floated over from Canada. Obviously they have no missing person report that matches up."

"It'd already moved back to a page eight story this morning."

He paused, spoke to someone else in the room, and came back on the line. "Detroit police resources are limited as I said. Unless the media makes it their business it'll probably die down quickly."

"I can only hope."

I TRIED DEREK again. This time his mother was out. Her perky voice on the machine begged me or anyone to leave a cheery message. Instead I did what I'd vowed not to do and drove down to Belle Isle again. The clouds overhead looked ominous, and the line of cars exiting the island was another warning of the coming storm. There were no boats on the river. Would Derek stick out a big storm here or run home?

He wasn't at his site. In fact, the site was only a remnant of its former self. The body parts were gone, of course, but other objects seemed to be missing too. I looked for the metal rocket—the hood ornament—from the car, but it'd disappeared. So too the dog's jaw and almost everything of interest. Even the doll's head had vanished.

"Looks like people have decided to have themselves a souvenir."

The voice had a discomforting familiarity. I turned around and saw Inspector Saad. "That's what happens when your artwork hits the front page and is easily carted off. I bet Tyree Guyton suffered the same fate over on Heidelberg Street." Instead of his slick suit and buffed shoes, Joe Saad had on khaki pants, a blue oxford shirt, and running shoes. I liked him better like this.

"Did you follow me?"

He shook his head. "Been down here all day with the harbormaster. He heads the police presence on the island."

"How many cops are stationed here anyway?"

He looked at me with renewed interest, and I could've kicked myself for asking such a pointed question.

"Depends. Six, ten, twenty. When the State takes it over that will probably change."

Was he being vague on purpose? "Have you found anything else? Learned anything new?"

"Only nasty stuff about you." He laughed on seeing my expression. "Guess that wasn't what you wanted to hear." He raised his eyes, watching the clouds race across the sky. I looked up too. "You must watch enough TV to know I can't share the kind of information…" His voice trailed off—either due to the wind or propriety.

"Were you going to say you couldn't share information with a suspect?"

The word "suspect" hung in the thick air.

He didn't answer, instead asked, "Do you know where Derek Olsen is, by the way? No one's seen him in the last twenty-four hours."

"Not even his mother." How long had it been since I spoke with the woman?

"Nope. But Derek doesn't always come home at night according to Mrs. Olsen. Has the occasional sleepover—probably when he's too strung-out to make it home, or perhaps when he gets lucky." He sighed. "I didn't see much sense in worrying her so I didn't push it."

"He probably freaked out when he saw all these people. Derek wouldn't like being the subject of such scrutiny. I don't know him well, but—" I looked around again. "If he sees what's happened here, he may never come back. His work would be his only reason to return and now it's ruined. Couldn't the cops stop it?"

But why would they? They probably saw Derek's work as a pile of junk—the work of a madman or murderer. I remembered how much respect I got from the cops on Belle Isle all those months ago.

Maybe he'd have to come back eventually though; where else would he be permitted to build structures on the shoreline. Because that's what he did. That was his personal art form. I understood this. It wouldn't be easy for him to change his medium now. Fuck with an artist and no telling what might happen to their work. It applied to me too. I'd heard of an artist whose studio burned down and he turned to writing novels, a more sustainable product, although a dubious choice in the current environment.

"Well, don't you take off," Inspector Saad said. "I'm sure we'll need more help before this mess is wrapped up. With Derek out of the action—even temporarily—you're our chief witness."

"Swell." I made a face. "Do you expect to wrap it up soon?"

I was looking for assurances that this would eventually end, and I could go back to my work. Not that I didn't appreciate the fact I'd gotten myself into this jam. But time was galloping by. Five photos to go, but I was sidelined till this case was solved. Maybe I'd have to solve it myself.

"I *always* expect to wrap a case up quickly," Saad said, starting back toward the road and his car. "Don't always get what I expect though." He turned around as he opened his car door. "Better get off this island, Miss Hart. There's a tornado warning in effect. Not the best place to sit one out."

We looked up at the sky simultaneously, noting the racing clouds, the strange color.

After he left, I looked around for a few minutes, wishing I had the proper camera with me. Nature seemed to be putting on a pretty good show and maybe a few nifty shots of a storm would diversify my portfolio, make me look like a harmless picture-taker instead of a lunatic. It was rare I didn't have my Canon along, but I hadn't expected to come here when I left the house. That idea occurred to me only after the call from Bill, when I needed to track down Derek and pin him to his structure if need be. I'd like to know exactly what he'd told Saad. Where the hell was he?

The park was being blasted by the winds from the coming storm; it looked pretty damned cool. Deserted plastic or paper picnic items and children's playthings were sailing across the sky like Dorothy's cow. A tablecloth hung from a tree limb, and several boats had broken away from their mooring at the Yacht Club and set sail. A table umbrella was inside out and looked ready to take flight. One or two park denizens were strolling around unconcerned and half-lit, but aside from them the place was deserted except for the stream of cars heading onto the mainland.

I was halfway to the car when I spotted Derek's geobag back in its old spot. He must have dragged it up there recently. On impulse, I walked across the field, covering my head to protect it from blowing debris. There was something odd about the bag. When I got closer, I saw what it was. Two legs and two arms poked out underneath, making it look like a giant turtle. Closer still, I recognized the outfit, especially the footwear—an untied pair of army boots. It was Derek underneath. Heart pounding, I crouched down and took his wrist. Nothing. He was already cold, rigid, silent. Why hadn't the intrepid detective found Derek? All of those cops roaming the island, looking for that torso, turning over every rock, but no one had turned this one? The irony of what I mistakenly thought was a body weeks before becoming one now was not lost on me despite my panic.

I slid back onto my heels and started bawling—wailing almost; nobody heard me over the wind. There was no way I could look at his death as unrelated to the course I'd set into motion. He'd paid the price for my ambition. I'd dragged him along with me like a human geobag. I thought of his mother's cheery voice on the phone, of how he'd tried to bring me a find worth photographing, of how he finally had. I cried until I knew I had to do something about it.

CHAPTER 20

Detroit Free Press: A man dressed in camouflage fatally shot and killed two people inside the Gratiot Avenue branch of Bank of Detroit today. It was the second deadly bank shooting in less than a week. The victims were Barbara Rousch, 53, from Eastpointe, a teller at the bank, and Ancil Battle, 28, of Indian Village, who worked for the bank as a loan officer. The gunman was apprehended by four police officers as he left the bank. (August 2011)

I T WAS INSPECTOR Bates, Saad's female partner, who interviewed me first—this time in a small room at the harbormaster's offices on the island. From what I managed to overhear, Saad was off on another assignment. It took Inspector Bates about thirty minutes to arrive. The lieutenant manning the office and I tried not to stare at each other. He must've been ordered not to engage me in any conversation because he seemed reluctant to say boo. I spent the time reviewing my activity over the last few weeks and came out smelling like the skunk I was.

I was soaking wet by the time I'd found a cop and dragged him over to Derek's body. The officer made sure he was dead, but left the rest of the spot untouched, putting a yellow crime scene strip around it. The strip blew away twice before he managed to secure it with a

rotted picnic bench and a tire iron and spare tire from his squad car.
Since Derek was still weighted down by the geobag, he probably wasn't
going anywhere; but the crime scene itself was victimized by the storm.
Any clues would certainly be washed or blown away.

I dried off my hair with another grungy towel the cop tossed me.
He also supplied me with coffee from the oldest pot I'd ever seen. It had
the burnt taste of Bunny's coffee, a concoction I'd first tried as a child.
It'd kept me from drinking coffee till college when I discovered it could
actually taste good.

"Probably don't wash the pot out often enough," the lieutenant
said, seeing my grimace.

I smiled and took a reassuring sip. The lieutenant poured himself
a cup and sat down in front of his computer screen. His coffee cup,
visible from my chair, featured a photo of a black kitten asleep in a
basket of colored wool. Had he inherited it from a cheerful woman?
Or maybe he was more secure in his masculinity than most men. He
turned around, found me watching him, and tossed over yesterday's
newspaper. The Tigers had lost to Cleveland, the problems in the
Middle East showed no sign of ending well or soon, housing starts
were down, as was the Dow, and there was another death in Detroit.
I tossed it aside, not bothering to read the story about the murder,
wondering if I'd photographed my last death.

The rest of the cops stationed on the island were out—scouring
the acres for clues or trying to cope with the weather. The storm was in
full force now, and I listened to the sounds of cracking tree branches,
fire sirens, a lonely foghorn. Alarm systems in cars went off regularly
too. The crackling of electrical lines was more menacing. What would
happen if the lights went out? Would I be required to sit here in the
dark? Had Derek been rescued from the underside of that bag yet? The

image of his frail body beneath such a weighty bag haunted me. If only I had never run into him that day weeks before, he'd still be alive. Or would he? Wouldn't finding those body parts have taken him in the same direction? I wasn't sure.

When she arrived, I saw Inspector Bates had taken on a completely different demeanor than with our earlier meeting. No more the placid female ceding to her dominant male partner. In fact, she looked irritated to be called down to the island, not offering me a cursory smile or greeting. It was all business and the officer with her, another woman, took on the steno duties, sitting right behind us.

We went over the circumstances recounted in my earlier interview with Saad a dozen times. I insisted again I hadn't encouraged Derek to scour the island for body parts, much less procure them through disreputable means. This bordered on truth. Finally, Bates moved on to today's events. Even to my ears, it sounded strange I'd hung around after speaking with Inspector Saad—even as the storm was kicking up. And, even more odd, that I'd managed to magically stumble upon Derek's body on an island this large when no one else had seen him.

"Well, it was the same spot where I first met him," I said for the tenth time. "I was worried and naturally I went back to the place since I knew he liked to sit there. He would drag a—"

"So you've said," Inspector Bates said, interrupting me. "Did it occur to you to tell Inspector Saad where Olsen might be found since you were ready to go right to it?"

"I didn't go looking for him—not exactly. I passed by the spot on my way to the car—after I'd given up. Sort of stumbled onto it."

"What was it you wanted from Derek today, in particular?"

"It seemed like a good idea to see how he was after Inspector Saad told me he was missing. And to make sure he wasn't going to pull some stunt and get us both into trouble again. I felt obligated to his mother. I knew she'd be worried…"

"And *did* he get you into trouble? Was that the problem?"

The questions went on and on.

Two hours later, Saad showed up and Bates gave him her seat, reassuming her earlier placidity, donning the facade like the familiar sweater you leave on the back of a chair.

I felt like kicking her in the shins, watching the intelligent face of minutes earlier turn bovine. But I turned my attention toward Saad instead.

"You know if I had anything to do with Derek's death, I wouldn't have run down a cop in the storm and led him to his body. I would've avoided the police. Avoided a situation like this. I would've headed home, putting as much distance between us as I could."

It was difficult to explain my actions, much less put the right spin on them. My words had never counted for so much before.

"I think if you murdered Derek, you'd have done exactly what you did," Saad said, shaking his wet coat out and hanging it up on a coat tree. "Run down a cop as quickly as possible. You saw me minutes earlier, unintentionally, of course, and once I could put you on the island at the right time, what choice did you have?" He shrugged as if I knew what he meant.

"What?" My tongue was thick and it felt like his words were coming at me through water. "What?" I repeated.

He sat down, using the same towel I'd used an hour or two earlier. "Well, it'd be useless for you to tell us you were elsewhere this afternoon once we'd run into each other. So why not look like the Good Samaritan and alert the cops?" He nodded to himself, satisfied with his scenario. "Knock Derek over the head with a fallen limb and then run for help."

"Is that how he died?"

"We don't know yet."

"Well, I didn't do it. No matter how it looks. I felt responsible for making sure he was okay, you know."

I knew a million people on TV crime shows, in novels, and in life had claimed this throughout the ages, but it was true. Surely some, like me, were telling the truth.

"I liked Derek. He was one of the few people who ever tried to help me." I was embarrassed to be saying this to a stranger. "Why would I kill him?"

"Maybe he was the only witness to what you were up to. You could've hired him to kill people, and later decided to get rid of him. Especially after you saw he wasn't going to keep his mouth shut. When you realized you'd picked the wrong guy to partner up with." Saad reared back in his chair and looked supremely satisfied. Each creak of the chair's base made me see red.

"You think I could handle a geobag? They must weigh a hundred pounds."

"I saw the camera equipment you tote around. What does that weigh?" He looked me up and down. "And you're a fairly tall girl. Muscular." He looked at my legs, my arms. I wasn't used to being assessed for my strength, and I flinched. "If Derek could haul one up from the shore, so could you."

"Woman," I said testily. "I'm a woman. I haven't been a girl in twenty years. Can I go now?" I added, getting up. "We've been through this till my head hurts."

"Yeah, I guess. Once we get information regarding how and when it happened from the coroner's office, we'll need to talk to you again."

He rose too. We both knocked a little water off his coat as we nudged by the coat tree. Saad peered out the window.

"About stopped out there." It was dark; most of the street lights were out.

"I guess no one would drive me back to my car? It's about a mile from here."

"Sure. We can take you back."

He motioned to a sergeant at the desk, who followed me out the door. We drove to my car in silence, both afraid to say a word.

I wasn't home more than twenty minutes when Bill called. "Know I said we should take a break from this wretched business, but I have another body." He laughed hollowly, dully. "Guess I felt obliged to call. Got me trained." He paused. "Besides, sooner this is over, the better. Weary of it as I am."

Despite extreme fatigue, I felt a shiver go down my spine. I'd been considering calling Bill, filling him in on Derek's death, but put that idea on hold.

Bill wouldn't be burying him; Derek was white and headed for a resting place in the suburbs. And he'd certainly be lying in the police morgue for days first, gone over by the entire staff probably. So Bill might not hear about Derek's murder and my part in it until the next morning when the papers got a hold of it—if I was lucky. I should tell him first, but once again I didn't do what I should. Was it because of my desire to add to my portfolio or my desire for Bill? To not tell him something he wouldn't like hearing.

"Be right down," I said, repeating the words I'd uttered so many times now. My energy level inched up a bit.

"I won't be here. I've got a dinner engagement with a client."

"Rattlesnake Club again?"

I wondered if he took clients there often. The staff seemed pretty familiar with him. How upscale had his business become? Or was it a woman?

"No. This dude wants Mexican. We're meeting at Evie's Tamales."

Evie's Tamales sat in the city's southwest corner—a good place to find mostly inauthentic Mexican restaurants, cheap and tasty, but slightly more authentic Mexican grocery stores, day laborers for the area's landscaping businesses, and a sampling of the city's most bona fide gangs, Bill grunted, and a few seconds later, hung up.

Ancil Battle, the dead loan officer, and I spent an hour or two alone, an unusual occurrence. If Bill couldn't stick around, he usually made sure one of his people was hovering over me. But today his personnel was tied up, and I had Ancil to myself.

I'd learned enough about the application of cosmetics to the "beloved" by now to make my own adjustments. I went for Bill's kit and touched up Ancil's lips a bit. They looked chalky and two small spots, probably errant cover-up, dotted the neck of his shirt. I managed to remove them and to get Ancil looking right. I doubted Bill had prepped this body. It seemed like a second-rate job. It was hard to say why, but it wasn't up to Bill's usual standards. The clothes were perfunctory, a gray suit with a pale peach shirt and tie. His shoes looked wrong for the suit, too square-toed. Ancil wouldn't be the star of my eventual show, but he'd have his place. His tiny moustache refused to lie flat, and I put a dab of hand moisturizer on it and brushed it. Being alone with his body, touching him with no one standing over me, I started to shake.

The vision of the other body I'd found a few hours ago at Belle Isle—Derek's—kept running through my head. What invasive procedures were going on with his frail body as I worked over this one? Whenever the image of his body, sticking out from under that bag like a turtle's, rushed back over me, I began to shake harder. But finally the work itself helped to steady my hands. I wondered what Mrs. Olsen was doing; how she was coping with his death. I thought of Derek's neighbor, the one who fell in the lake, and the dog who returned to the spot. Who was around to mourn Derek? I knew so little about him.

Ancil Battle was another guy in the wrong place at the wrong time. At the start of this project, I'd expected to photograph men who died because they were running drugs, in a gang, stealing cars, in a gunfight. But the majority had been defenseless men unfairly slain by disease or circumstance. Well, Bill and I would see they fared better than the average murder victim. Bodies didn't bother me per se, no. But the random and senseless accretion going on in Detroit did. I wonder how Mrs. Battle, if there was one, would feel if she saw me sharing these intimate moments with her husband. He looked like a man with a spouse—cared for and loved. Or perhaps there was a mother at home.

When I'd finished with the preparations and had taken an adequate number of photos, I sped back home, crying again. I didn't realize I was weeping until I turned on the windshield wipers and noticed rain wasn't the problem. *Suck it up, girl. Be an artist.*

Bill'd be out for an hour or longer so there was no sense waiting around for him or his call. I took a bath, worried more, and popped a Xanax. As I waited for sleep to come, the guy upstairs started to run on his treadmill. The pounding in my head was almost as bad. I looked up into the mirror and what I saw wasn't pretty. I got out of bed, ready to run up the stairs and ask Ben to give it up. The mirror seemed to vibrate with the force of Ben's feet, looking at one point like it had shifted slightly. But before I could rise, I fell asleep somehow.

CHAPTER 21

*"We photographers deal in things which are continually
vanishing, and when they have vanished there is no
contrivance on earth that can make them come back again.
We cannot develop and print a memory."*
Henri Cartier-Bresson

"DO YOU KNOW you're in the *Free Press*, Six? Not one of your delightful photographs of implosions or corpses—but an endearingly grisly item nonetheless. The story didn't give your name, but it's you, right? 'An area photographer on Belle Isle as yesterday's storm broke discovered the body…'" His voice tailed off.

"Oh, swell. Nice piece of news to wake up to." Thank God it was Diogenes on the line and not Bill. "No name mentioned, right?" I thought he'd said that, but I was half-asleep.

"Right. I know you don't get a newspaper, so I thought I'd better call. Helping the police with their inquiries, huh? That's what the article says. 'An area photographer, on Belle Isle as yesterday's storm broke, discovered the body and is currently helping the police with their inquiries.'"

This was the phrase I'd dreaded hearing and here it was in the newspaper. Di paused. "You actually found his body? The kid you mentioned, right? Eric?"

"Derek. Derek Olsen."

"I knew it was you right away. What the hell were you doing on Belle Isle in that storm? The restaurant still doesn't have power back. Didn't have an appointment to fix you up, did we? Turkey Grill time? Didn't get any messages."

"I was down there poking around."

I wished he had fixed me up though. This news, when paired with my sins from the night before, immediately produced a headache that made daylight lethal.

"Poking around? Doesn't sound plausible. Not in that storm. We all ran down to the basement and huddled together for the duration. Sirens were going off, for God's sake."

"I was already there when it blew in." I took the phone into the bathroom with Di still talking in my ear. Babbling on about how crazy I was not to have an attorney, how stupid it was I couldn't tell Bill I loved him. That I was willing to settle for—well, whatever it was I settled for.

"This was the kid you told me about, right?" he repeated. "The freaky guy who builds sand castles from found objects?"

"Sculptures. Yeah. I was down there. Doing, I don't know what," I repeated. "Maybe looking for him; I don't know. His mother—well, she's the kind of woman who makes you want to do good by her." I laughed nervously. "So I was poking around the spot where I last saw him. And there he was—under one of those bags the Parks Department uses for erosion. Probably the same one he dragged up to sit on." The vision of him there came back to me. My brain had photographed it more saliently than any camera could.

"From what you've told me so far, I thought he was probably the kind of guy who crawled out from under a rock." Di could usually get away with sarcasm, but today he caught himself. "Lord love a duck. I don't believe I said that. That was nasty. My need to make a joke when I'm talking to you can outpace good taste. Or humanity even. That's the kind of relationship we built as kids. Maybe it's time to change it."

"Except he didn't," I said, ignoring the apology and the observation. "Crawl out. He was splayed like road kill."

I could still picture him with all four limbs extending. Funny how many of my recent days had been about arms and legs. Or hands and feet.

"Squashed like a roach," I added.

"Enough analogies. I got the idea from the newspaper's photo. You'll flip out when you see what a piss poor photo it is. Should have let you take it."

"Now that wasn't likely to happen. I was holed up at the harbormaster headquarters with an interrogation team by the time the photographer arrived, I guess." I thought about it for a minute. "Same damned cops as last time. The other day, back at my place, it was a fairly polite interview, but yesterday it was an interrogation. No chitchat, no niceties."

"Poor baby."

"Can I get back to you later? We could actually talk about your life too. Topics other than what's going on in my part of the world. What're you doing after you close tonight?"

"I can probably get out of here by nine or so. It's Tuesday."

"How about Greektown? Apollo's?" I stifled a chortle, knowing his thoughts on Detroit's Greek cuisine. He grumbled a bit but gave in. One of his biggest gripes was that every restaurant in Greektown served the same terrible Americanized version of Greek food. "It's been bastardized over the years, but a semi-ambitious chef could make a trip to Athens and reinvent their menu. French and Italian chefs do it all the time. But not those guys. They sit on a menu invented in 1935 like it was handed down by…Plato."

I always countered with the argument that Detroit's American Greeks were used to their own version of the cuisine and would fight any change.

"It'd be better to risk losing a few customers. At least they could take pride in their kitchen. Half of them serve canned peas and rice with each entrée. When was the last time you ate canned peas anywhere else?"

After hanging up with Di, I thought again about calling Bill. He'd probably seen the *Freep* by now, and if he hadn't, I'd have to tell him about it. Either option seemed unattractive. Maybe I should put distance between us. He probably wouldn't notice my absence. When did he stop noticing me? I slapped the *poor me* thoughts out of my head and thought about what to do.

I decided to take a look at the photos I'd amassed for my show so far. Maybe it'd take my mind off what I saw yesterday. Derek. Would he have come to this end if I left him alone? Possibly. He did poke around on the island looking for stuff to hang. But certainly I pushed him into more dangerous territory. This was a consequence of allowing more people into my life. They went and got themselves killed.

I hadn't looked at my output in a week or two. I put the extra leaves in the dining room table up, pushed it against the wall, and propped the pictures up. In some cases, I wasn't positive the shot was the one I'd eventually use. I had several acceptable choices for a few of the men.

Rodney Jones, the rugby player. I'd probably use the photograph in the show out of sentimentality, but its quality was not nearly as good as the rest. Not with its graininess and the glossy background from the prep room that made it shimmer. What made it stand out, however, was the sheen and flamboyance of the rugby uniform and Bill's hand in making Rodney look more vibrant than a corpse had any right to look. There'd been no trauma to his body. He looked perfect—if dead. If I ever put together a book, it'd be good enough to include.

Willis Dumphrey, the bartender from Slack's Shack, elegant in the ex-mayor's tux. This might be the best photo overall, though I still hadn't found the right location at Bill's place in terms of lighting and angle when I shot it. It looked a bit tentative. But Willis, unlike most of the other men, had come into his own. His face was filled out. He looked confident and peaceful despite his sudden death.

Ramir Obabie, the guy who overdosed. Bill did the best he could with Ramir, but a lifelong drug habit took its toll.. I remembered Bill saying he'd dressed him for his last dance—saying he liked dancing. I'd bet it had been a long time since this man had the energy to dance.

Barry Johnson, the paralyzed victim of West Nile virus, dressed in a stock car racer's colors. In his photo, you couldn't tell he'd spent his last years in a wheelchair. It felt inauthentic—a pretense that he'd died in a car race. I couldn't photograph him in his chair, but this charade—that he was still a virile man—well, I'd never have allowed it had he been my son. It looked like his parents were ashamed of him. Or was I just thinking what would've worked best for me? Whereas they were thinking how he wished to be remembered.

Cajuan Grace, the photo I was forbidden to use, looking like a handsome but angry rapper—even in death. The baseball cap, worn at an angle, of course, had been cut and pinned to the fabric lining of the casket so it would lie flat. Bill told me later the photographer they'd called in asked them to dress and redress him half a dozen times—each outfit different.

"I almost threw the guy out," Bill said, "but his sister calmed me down. Said Cajuan himself went through such a routine each time he played a concert, said he was more worried about his clothes looking right than he was about the music."

Albert Flowers in his marine uniform. Wearing a pair of glasses at his wife's insistence. I removed them for a few of the shots, but went with this photo with him wearing them in the end. For a youngish man, he had deep pockets under his eyes.

"Wife says he hated those pouches," Bill said. "Never took his glasses off because of it." Albert was right to think he looked younger in glasses.

Peter Oberon, the fireman, also in uniform. His crushed chest was padded into normalcy. He had the look of a hero. His bear-like body probably cost him his life.

Wylie Edwards, the Jackson kid whose truck was hijacked along with his life, looking younger than his years. Ted might not be willing to include him. He didn't fill out his clothing and didn't begin to fill out his bone structure. His mouth looked like a set of braces had been recently removed, a bit unnatural still, but resigned. All the deaths had been unfair, but his seemed the most so.

Ancil Battle, the loan officer. His photo turned out better than I expected. A solemnity that caught the eye. Watchful, careful. He probably would've moved up in the bank quickly. A black man with a good education and nice looks—but here he was with the rest of them. There was no escape in Detroit.

Nine dead men. I worried incessantly that the photos wouldn't be distinct enough—a dozen black men of a similar age, all dead, all lying in a casket, each shot from the same angle. Would they be like the shopping carts? But Bill helped out by giving each a unique look through his attire. It was eerie, unsettling, and I loved it. I loved Bill's work, but did he love mine? Did he believe in this project? Why was I still holding out with him over Ted Ernst's part in it? How long had it been since he offered me a compliment on any of the photos? My approval or appreciation of Bill was evident in the work. I'd made it an essential element in the photographs. His appreciation had yet to be won. Did he see my work as more than reportorial—like that first picture of the soccer player? Or exploitative—as he hinted more each time? Was I like the photographer in *Wisconsin Death Trip* to Bill? Cataloging death for the record. Artless and automatic. Hardly more talented than the guy he brought in when people requested a photo.

Shrugging off this unsettling thought, I went over and got the best photo I'd shot of the hands and feet Derek had found, one of the ones I'd enlarged before Inspector Saad took the contact sheets away, and set it alongside the others. I knew I wouldn't use it, but it was also about death, perhaps a more potent look at it. Standing there for a minute or two, I noticed something for the first time. I walked across the room, and it became clearer still. I went to the worktable and pulled a magnifying glass out of the drawer. How could I have missed it? That oblique illumination I'd mustered through the use of Derek's lanterns had cast a shadow in the right spot, creating a contrast. Damn. Now what?

CHAPTER 22

Detroi Free Press: Father Walter Bertram, age 39, of St. Alban's Church, died Friday of an AIDS-related illness. Rev. Paul Patterson, who runs Sanctuary House in Detroit, identified the priest's illness openly at Father Bertram's request in an attempt to make the public aware of the epidemic of AIDS among priests. "Most affected priests suffer in solitude, often not seeking treatment due to the stigma attached to the disease for those in the priesthood," Rev. Patterson stated. Six out of ten priests, responding to a recent survey, said they knew fellow priests who had died of an AIDS-related illness. One-third knew of a priest living with AIDS.

(August 2011)

DIOGENES WAS LATE. I sat in the Apollo Restaurant impatient and nursing a glass of red wine, the kind made from retsina—whatever that was. I had the impression it was a substance closely related to paint thinner. It'd probably provoke a headache within the hour, but the waiter was so pleased with my choice, I didn't have it in me to send it back. After the same waiter's third or fourth inquiry as to whether I'd like an appetizer I gave in and ordered the flaming cheese dish, saganaki.

"*Opa*," the waiter shouted, bringing it to the table seconds later, a dark-eyed hand-maiden at his elbow to assist him, both of them appearing vastly relieved I'd ordered Greektown's signature dish.

Patrons at nearby tables smiled their approval; a light applause broke out. I watched politely as the waiter held the blazing platter up, setting it down on the table carefully, as though the cheese was sacred: a holy Greek ritual. The handmaiden flourished a lemon and a lid, making sure the flame died without incident. This ceremony took place repeatedly at the Apollo and at the half-dozen other Greek restaurants on Monroe Street. It didn't disappoint. On inspection, I wasn't sure the waiter was Greek; Russians and Eastern Europeans seemed to have taken over serving food to Detroiters. His accent was certainly suspect, and I thought the girl had called him Serge.

Di arrived at ten, a dangerously late hour to order a legitimate dinner on a weeknight in Detroit. But the staff seemed to know Di, and the waiter took the order without the frowns and head-shaking usually accompanying attempts to dine late. My stock always rose when a man accompanied me, especially a well-known Detroit mortician or chef. If only I was half as famous as my escorts. Di picked up the menu and ordered for us both, selecting items he deemed semi-authentic.

After the waiter scurried off, he said, "So what's up, my little jailbird? Any more run-ins with Detroit's finest?"

I filled him in more fully on the events at Belle Isle.

"I'm flabbergasted they let you take off after this last incident. Who has a better motive than you to get rid of old Eric?" I started to correct him but he jumped in. "Right, Derek. Wonder if they're following you? The cops. Isn't that what happens in *Law and Order*? Don't the cops let you leave the station so they can follow you to your lair and bring down the kingpins too? Who's your kingpin, Vi?"

"I feel pretty damned horrible," I began, "though I'm positive he'd have acted no differently once he saw those—body parts." The distance I'd kept between me and other people my whole life had been healthy. Now it'd closed in, and I was nauseated most of the time.

"You should feel guilty! He was trying to get into your pants, no doubt, and figured it'd take severed body parts to do it." This was said with the dose of irony Di seldom left behind. He took a sip of my wine and blanched. "How do you drink this stuff?" He slapped the glass down on the table. "I bet our young Derek believed he was going to get laid. That's how boys in their twenties think. Give the lady a severed hand and she'll give you a hand job. Need I add a similar maxim about toes?" I shook my head, and he slid the half-eaten plate of saganaki across the table, frowning. "Are you eating this artery-clogging cheese, for God's sake? Good rule, Vi, if it congeals on the plate, pass it up."

"I think you're crediting me with way too much influence. The kid had pretty weird stuff hanging from his concrete slabs long before I came along. He would've found those body parts and mounted them regardless. You didn't see the dog's jaw or doll's head." I took another bite of the saganaki. "It was more a meshing of two minds. Derek's and mine, I mean." I was saying these things but didn't exactly believe them.

"Did you say 'a messing of two minds'?"

We looked up together as the waiter brought us sea bass with steamed spinach and lentils. Di took an experimental bite and smiled up at the waiter, who beamed his relief. A little more lip and teeth than was absolutely necessary too if I read him correctly. Di didn't pick up on it though. He was boringly faithful to Alberto. Had he ever strayed? Was I missing that specific gene, the quality that made you stick it out through thick and thin? Well, what example did I have in my father?

After the waiter left, Di said in a low voice, "Food's passable and not unhealthy so let's be thankful. Why do you choose this place so often?"

We looked around at the battered wood paneling, the dog-eared posters of Greece, the dusty fan spinning motes above us, the waiters in ancient tuxes and yellowed white shirts. "Can't be the ambience and I doubt it's the food." He squeezed lemon over his spinach and held out what was left.

"No thanks. As you should know by now, twenty years into our friendship, I'm pretty indifferent to food. Place is cheap and midway between us." I looked around pointedly. "And it's not pretentious—like other area establishments that will remain nameless. Plus it has the added value of making you crazy."

"Well, it makes me physically ill to hear that you take good food so lightly. Let me pick the restaurant next time. I'm sure I can find a new spot to tickle your taste buds."

I took a bite of the fish. It tasted fine if dull. Fish was fish, why pretend otherwise?

"Something else, isn't there? You have a distracted look on your face." He reached across the table for my hand. "Romantic troubles, sweetie? Bill giving you a hard time? Holding back in the bedroom now he's supplying bodies?" Di let go of my hand and sat up straighter. "Mixing love and business, especially your kind of business, is dicey. Bill's probably looking for a woman who takes his mind off the corpses, not a girl who's turned on by them." He sniffed. "Smells like you're beginning to bring the odor home with you." He looked at me suspiciously. "Where were you before coming here?"

I sniffed too, detecting only garlic, and shook my head. "At home surveying my recent work if you must know. And I was damned impressed with myself."

Di was examining a piece of fish—probably for bones—so I tapped his plate with my fork to get his attention. "Things aren't going well at the moment with Bill and me, but that's not the immediate problem." I put down the fork and reached for my bag, pulling out the photo I'd brought along. "Look at this, will you?"

Di took the photo and did a double take. "Couldn't you have warned me what was coming across the transom? Jeez! I thought it might be that boy toy chef in Troy you photographed." He looked again, turning greener. "You might be used to this stuff by now, but I only see severed hands and feet when I butcher animals. These," he made another face, "are clearly human remains."

"I thought you knew the kind of pictures I've been taking, Di. You're the one who brought me that appalling book."

"The bodies in *Death Trip* were intact, centuries old, almost fictional, certainly mythical. I hardly believed in them at all. This photograph's in a whole different realm."

He put the photo facedown on the table, pushed his plate away, and took a deep breath. Pulling a pair of tiny glasses from his pocket, he looked around furtively as he put them on, flipped the photo over, and took another look.

"Lord, girl, it's a wonder the cops didn't cart both of you away after seeing this." He whistled softly. "Don't know what's worse, Derek nailing these body parts on his concrete or you taking a photo of it. Quite a pair, aren't you? Any wonder the murderer disposed of him? Probably thought your boy saw the whole thing go down." He looked up. "Do they use that phrase anymore in criminal activity? *Go down.* Seems to be only a sexual reference nowadays."

"Back to the picture," I said, tapping it gently.

"Must've happened right on the island."

He still wasn't looking at the right spot. Perhaps it took a practiced eye.

"You don't see it, do you? I don't think the cops noticed either." Di looked at me with a puzzled look, clearly at sea. "I didn't see it at first either. Look more carefully, Di." I pulled the magnifying glass out of my bag and passed it to him.

"I can see the body parts, as we seem to be calling them tonight, pretty damned well without any help. Don't need to look at the saw marks, do I? Isn't that what was used? Some big-assed hacksaw?"

"Nobody's shared any information with me, being I'm their number one suspect. But that's not what I'm talking about. Look at his ankle. The right one." I pulled the photo away from Di and pointed to the spot.

"What the hell is it?" he asked, taking the photo back and using the magnifier now. "Is it a tattoo? Sure looks like a tattoo."

"I thought so at first, but I think it's the mark or tracing a tight ankle bracelet makes on your skin if you wear it all the time. You know, like a watch makes on your wrist. It's lucky there was enough light to get the impression on film."

"It is a man, right? What kind of man wears an ankle bracelet? And I ask that question coming from—well, where I come from."

"He's a man all right. Look at the size of those feet."

His feet were huge. Probably a size thirteen or fourteen.

"Difficult to judge size with nothing to compare them to. Maybe they look big because it's an extreme close-up."

"Trust me, those babies were big. I saw them firsthand," I said. "Could the ankle bracelet be a military accessory? Sort of a Green Beret emblem or logo?"

"Do you think I know squat about the military?" He looked into the air for a few seconds. "Wait just a minute. Could what we see here be the tracings of a home detention tag? I'm not sure if those things leave marks though. Seems like that would be a violation of civil rights. Marking you for life like that. What did the inspector have to say about it?" Di put the picture down but picked it up again, wincing. "No marks at all on his hands. So he wears ankle bracelets but no rings or a watch?"

I shrugged. "I don't think Saad or any of his people noticed the marks," I repeated, lowering my voice. "At least, not as of yesterday. They might've taken a better look at my photos by today though. Now that another death's occurred."

"So how do you know the marks weren't on their pictures too? The ones the police photographer shot?"

"Saad happened to fan a bunch of police photos in front of me and I'm almost positive there were no marks on the ankle in those shots. He'd blown them up bigger than these. I would've noticed."

"How do you explain it?" Di was whispering too. "No marks on their copies."

We both looked around; the place had suddenly grown eerily quiet. But a second look confirmed it was quiet because it was empty—empty except for our waiter, who was trying to look nonchalant as he dozed, head on hand, at his service station.

"I think the marks or imprint must have dissipated or faded by the next day—if that's the right word for it. Disappeared. Probably twenty-four hours or more had passed by the time the police photographer got there with his camera." I looked at him. "*Is* that the right word? Dissipated?"

"Has to be what happened whatever you call it. Do you think

whoever killed the guy ripped the bracelet off so he couldn't be identified?"

"Well, duh! If this fellow's murderers went to the trouble of hacking him up, they'd do that, wouldn't they? Wonder if any teeth were missing. They always seem to identify people from dental records. Maybe they yanked them too."

"They only go to dental records when they've an idea about who it is. You have to know which dentist to consult. Right?"

"No huge dental database to check with yet?"

He shrugged. "Don't know. So what're you gonna do?"

I steepled my hands—hands that were sweating. "Am I wrong or is it to my benefit that the guy gets identified? An ankle bracelet's impression may help. How many men wear them?"

"For a minute, I thought you were thinking of Derek. I thought maybe you wanted to see his killer brought to justice. "

"Fuck you. Goes without saying. The two go hand in hand." I couldn't seem to stop talking about hands. "Seeing him dead nearly wiped me out."

"Sorry, Vi." And he did sound sincere for once. "Guess you two were closer than I knew."

I wished it were true. I wished I'd given more thought to what Derek had been up to on Belle Isle. I lost track of him, but he'd kept going with his own project—an offshoot of mine. That's the thing about being an artist—if that term doesn't sound too lofty. It takes over your head.

"Look, I've had to look after myself my whole life, so by now it's instinctual, second nature. But it's not sociopathic. I liked Derek well enough, but remember I only saw him a few times. It's not like we were bosom buddies."

He reached across the table to pat my shoulder. "Sorry, kiddo.

Anyway, getting back to the ankle. How many men would let anyone know they wear such an ornament? At least once you get out of certain communities." He pulled his plate back and took another bite of his fish. "You know, come to think of it, I've never seen a gay man wearing an ankle bracelet—not that I examine many ankles. I don't think the bracelet has anything to do with him being gay or straight." He picked up the photo again. "You can barely make out the pattern, but it looks like a row of heads. Or skulls. Like you might see on a tattoo. Though clearly it isn't a tat or it would be on the police photos."

We both grimaced involuntarily and studied the photo again.

Diogenes looked up. "Actually, Violet, it seems like an item *you* might wear. Or have worn in your younger days. Gothic. Might you have loaned it out?"

I threw a napkin at him.

CHAPTER 23

*"The still must tease with the promise of a story
the viewer wishes to be told."*
Cindy Sherman

I WAS HEADED TO the police with my discovery when one of Bill's assistants called to tell me about the death of a priest. I couldn't let this one get away—despite my mission and never mind the pun. Ted hadn't been on my back about the number of finished photos lately, but I was expecting his call.

"Mr. Fontenel didn't tell me to call you," the woman in Bill's front office said, "but he's been busy with his mother. I think he plain forgot." Alice paused. "Father Bertram fits your criteria, I think." She cleared her throat, obviously uncomfortable with the project and her role in it. "Anyway, the viewing hours start at noon so you'd have to get over here right away."

I hung up and made my usual dash downtown, wondering if Bill had intended for me to point a camera at this guy. Whose approval would he get? Did he have a contract with the parish? I doubted it, but a wasted hour or two and a wasted photo wasn't the worst thing in the world.

Father Bertram was a priest and was dressed like a priest—a priest back in the days when they didn't dress vibrantly; the first man devoid of even a touch of color. I was starting to shoot when a voice behind me said, "I beg your pardon." His tone implied disapproval, and I whipped around.

Another priest, this one very much alive, stood in the doorway. "I don't think we requested that any photos be taken of Father Bertram. Or did the diocese call without telling me?"

This priest was white, much older than the fellow in the coffin, and more than a bit hot under his stiff collar. "I'm talking about the guy you're looking at," he said, seeing what must have been the puzzled look on my face. "Do you know his name?" He stepped closer.

I hadn't met a single person related to any of the men I'd photographed until now. Bill had seen to that. So I was more than a little shocked. I didn't know the dead priest's name. Had Alice told me?

I evaded his question, saying, "Someone must have okayed a photograph. Maybe his family?"

The priest shook his head. "I'm the closest thing he has to a family. You don't look like you're taking a photo for the record either." He looked at my equipment. "Not with this fancy gear. What's this all about? Newspaper send you out here? *Free Press*? *The News*?"

"Why? Is he famous?" I looked down in the coffin. "First black priest in Detroit? That it?"

"Not even close. First black priest was Father Clarence Williams, I think. Quite a bit older than Wally. Father Walter Bertram," he corrected himself. He came over to the casket and looked down at Father Bertram, shaking his head. "Maybe it'd be better if we spoke our minds instead of exchanging inane and time-consuming questions and responses. I'm Father Francis Talley."

We were both silent for a few seconds, looking down at Father Bertram.

"Violet Hart."

"Why are you taking Wally's picture. Ms. Hart?"

"Bill Fontenel—that's the funeral director here—gave me permission to take photographs of his...clients. With the family's permission, that is." I looked around wildly. "Must be a signed contract filed away."

But in my heart, I knew it was all a mistake. Bill never intended for me to take photographs of this priest. Who would he have asked for permission? This would have been a big deal, and he would've told me. I kept talking anyway.

"I'm a professional photographer, Father. This is the tenth photograph in a series I'm doing."

"A series? Why would you want to do that? Take pictures of the dead?"

He put a hand on Father Bertram's arm, squeezing it gently. And then he bent over and kissed the priest's cheek, brushing a tear away.

"Look, I'm sorry. I'll leave you alone with your friend. I don't need to take this photograph." It was a damned shame that old Alice had screwed this up because I'd probably never get the chance to photograph a black priest again.

Father Talley straightened up. "Answer my question first, Ms. Hart. Why are you taking pictures of the dead?"

Why indeed? *Because I was suddenly reminded of how mediocre my career was,* I thought of saying. *My time is running out. I wasn't even living a real life. I'm alone in the world and I'm feeling it more every day. I need some success. I need to produce work that matters. If I'm to miss out on a personal life—at least there'd be a professional one. Because* *black men are dying here every day.* Would saying that seem like I was hustling him? Was I trying for the magic words that would win his approval?

"I'm putting together an exhibit. If I can get enough pictures, that is. All of the photos are of young black men who died in Detroit over the last year."

"Who'd want to see such a thing? Have you also considered your work might look exploitative?" Yet his words didn't seem accusatory, merely interested.

"I've thought of that." Hourly, I could've told him. "But I hope people will find the photos compelling. I don't know if you've been to any of Bill's funerals, but he dresses the deceased like they're going to an important event. Tries to match their final wardrobe to their personality or profession—to make it special. You don't forget his funerals quickly."

Lately the bodies wore uniforms or business dress. The high fashion of earlier days had been drained away. I badly needed those peacock colors again. But not today, it seemed. And saying the words aloud now, it did seem exploitative, ridiculous. Peacock colors, indeed.

"You're pulling my leg, aren't you?" Suddenly he got a strange look on his face.

"Are you okay?"

"I'm fine." He walked over to a chair and sat down. "I might be willing to sign one of those contracts you mentioned. Sit down, please."

I did and he leaned over until his mouth was inches from my ear.

"Are you planning to explain the causes of death in your show?" I stared at him, not getting his meaning. "Explain how each man died," he said slowly.

"You mean like placing a placard beneath the photograph?" He nodded. "I hadn't planned on it."

I didn't like that idea at all. It turned the work into photojournalism, my bugaboo. What I steered clear of. "It's more about the art than politics. I'm not good with words."

"Can't it be about both? I understand your interest in this as an artist, and I'm not saying a long accounting of their deaths is necessary, but wouldn't it be effective to document how these men died? Perhaps include their name, age, the date, and cause of death." He stopped, lost in thought. "People are going to wonder about it anyway, aren't they? I think you almost have to include it. Certainly a catalog would contain such information. Otherwise a lot of the power of your images is lost." He narrowed his eyes. "What's it all about if not that?"

I didn't like to say it, but for me it was about creating art. It was about composition, shadows, angles, color. A piece of art was important in its own right—without making a statement. It wasn't superficial or exploitative or any of those things. I wasn't going to say a picture's worth a thousand words though it was.

I wasn't a Catholic, but telling a priest I was using these dead men for my own purposes took more guts than I had. "I could, I guess. But not the names. A lot of the families didn't want the name specified. I'm not sure how they would feel about it."

I didn't like this idea at all. Ted probably wouldn't go for it either, perhaps diluting the power of the image with words, making them, in effect, even more like morgue shots. Words rarely complemented art; they usually watered it down, made it too obvious, sapped its strength. Told the viewer what to think rather than allowing him or her to discover it for themselves.

"Father Bertram died of AIDS," Father Talley said, tapping the casket.

I nodded, not getting his implication.

"Look, I don't want to get on my soapbox now, but a simple photo with his death listed as a consequence of AIDS might help the issue. People think no one dies of AIDS anymore in western countries. And I bet there are other issues in your portfolio too. Other deaths needing explication."

"I see what you're saying. That *priests* die of AIDS too."

"Not too, Ms. Hart. More. Priests don't always get treatment fast enough. And the church doesn't do much to help. We'd all rather pretend celibacy is universally practiced, that priests are never gay or sexually active." He stopped and lowered his voice. "I'm not talking about sexual abuse here—not pedophilia. This man never laid a hand on a child." He sighed. "Homosexuality in the priesthood is an especially sore topic—as I am sure you know. And a black priest dying from AIDs highlights the dual problem of it affecting both populations at a statistically higher level." He stood up. "Look, I'm going to the office to sign your contract in the hopes you'll do the right thing." He headed for the door. "I don't see any reason not to sign it either way. Can't do Wally any harm now, can it? There'll be very few people to mourn him—he's been sick for a long time and nursed in out of the way places. They hid him like he was....Well, never mind. Perhaps this will help in some small way."

I felt like a character in a Spike Lee movie as I watched him depart. Okay, I could certainly do what he wanted. It wasn't much to ask.

CHAPTER 24

"Photography is a small voice, at best, but sometimes one photograph, or a group of them, can lure our sense of awareness."
W. Eugene Smith

WAS PLANNING ON heading straight to the police station with my new information, but when I'd finished photographing the priest and looked at my cell, I found a message from Ted demanding, more than asking me, to meet him at my flat or his shop. This had to be about the contract his attorney drew up, the document asking—no, coercing—Bill into stating he'd never demand a share of any profits derived from my work with him.

The document was still in my handbag, ready for the increasingly unlikely possibility Bill would return to his formerly docile self. The days when I couldn't get him out of my apartment, my bed, were a fading memory. Now I was lucky to get him into bed—and, in fact, hadn't in quite a while. Why? Was I ducking him as much as he was ducking me, not wanting to tell him about my arrangement with Ted? About the contract I needed him to sign?

I hurried home, noticed the photos were still sitting out, and decided to leave them. It couldn't hurt to have Ted see the pictures as soon as he walked in the door. Maybe they'd take a bit of the starch out of him, derailing this obsession with contracts. We could discuss the idea of a contract once the material for the show was nailed down.

My apartment had become an absolute rat hole thanks to the constant rush of my life since I started taking these pictures. I made a small effort at orderliness. The collection of masks, the first thing a visitor saw, was covered with a film of dust—and not a fine coating. And when was the last time I'd had a moment to run the mop across the floors or do a load of wash? My hair needed trimming; I hadn't shaved my legs in a week, maybe two. It was just as well no one wanted to climb into my bed lately—maybe this was why. Perhaps I was also covered by a film of dust. Di had suggested I smelled. I sprayed myself lavishly with a five-year-old bottle of Vera Wang and hoped it'd do.

Ted looked ready to say something the moment he stepped across the threshold, but on seeing the photos fell silent. "Nine photos?" he asked breathlessly. "Didn't know you were this close to finishing…." He stopped mid-speech, walking over to the portrait of the firefighter.

I could tell Ted especially liked that one. His eyes zeroed in as I told him, "Ten actually. I took a few of a priest an hour ago."

"A black priest under forty? How'd he die?" He turned around, immediately interested.

I didn't want to get into the AIDS issue with Ted—I was sure an offensive comment would quickly follow. "Bill wasn't there to ask." Ted still seemed expectant. "I can't always tell the cause of death, you know. Bill makes each man look perfect."

He nodded. "Well, these are sensational, Vi."

He stood in front of Wylie Edwards, the kid who'd been hijacked and then dumped at the casino. I followed him around, anxious despite my pride in the work. Although Ted's approval might mean the most to me professionally, I wished Bill had looked at my photos the way Ted was doing now. Just once couldn't Bill Fontenel have said my work was good?

"Don't know about using this picture though. What's he? Sixteen?" Ted squinted and held the photo up to the light.

"Twenty, I think." Was it twenty?

I definitely intended to use Wylie but didn't say a word. It was important to have one or two photographs reminding the viewer of how fleeting life is—especially life in Detroit. Maybe no children would be in the show, but boys, at the moment they became men, were important. I'd go down in flames over Wylie.

"Looks younger than that. We'll see."

Ted continued to stroll around the room, coming back again to the firefighter. "I like the one of the fireman. That's what he is, right? And the race car driver's pretty cool too."

A small frisson of revulsion bubbled up inside me at the word "cool."

"I think they prefer to be called firefighters now with a few women in their ranks." I took a deep breath. "I may not be able to use the rapper. Cajuan Grace. Family didn't sign off."

A vein in Ted's forehead throbbed. "Why'd you take the shots then? Pity, because its absence would be a real loss." He seemed to have forgotten his earlier dictum on the use of celebrities. Cajuan was a star—even in death.

"Once I saw him, I had to have it." I remembered the day. "I think I told you—the family had their own photographer coming in. A fancy-pants guy from New York or LA. Taking photos for a tribute book. It may be out by now. A money-maker even after death—Cajuan was." I walked over and took the photo from him. "Maybe Bill can get them to change their minds. An exhibit could only help promote their lousy tribute book. Don't you think?"

Ted whirled around, not answering. "So how did Bill react to signing off on the contract? You did bring it up with him, didn't you?" I stood silent. He slapped a hand on his forehead. "Weeks have passed. We're almost ready to go. What the hell are you waiting for?"

"You can't imagine what's been going on, Ted."

I know I sounded like a whiny little girl, and for a second or two, contemplated filling him in on all of it: Derek's death, the police investigation, the hands, the feet and the head, but chances were it'd turn him off, make him think that staying away from me was his best alternative. No money had been invested in a show so far. He'd suffer only a minor disappointment. Whereas I had so much to lose, having given myself over to this project for months now, hardly taking on enough assignments to keep afloat. I was living off my meager savings as I poured all the time I had into this. This and its consequences: my involvement with the police.

Notoriety only went so far in the art world; Ted wouldn't want to tie himself to someone under suspicion in a murder case. The liberal sensibility of the art world didn't extend to exploitation and that was precisely how my relationship with Derek might come across, especially when paired with the dead black men.

Ted didn't read the newspaper because otherwise he would've known about it, maybe figured out my involvement. Perhaps only Di among my minuscule coterie knew it was me poking around on Belle Isle. That it was me discovering bodies in a storm. Bill hadn't called either. Nor my mother. Maybe no one would ever have to know. Now that I had the photo with the marks on the ankle to take in to Inspector

Saad, maybe the police could wrap it up in a day or two, and I'd be free to finish my work.

"You're telling me you haven't approached him yet?"

Ted was talking again and I snapped back to life. He gave the monumental sigh I expected and sank onto the sofa.

"You've taken the tenth photo and you haven't brought it up with Bill. Guess you didn't get it when we talked about this before. We're not doing a show without his signature on that piece of paper. No way." He threw his feet up on the coffee table and screwed his face into a scowl. "I know you're not a businesswoman, but surely you can understand my position."

"I am so a fuckin' businesswoman, Ted. Just because I don't have a storefront or office space doesn't mean I haven't supported myself with taking photographs since art school."

I walked over to the table and began collecting the pictures, handling them like a sulky child taking her marbles home. "Look, I'm afraid Bill will cut me off before I have enough work for the show if I bring up the contracts. At this point, what's the harm in waiting? It'll only be another week or two with any luck."

Ted didn't blanch. "It's because you're screwing him, isn't it. That's what's fuckin' this up. Pardon my excessive use of the word."

We were a pair all right, both of us in it for ourselves—not terribly interested in the other one's stake despite our parasitic connection.

"And I've got to start advertising, there's the harm," he said without the slightest hitch in his speech. "I don't want to sink more money into your work—into this show—if it's not going to pan out." He began to pace. "My attorney says Bill will eventually come after a share of the money if we make any sort of splash. As soon as Bill sees you're earning more than room and board from your work with him, he'll think of it. Someone will put the idea in his head if he doesn't come up with it himself." Ted stood stock-still. "We're all of us businessmen."

"Is that a line from an Arthur Miller play? You don't know Bill..."

He didn't let me finish. "And I'm damned tired of hearing you saying, 'You don't know Bill.' It's *you* who doesn't know how he's going to act about this. He's not a charitable trust. He's as much into making a killing as the next guy."

A killing? I could hardly take it in. Ted headed for the door a few minutes later, looking up at my collection of masks on the way. "Well, I finally figured out why you collect masks. It occurred to me last night as I was falling asleep."

I didn't answer.

"The masks tell me you have a face you don't show." He drew himself in, pontificating. "And that mirror over your bed—"

Now Ted was going to present me with the golden apple.

"Unmasks the poor sap beneath you."

"Is that Jung or Freud?"

"It's Ernst," he said. "And now that I'm thinking about it, these photos"—he waved his hand at them—"pretty much look like death masks."

"You got me, Ted. I'm all about the masks."

I tried to make it light but he didn't smile, pressing another copy of the contract into my hands as he left. I tossed it on the desk and picked up the phone to call Bill.

He wasn't in. Maybe he was up in Saginaw with his mother? There was no putting it off. I'd have to go see Inspector Saad. So that's where I went, wondering on the way if I was all about the masks.

CHAPTER 25

Detroit News: Ten-year-old Levan Dorris died today as he played
with his younger sister on the floor of his bedroom. An errant bullet,
presumably fired at a man sitting on the porch next door, entered his
room through the wall and fatally lodged in his skull. He was declared
dead at St. John's Hospital at 8:45 p.m. It is believed the intended
victim owed money to a local drug dealer.
(September 2011)

MIRACULOUSLY, INSPECTOR SAAD was in his office and willing to see
me immediately, which probably made me a prime suspect. "I was
going to come over to see you today," he said, motioning for me to
sit down. "I have news."

"Did you notice the marks too?" I said, without preamble. "I didn't
see them until I got out the magnifying glass yesterday."

Was it yesterday or the day before? The days were starting to run
together. Sleep, the usual demarcation, had been scarce.

"Suddenly, they leaped off the paper," I said in a rush. "I don't know
how I missed them."

"What marks?" Saad looked completely baffled.

So no one in the police department had spotted the ankle tracings on my prints? Maybe they were still working from the contact sheets or their own pictures. Maybe no one had printed them out, blown them up. I pulled the photos out of my handbag and handed them to him.

He looked at them blankly. "Guess I don't have your eye for detail," he said, looking up. "Could you help me out?"

"The marks on his ankles," I said, jabbing at them in my excitement. "I think he may have been wearing an ankle bracelet as crazy as it sounds. What man wears an ankle bracelet? And a man with ankles as thick as his—who'd want to show them off?" Saad looked at the photo closely now. "I'm almost positive those marks were gone by the next day—when your photographer took his pictures," I continued. "Like the marks a wristwatch makes? They disappear pretty quickly."

He continued to stare blankly at the shots. Did he get it?

Saad finally looked up. "Nice piece of evidence, Miss Hart." For the first time, he seemed pleased rather than wary of me. "Very nice."

"Maybe there's a man who wore an ankle bracelet in your files."

He smiled. "I'm going to share some information with you, Miss Hart. You were kind enough to bring this in and now that we know you couldn't have murdered Derek Olsen, I'm gonna let you in on it. We've been busy too."

"You know how Derek died?" I felt like the breath had been knocked out of me. I'd forgotten about Derek's death in my excitement over the photo.

"He was strangled by a person with brutal strength. Broke almost every bone in his upper neck and jaw. Popped two teeth out of his mouth as well."

I cringed, thinking of his fragile physique. The word overkill came into my head. That's what it literally meant. It was horrible to think about it.

"Plus the geobag covering Derek weighed over one hundred pounds," Saad continued. "You'd have to pump up pretty good to handle that kind of weight. How big are you? One thirty-five, five-ten? We can rule you out."

The image of an enormous ogre coming up on Derek and lifting him off the ground suddenly swept through my head. The pounding in my ears took my breath away. I tried to tell myself again he'd have found and mounted the hands and feet anyway, that I hadn't sent him off to his death. But I couldn't persuade myself and never would.

"You okay?" Saad asked, rising. "Looks like you're gonna keel over. Let me get you some water." He motioned to an officer outside the door,

"I'm okay," I said, waving him away, but gulping down the paper cup of water when it was handed to me." I slowly recovered. "Any idea who?" I asked.

"Catch your breath first. For an olive-skinned girl, you went dead white."

"I'm fine. Tell me what you think."

"Okay," he said, picking up the clearest of the photos again. "This photograph you've brought me is a good start in identifying the victim—where he came from." He handed it back. "Those marks on the ankle *are* from a bracelet, and I recognize what sort of bracelet it is." He paused, theatrically dramatic. "A little history here, Miss Hart?"

I nodded.

"A few years back," he said, settling back into his chair, "paroles were given to gang members on the condition they wear an electronic ankle tag after their release. The bracelet ensured they wouldn't return to the gang since parole officers could track them through the tag." He cracked his knuckles. "Had other uses too, of course, but keeping parolees away from the gangs was its biggest asset. Especially in cities like LA—ones with heavy gang activity. Chico State pioneered the idea, I believe."

"That's what was on his ankle? Marks from an electronic bracelet?"

So Di had gotten it right. It was puzzling though because the marks looked too delicate. Not like a mark an electronic tag would make. That kind of tag would probably show up as a rectangular mark, an indent almost.

"Not quite. Let me finish," Saad said. "The device uses GPS software to monitor movement, and the parole officer can sit at his desk in a remote place and follow the parolee's activity. These babies were worn by sexual predators long before anyone came up with this new use."

"Must be expensive to monitor every paroled gang member?"

"Yeah, one of the problems. But it does work if a department's flush. Before the economy went south, the feds were willing to cough up the necessary dough to subsidize it. More than a few of those jokers are back in the slammer because of the program. Thanks to this invention, gangs were frustrated in reclaiming their most lethal members. See, these guys migrate back to their gang like homing pigeons if there's no penalty—no way to stop them. The gang's their family—their lifeline. Their best chance of survival unfortunately. An ex–gang member doesn't get much slack with rival gangs. But we slapped them on these head bangers when we could, and they had to keep their distance, stay out of trouble. Not that they couldn't get in touch through other means, of course, But not face-to-face contact."

"Another electronic success story?"

"Let's return to our guy. Or to the ankle, at least. We don't have a specific suspect yet. The marks you see on this ankle are not from a GPS monitoring bracelet."

"Then—" I began.

"Then why am I telling you about them?" He rose and went over to a file and pulled out photos of his own. Several showed the ankles of men wearing bracelets, but not electronic ones. "Gang bracelets," he said. "The little fuckers, pardon my French, are mimicking the GPS ankle monitors by wearing jewelry they designed." He shook his head in disbelief. "Like they adopt prison garb, the prison haircut, prison lingo."

"What are they made of?" I asked, frowning at the prints. I didn't see the skulls from my photo on any of the bracelets in this batch.

"This particular gang uses bracelets made from actual dog's teeth. Nice, huh?" He stiffened. "Whenever we find a dead dog in certain neighborhoods, his incisors are missing. Another gang makes their ankle bracelets from human hair. Girls dragged into alleys and assaulted for their hair. Nice how our boys find a way to make group endeavors inclusive of neighborhood women and animals as well as violent. And all of it to mock our attempt to interfere with their activity." He paused. "Or it was at first. Now it's taken on a life of its own. We see new bracelets all the time. Each competing with the others for goriness, cleverness, mockery."

"What gang was this?" I motioned to my photos.

He shrugged. "New one on me. Maybe not local."

"But this guy, our Big Ankles, was probably killed by a rival gang and chopped?"

"And Derek was most likely killed because whoever took out Big Ankles, as you put it, thought Derek saw it happen. Or at least saw part of it. They might've seen Derek's mounting of the body parts as a sort of warning. Gangs like to mount warnings with graffiti. Derek's work comes a little too close perhaps."

"Well, he didn't witness a crime. He found those hands and one foot on the beach. The other he had to swim after."

"Means the murder probably took place on Belle Isle or it wouldn't worry them. Or the murderers themselves probably dumped the body parts there if it happened elsewhere." Saad stood up, finished. "Thanks for coming in today, Miss Hart. We do appreciate your help, your skill as an observer. Probably would never have noticed those marks on our own. You'd make a good crime scene photographer."

"So I'm cleared?"

"Unless you get yourself into trouble again." He smiled. "You were never a serious suspect. But you do see how you set this into motion? At least some of it."

"I don't think that's fair," I said, bristling. "Even if Derek'd never met me, he would've still found and hung those hands and feet. He was looking for crazy stuff when I met him. Had a dog's jaw up long before he came across me." I tried to believe what I was saying—if other people believed me maybe I would too.

"I can't persuade you to stop taking those pictures."

I shook my head. "I don't want to take up your time with an explanation, but it's important to me. Really important. I'm nearly finished—if that's any help."

"I guess I can't completely cross you off our list in that case. Taking those pictures means you'll be awfully close to murders. You bear watching."

"So watch me." I flashed him a half-hearted smile, more out of habit than pluck. "Being watched isn't the worst that could happen."

"One more item—before you take off." Saad opened his attaché and removed a file folder. "Over the last week, we've talked about your mother a bit. Waitress, right?"

What now?

"But your father's not local—as far as you know." I nodded. "Turns outs though it's got nothing to do with any of these deaths, I looked into him too—before I knew you weren't a suspect. Seemed like you were evasive about him up at your flat and that always gets me interested. Lots of blind alleys and rabbit holes, but once in a while…. And it's pretty simple with the Internet and the systems we have access to. The Patriot Act and the associated legislation have been useful to cops."

"My father?" I felt a bristle of anger as it registered. "I haven't seen him in more than six years."

At our last dinner together, he'd called me Bunny twice and never realized it. He never once looked me straight in the face, flirting with the waitress instead. Both of us were thankful when the check arrived, fleeing quickly in our eerily similar cars—two blue Saabs: his ten years old, mine eight. We'd also both ordered steak rare.

"I can tell you two are related," the waitress had said that day, smiling. "Spitting image of each other."

Again my father looked away. I shivered now, remembering it. What was it about me he loathed? What had I done as an infant to send him away? Why did he hang around after Daisy's birth but take off after mine? It was a short piece of film I ran in my head when I felt especially brave. The entire library of Hal Hart films probably would run less than an hour.

"Hal Hart. Trumpet player, right?" Detective Saad rifled through the papers in his hand. "Mother met him in the Berkshires in the late sixties?"

I was completely blank on where this was going. Last I'd heard, he was on the west coast polishing his horn. I nodded.

"You never told me your father was partly black. Is that what draws you to black men? Why you've been focusing on them in your work?"

The words came out of Saad's mouth in a rush, like he hadn't been able to come up with a way to say it more indirectly.

"Or did you even know it?" He looked me in the eyes. "Didn't know, did you? What got me to thinking," he continued, probably seeing I was unready to open my mouth, "was that although you indirectly admitted to sleeping with a black man, and more than one black man, and although you took pictures of black men—you never said you were partly black yourself. Which would've explained a lot about your... habits. I thought you'd have told me if you knew. But maybe I'm wrong." He kept trying to rephrase it as I sat and stared at him. "It seemed likely you would've mentioned it. Or am I mistaken?" He raised his shoulder, asking. "Violet?"

I sat still for half a minute more and then blurted out, "My father's not black. How did you even come up with this idea?" The chair squeaked with my quick movements and we both jumped. "Hal Hart's a fairly common name." I knew that from my years of searching for him as a teenager.

"So you didn't know. I thought not. Did you know that after a while he started spelling his name H-o-w-l instead of Hal?"

"What?"

"H-O-W-L." He spelled it—like the Ginsberg poem. "Guess because he was a musician"—Saad handed me the papers—"and liked the artsy tie-in. Made his name memorable. Or something like that."

The file was mostly newspaper clippings, flyers for musical events, that sort of thing.

"Look at this picture in the *Philadelphia Bulletin*, for example." He poked the pile with his index finger, shaking his head impatiently until I came up with the right one. "And he didn't just change Hal to Howl.

It's Howl Heart. H-E-A-R-T. Changed the spelling of his surname too. Took an ordinary name, a very ordinary name, and made it memorable. Looks great on a marquee or in a newspaper headline."

"This is ridiculous."

Surely I'd have heard if he'd changed his name. I saw him a few times after his long absence following Daisy's death. And Bunny—she'd have to have known.

"Not so ridiculous. Think of Count Basie, Cab Calloway, Dizzy Gillespie, Jelly Roll Morton, Fats Waller. Names chosen for their bang. Picked for their memorability—of how they'd look on a marquee, an advertisement."

I looked at the first clipping closely, a grainy, black-and-white photo of a band called The Jazz Daddies. My father, trumpet in hand, was in the back row. He didn't look black—wasn't black. It was ridiculous.

"I don't get it. How does this photo or his new name make him black?" Some of the musicians looked black, but others didn't.

"Read the caption." He poked his interfering finger on the page again.

I read it aloud. "Billy Baldwin and his year-old group, The Jazz Daddies, will appear for six performances at the Latin Room on South Street over the Labor Day weekend. The all-Negro band plays jazz, Dixie Land, and be-bop." I peered at the photo again, trying to see what Saad saw. "Maybe he was sitting in for the regular guy. Musicians do that all the time. Keeps it fresh."

"Look at the *Star Ledger*." I thumbed through the pile, hands shaking. "It's the Newark paper." I found it. It was dated earlier than the last one. 1962. Here the group was called The Dark Lords, and my father was again in the back row, trumpet held up.

"The story doesn't identify the group as black. Or Negro. Whatever they were calling it that year."

"Paper didn't have to print it, Violet. The club was in a 'colored' neighborhood; folks in Newark would've known. There's ten more news clips like these two." He took the pile away. "Did you ever have an inkling growing up? No one dropped any hints?"

"He was gone nearly all of my childhood. I looked for him for years before I gave up. Haunted libraries and telephone offices with directories. Called strangers like a pathetic dolt. But no one ever told me he spelled it like that: Howl Heart."

I could still remember sitting in those libraries, my index finger trailing down a column of Harts, but stopping long before I ever came to Heart. There would've been Hartleys, Hartmans, Hartwicks, Healeys, Hearns. Heart would have been in another column entirely. Suddenly I remembered the day a man on the phone had told me he was black. Had he been my grandfather or an uncle?

"Was it some kind of a stunt?" I didn't know my father well enough to answer my own question. "Changing his name?"

"I doubt it. He finally changed his name legally to Howl Heart in the eighties. When a band he was with was nominated for an award. Guess he thought he'd established himself well enough under the new name to petition for a legal change. Probably why you never found him."

I shrugged, speechless.

"And you can see why he never brought the name change up when he reappeared from time to time." Inspector Saad sat up straighter, his chair creaked. "I thought you had the right to know—once I knew. And I have to say, I wrestled with telling you. Wasn't sure about it. You should probably talk to your mother. She must've known her husband was half-black." He paused. "Not that it's a big deal, of course. But still, she should have mentioned it to you. Did you ever tell her you looked for him? Looked through those telephone directories?"

"She'd have gone crazy. I could hardly mention his name around her. Talking about him was a betrayal. Once Daisy died, and he didn't even show up for the funeral…"

"Daisy?"

"I had a sister. I thought I told you. She died. Fell down the stairs when I dropped my roller skate on a step and didn't pick it up quick enough." I could see him swallow.

I wasn't at all sure Bunny knew her husband was black. Suddenly, I got angry.

"Were you looking for a reason why I only photographed black men? Why I sleep with them? Are you making use of some police academy course in psychology?" I fanned my face with the pile of clippings, wondering if it was as red as it felt.

"It did occur to me," he said. "But I'm no longer interested in the psychology of your lifestyle now that you're not a suspect. Thought you deserved the truth. Do what you like with the information."

Sure, throw it out on the table but deny any evil intention. But though the words were harsh, his voice wasn't, and I knew he felt sorry for me. The poor fatherless girl.

I handed him the pile of news stories, lashing out at him. "Well, what should I do with this information? Take out an ad in the *Free Press*? Is it big news nowadays? And in Detroit?"

"I might think it was big news if it were about me. It must bring up some questions. Answer others."

"Let me see the rest of those clips."

He handed them back, and I went through them one after another. "Can I take these with me?" I said after a while.

"Well, that was my plan. Whether it was a good one, I'm not sure. They're copies. You can have them." He started to put a hand on my arm, but the look on my face must have stopped him.

MAYBE I'D ALWAYS known on some level. Perhaps it was my photographer's eye. Had I missed hints or shoved them away; had my father alluded to it in his oblique way the few times we'd met? Maybe I'd known, but because Bunny never acknowledged it, nor anyone else, I didn't absorb it, at least not consciously. Was it the reason my maternal relatives had nothing but smirks and religious material to give to me? Was Daisy's lighter skin and waspish features a reason to hang around and mine a reason for my father to leave?

All I knew was that it should've been a bigger surprise than it was. It should've rocked me, but instead I was mostly irked. Howl Heart, indeed. Did the spelling make finding him in the eighties impossible? It was the last name that derailed me. Did he change his name partly to keep me away? I doubted he gave me much thought—music drove his car. Not much else mattered. Sounded a bit familiar.

CHAPTER 26

"Above all, life for a photographer cannot be a matter of indifference."
Robert Frank

I CALLED BUNNY LATER.

"He was certainly not half-black," said Bunny, sounding outraged. "Look, maybe it was the sixties, but the sixties you're thinking of came much later in places like the Berkshires. I'd never have dated a black man there or then. My goose would've been cooked if I had, sad to say. Anyway, all the girls in Lennox that summer dated Hal. He was real handsome, a good dancer, had some dough. Never heard one of them suggest he was colored." Bunny sighed, like the air had gone out of her. "Sorry, black. The world was different. Restaurants in the Berkshires didn't hire black waitresses. The only black woman I knew cleaned the place after it closed at night. Black men pumped gas, cleaned toilets, or shined shoes. Oh, it might have changed in New York, LA, or Chicago, but not where we came from."

"You talk about Massachusetts as if it were Mississippi," I fired back, annoyed with my mother as usual. "If that's the case, he definitely wouldn't have told anyone he was black. You're giving me the very reasons he'd hide it. Any wonder he didn't tell you?"

I could picture him playing in the orchestra pit for a summer run of *South Pacific*, a show about racism, and having to keep his color quiet. For the first time, I felt sorry for him. "Didn't you ever meet his family?"

Bunny was silent for a long minute, remembering. "They didn't come to the wedding. Sent us a gift and a card." She paused. "Hal claimed they were old and not well. They lived in Oakland, or somewhere out on the west coast, and couldn't make a long trip. Weddings weren't such a big deal in the sixties. Back then, an aunt with a brownie camera took pictures. A few people, a meal of casseroles, punch, and a white cake, a nice dress. Didn't seem odd at the time. I was relieved not to have to put up a lot of strangers, to spend my tips on fancy food, flowers."

"Did he ever show you a picture of his family? He must have. And what about the way he spelled his name?"

"I saw a few pictures. His mother and a sister, I think. No way they looked black. Of course, they were black-and-white pictures and lousy ones at that." Bunny stopped suddenly. "Look, I knew he used 'Howl' professionally—sort of a joke, something to catch your attention. But it's Hal Hart on the wedding certificate. He never suggested I change my name to Heart." Bunny was still talking. "My family would've come down on me like a ton of bricks if they thought I was marrying a black man. You know what they were like. I think you've got it wrong. I would've known it. Sensed it. He was on the road most of the time, but we were together for nearly seven years."

I was silent for a minute. I'd thought the same thing an hour or so ago—thought I would've known it. But why would either of us have known it if he didn't tell us—if he was light-skinned enough to fool virtually everyone? What would've tipped us off?

"I bet it's why he left," I said. "Maybe he was afraid I'd turn out to be too dark to pass. He got away with it once with Daisy—she looked like you. But he couldn't chance it with a second child. You might find out he was black. It was too late for it all to come out—easier to disappear."

"Why didn't he come back when he saw you didn't look black?" My mother's voice was more puzzled than argumentative.

Maybe marriage didn't suit an itinerant musician. Maybe being a family man didn't either.

"I'm a lot darker than Daisy was. I could be a light-skinned partially black woman." I realized that's what I was, and a calm descended.

"There's that," my mother finally said, probably relieved that his desertion had finally proven to be my fault. "Daisy was porcelain. Like me." She sound satisfied for about ten seconds. "I don't ask you about him much, but do you still see him now and then?"

"You don't ask at all."

"But do you?"

"It's been at least five years."

"So he could be dead for all we know. He'd be well into his seventies. Hal in his seventies. That's plain weird."

"Seventy-six. And he's still alive. It's pretty easy to keep track of people now." I closed my eyes and pictured the apartment building I'd seen on Google Earth. I could nearly look into his window.

"You gonna call him and tell him you know?" Her voice had gone soft.

"I don't know."

CHAPTER 27

"Once photographed, the subject becomes part of the past."
Berenice Abbott

READ THE KID'S death notice in Ben's newspaper upstairs the next morning, crouching in the hallway and turning the pages furtively. It finished with the sentence, "Visitation Monday 3-9 p.m. at the Fontenel Funeral Home." I folded the newspaper up, returned it to Ben's perky green welcome mat, and crept back downstairs. Although I would never see this kid or photograph him, I could picture him at Bill's. Imagine Bill preparing the body. This one would be dressed as simply as possible.

I'd been looking for a story or obit about Derek's death. Or other deaths, of course. This was what it'd come to now—checking death notices to see if Bill was freezing me out. I was sick to death of the whole project. Sick of what I'd faced again and again over these long hot months. Discovering my limits involved a lot more angst than I'd expected.

Other than a few rushed phone calls, I hadn't seen or talked to Bill in several weeks. I also had the impression his employees had been ordered to brush me off when I called.

"He's up at his mother's place, Ms. Hart." Or, "He's tied up with a bereaved family."

Maybe I was paranoid, but it wasn't only about getting the last photographs; I genuinely missed Bill. Could it be I was falling for him? Or had I fallen for him a long time ago? Had I finally succumbed to a man's charms, or was I merely a sore loser, imagining him with another woman? Bill liked sex too much to go this long without it; maybe he'd always had other women and I'd been too obsessed with my own work to notice it.

Months ago, long before any of this business started, a client particularly appreciative of my photographs of her son's bar mitzvah, gave me a gift certificate for products and services at a spa at Somerset Mall—the Red Coat, Red Hat, or Red Door Spa. Something like that. I rummaged through drawers looking for it. A ritzy spa in a ritzy store at a ritzy mall. The city of Detroit was without a major mall, and in recent years the ones located in the inner rim suburbs had also been deserted or turned over to Dollar Stores and cheap clothing and shoe franchises.

Right now, I needed the amenities a day at a spa would provide, despite my misgivings and the time involved—I wanted a day filled with coddling, of letting a nameless stranger put his hands on me. A good male masseuse might pound or rub some of the anxiety out. I found the certificate in the last drawer I opened, checked the expiration date, and saw the amount was for $500. What the hell! Maybe Bunny would come—a real mother-daughter day. Truthfully, I'd no one else to ask. My uncomfortable conversation with Bunny from the night before needed healing. I was blaming Bunny for my father's sins. She was a victim of his subterfuge as much as me. More. Maybe there was more to be learned over the course of a day of soft music, candlelight, skilled hands.

"Neither of us is going to be comfortable at that place," was Bunny's first comment once I got her out of bed. It was only seven, early for a waitress on the late shift. Bunny grew quiet for a minute. "It's hoity-toity land out there. Sure you got enough dough-re-me for both of us? I can't afford to chip in."

"I've got enough. My treat, head-to-toe."

"Head to tip, you mean?"

"Yes, Mom. Including the tip. I'll make appointments at eleven if I can. They shouldn't be too busy on a Monday." After listening to several more potential deal-breakers from her lips, we began the long process of hanging up, eventually agreeing to meet at 10:45.

"In front of the glass elevators," Bunny said. "On the north side. Near Macy's."

"Macy's?" I didn't know Macy's had landed in Michigan.

"Used to be Marshall Fields and before that J.L. Hudson's." Bunny paused. "But for God's sake, Violet, it's been Macy's for like—oh, about fifteen years. Don't you ever shop anywhere but resale? If you bought new clothes once in a blue moon, you'd know the names of the major retail stores. Personally I hate Macy's. Same merchandise as Marshall Field's but higher price tags. New York stores think they're grand. Folks in the Midwest get to pay for their parades and fireworks."

Bunny hung up without waiting for a response. I wished I'd had a chance to remind her I'd been brought up on resale; new clothes felt wrong next to my skin. I liked things better when the threads were a little loose, the color mellowed.

I decided to leave a bit early, hoping to buy a new dress I could tolerate. I cruised Saks, Neiman Marcus, Nordstrom's, and Macy's—all stores I detested—before finding the perfect dress in a smaller shop. I could ill afford the prices, but the situation demanded it.

The dress was a pewter-colored sharkskin number. It fit like a second skin to the waist, and below it got tighter still before ending at the knee. The salesgirl, perhaps twenty-two, was all atwitter over the fact she'd sold the dress, one seemingly destined to end up on the sales rack.

"Only looks good on a woman like you," she said, helping with the zipper. "You know, a tall, dramatic-looking woman with the right complexion. The color makes the rest of us look washed out. I tried it on once and couldn't find myself in the mirror." Here it was then, my coloring was different than the rest of theirs.

After paying for it, I ran down a pair of strappy black heels on the sales rack at Macy's, and a beaded, black choker reduced to $39 in the jewelry department. The whole ordeal had been accomplished in forty-seven minutes. My credit card hadn't had a workout like this in ages. Bill would have to take notice. Something had gone wrong in my grand plan of avoiding feelings like this, of maintaining the upper hand in romance.

Bunny was waiting at the elevator.

"What did you sign us up for?" she asked as we walked toward the store. She looked critically at her hands. "They could start at the bottom of me and work straight up." Looking around nervously, she added. "I'd rather be at the corner beauty shop. Joyce's. I feel totally out of place here. You should only come here after seeing Joyce first."

We both looked up as a perfectly groomed woman headed toward the back of the shop. "What could she possibly be having done?" Bunny fretted. "See what I mean?"

"Maybe she broke a nail?"

Bunny was right. Perhaps I should've worn the sharkskin dress for our appointment. That would've won respect.

At one point, an hour or so into it, we lay side by side covered in goo.

"We haven't been together this much since you were in fifth grade," Bunny said. What sounded sentimental was really observational. "Remember the time you invited those girls over to watch Michael Jackson's new video. What was it called?"

"'Thriller.'"

I'd been thinking about it too. I was the first kid in our neighborhood to have MTV since Bunny was a TVholic. We may not have had many clothes, but we had cable. Having MTV early made me briefly popular. Bunny threw me a big party for the "Thriller" debut, doing a campy version of the moonwalk for the giggling girls. I could never decide if the girls found Bunny ridiculous or fun, but any attempt to exclude Bunny from the festivities was eventually overridden by me when I couldn't think of how to entertain my guests. Sooner or later, I'd sneak out to the kitchen and beg Bunny to take over, exhausted by my own feeble attempts to host a party.

Bunny obliged, and I found myself resenting her ability to make fun. Had those girls with their stiff, blown-back bangs, stone-washed jeans, and knee-length sweaters been more Bunny's pals than mine? Once the MTV craze dissipated, or when the other kids all had cable too, Bunny couldn't hold their interest either. At some point, Hart women lost their allure.

"Didn't he seem like the coolest guy?" Bunny was saying. "Those girls were all in love with a black guy, but then he went and made himself white. Funny, huh?"

I was taken aback by Bunny's words. Our conversation of the night before about my father had made no impact on her. Bunny didn't hear the eeriness of her own words. Hal Hart had made himself white for a long time.

Thirty years later and color had still mattered to Michael Jackson. Imagine photographing his face. It would be hard to make it look like more than smoke and mirrors. It suddenly occurred to me; he'd looked much like Bill's dead men—his eyes seemed like opaque marbles— even before he died.

Three hours later, we walked out of the spa: smoothed, waxed, kneaded, buffed, polished, and laughing. It was among the best days we'd ever spent together. Maybe the bilious water of our joint past was now under the bridge. Now we had an explanation for Hal Hart's desertion, one that didn't fault us. Soon I'd find good old "Howl" and make him acknowledge it. I'd know when the time was right.

I'd tell Bill too, couldn't wait to see his face, in fact. "I am not a white woman exploiting black men. You had me wrong." That's what I'd say. But I'd probably still seem white to him.

"Let's stop for a quick bite at P.F. Chang's," Bunny suggested. "My treat."

We were headed toward the restaurant, passing Crate and Barrel's three-story fortress, when I saw Bill coming out of Tiffany's. He had an attractive woman on his arm—an African-American woman. I quickly nudged Bunny into Crate and Barrel, heart pounding as I waited while the couple passed. They were laughing, the woman leaning into Bill in an intimate way. I watched frozen as the woman reached up and adjusted Bill's Panama hat. He'd lost weight; he looked good. I continued to watch in stunned silence as Bill and his companion made their way across the floor to a Caribbean-style bistro and disappeared inside.

"So did you want to get something in here? Is that why you pushed me in?" Bunny was asking me when I could hear again. "I could use new placemats. What do you think of these? Violet, are you listening? What about these?"

CHAPTER 28

Detroit News: Derek Olsen, age 23, of St. Clair Shores.
Suddenly. Beloved son of Susan and the late
Robert. Beloved brother of Amy and uncle to
Conor and Madeleine. Visitation 3-9 Tuesday
at the Charles Barton Funeral Home in
St. Clair Shores. 32907 Jefferson Ave. Funeral
Services Wednesday at St. Nicholas' Catholic Church.
19045 Mack Ave., Grosse Pointe Woods. Interment
at the Overlook Cemetery, 33300 Gratiot Avenue,
Roseville, MI.
(September 2011)

I MADE A QUICK excuse to my mother and ran for the parking lot.
People made way for me as if I were a careening bus. I wasn't crying
yet, but was damned close to it—had a funny, unfamiliar taste in my
throat; my heart pounded.

So he'd chosen an African-American woman to stroll through
the mall with. He chose a black woman to hang from his arm in
daylight and in a public space. Had we ever been together in a place
like Somerset Mall, where people might see us? Or was I only for the

nighttime when we were unlikely to be spotted?

Did it always have to be about race? If I lived in Seattle or Minneapolis instead of Detroit, would I be free of it? Or was it about Asians, Somalians, or Bosnians in other places? Would there always be someone to look down on or up to because of where they came from, the color of their skin, the shape of their eyes?

Who *was* the woman on Bill's arm? Looking like she belonged there, like she'd been with him forever. There was something familiar about her. Then it hit me: she might be the sister of the murdered rapper, Cajuan Grace. Their faces were nearly identical. I had spent enough time with Cajuan to recognize that bone structure, the high cheekbones, for instance. Hadn't her name been dropped on several occasions: was she the one who knew about diabetes; the one he'd asked about photographing Cajuan? Maybe I saw her hanging around Bill's at the time of the burial and maybe once more recently. Hadn't I heard him talking to her on his cell a few weeks ago? Had he mentioned her to me a couple of other times? A nurse maybe? More than a couple times, now that I thought about it. What was her name? It was horrible not knowing who she was. I'd google Cajuan's obit as soon as I got home. One of the articles would've mentioned her—survived by a sister. Why didn't I read the newspaper?

Damn, and double damn. How long had this been going on? I tried to remember when the feeling of what—remoteness—began. It'd been gradual. Events always seemed to intervene in our relationship. I'd been in a perpetual rush lately too, barely any time to think about our quasi-estrangement. Hard to remember what Bill knew about Derek Olsen's death, for instance. When was the last time I spoke to him? Filled him in on what I was doing? Would there ever be an opportunity to share the news of my father with him? How would he react to my new "blackness"?

One fact was certain—I'd have to find a way to see him that didn't involve death—death in any form. Remind him of what we'd had before all of this began. Remind myself of it too. In certain ways we'd become closer through sharing this project. Gotten beyond the pure sexuality of the first months. Could there be more? Was that why that dame was on his arm—he wanted more? More than I gave him? Maybe he thought he could only get it from a black woman?

With the lane closures on I-75, it took more than forty-five minutes to get home. Jumping out of the car, I noticed the shopping bags in the backseat and wondered if I should head right back to the mall and return my wasted purchases. The amount spent on the dress was staggering and with the way my life was headed, there'd be no money from a gallery show to balance my checkbook. When and where would I ever wear a dress like this now? Still, it wasn't over yet. There was the remote possibility Bill's relationship with Ms. Grace—if that was her name—was more friendly than romantic.

Suddenly, it struck me. Bill and the woman were coming out of a jewelry store. Tiffany's, for God's sake. Could it have progressed that far so fast? Progressed to the point he was buying expensive jewelry? Perhaps THE jewelry.

Bill had never given me more than token gifts. I only remembered a DVD of *The Departed* and an inexpensive necklace he picked out at the art fair in Ann Arbor last summer. For Christmas, he took me to Chicago for the weekend. Out of the way, as usual.

It was because I was white; I knew it in my heart. He'd never taken me seriously because I was white. A convenient woman to sleep with till the real thing came along. Was the real thing the woman at the mall today? Once he knew I wasn't 100 percent white, would that make a difference?

Before I could settle into a full-blown pity fest, the phone rang. I leaped for it, thinking whatever distraction it might bring had to be better than this. The voice saying my name was vaguely familiar—a woman's voice.

"Ms. Hart?" the voice repeated for the third time.

"Mrs. Olsen?" I assumed Mrs. was the title she'd prefer. I mumbled the words the cops from *Law and Order* always said. "I'm sorry for your loss, Mrs. Olsen. Derek—well, he was a terrific guy. I didn't know him for long…"

"Thank you, Violet," Mrs. Olsen interrupted before I could finish my thought. "I hope I can call you by your first name, knowing how close you and Derek were."

I didn't correct this misconception since Mrs. Olsen sounded far too shaky for any disappointing clarifications. Maybe in Derek's world, I *was* a close friend. Mrs. Olsen was still talking, telling me Derek's body had been released—it was now being prepared for the funeral.

"Would you be willing to take his picture, Violet?"

Take his picture. Had Derek told his mother?

"The photographs I've been taking have all come from the Fontenel Funeral Home. I made an arrangement with the mortician there. The men have all been African-American."

"I want a photograph for myself." Mrs. Olsen cleared her throat. "Derek told me you took pictures of dead people. Art photographs. At first I thought it was a little odd, but Derek seemed to think it was a good idea. I think he'd want you to take his picture."

"You might find it painful," I said, not warming to this idea at all. "I'm not sure Derek would want it for himself either. He liked the idea of it—the art aspect. He never saw any of the photos, you know. He might not have cared for them. You might not either. It takes some getting used to."

"Even if I never look at the photograph, I'll know it's there. We'll have it, at least. I can't remember when we last took a picture of anyone besides the grandkids."

Bill told me how many of the parents of the dead men had said this—that they had no recent pictures. Instead of producing prints, the images from cell phones or digital cameras sat on people's hard drives now. Or never left their cells. Sorting through cold technological devices was more difficult somehow than flipping through an album.

Mrs. Olsen paused. "You know it's only his sister and the grandchildren besides me. Have you met her?"

"No, I didn't get the chance." I still couldn't tell Mrs. Olsen I'd only been with Derek three times, and he'd never mentioned a sister. We'd never shared a meal, or a cup of coffee. Our time spent together couldn't have exceeded two or three hours and most had been spent burying the animal fetus in my neighbor's garden. "Tell me where they have him—the name of the funeral home, I mean."

"And you'll stay for the viewing? I'd like to have you there. I know he'd want that." Mrs. Olsen was starting to cry now. "He didn't have too many friends, you know. He was popular as a kid, but once his troubles started—well, you know. He got—unpredictable—in high school. People flee from a child like Derek, especially teenagers. They thought Derek was cool for a while. The way he'd do the unexpected. Like urinating in a water fountain or skateboarding holding onto the back of a truck. But, well, they figured it out. I can't say he didn't scare *me* at times. Once we got him on the proper medication, it got better." Mrs. Olsen sighed with a momentary relief, probably forgetting for a second or two that those better days had come to an end.

"I'll be there." I'd never been to the funerals of the men I photographed. "I'll call the funeral home and find out when's a good time for me to take pictures." I wasn't sure if other morticians worked as efficiently as Bill. Or if I'd have a hard time gaining access to Derek. "You might want to call and clear it with them, Mrs. Olsen. They may not be used to someone photographing a…"

"I sent his best suit over with a courier, but it may be too large for him now. It's actually from his high school graduation—well, he didn't actually graduate. He's lost weight now, living like he does—did—food got short shrift." She sighed. "I should've kept him at home, even during the day."

"They'll make the suit fit. They know what to do. It happens a lot. People can change quickly."

I hung up as soon as I could, not able to listen to Mrs. Olsen anymore. She was, thankfully, unaware of my part in Derek's death. I hoped her ignorance would continue, but I felt like a hypocrite going along with the fiction that we were close friends. Even if it was a merciful interpretation of the events.

No good could come from telling Mrs. Olsen I used her son's illness to try and procure subjects to photograph. Sent him out looking for exactly what got him killed. No one's interest would be served by hearing that. If I was acquiring a more active conscience, it didn't sit well. I could feel pushing from each corner.

My familiarity with corpses did little to prepare me for Derek. This was the first time I'd looked at a familiar face, now dead, through a camera lens. Whatever Derek went through in the last few days had changed him; he looked older than his years.

And whoever prepared him for burial at Barton's Funeral Home didn't have Bill's touch or care. I'd rushed into the mortuary out of the rain, where a sullen secretary met me and pointed me in the right direction, gesturing wordlessly to a place to stash my umbrella. I shook my head like a wet dog, soliciting darker looks and a quick search for a towel to wipe it up.

Derek's graduation suit looked huge on him despite my assurances to his mother that this sort of problem was easily solved. I tried to adjust the jacket, but it was a two-person job and I went for help.

The Charles Barton Funeral Home, in a far better neighborhood than Bill's place, didn't have much to recommend it. The interior furnishings looked cheap and indifferently selected, and the rugs were threadbare. The prep room must have been located right beneath the room where Derek lay because I picked up its odor whenever the air-conditioning came on. I hadn't fully realized how much care Bill took with his business. More than the corpses got his attention. Black people took death seriously, perhaps because it loomed larger in their lives. They'd never put up with a shabby place like this one. They'd see the paucity of nice touches as a sign of disrespect.

I found help quickly, a young guy who seemed willing to give me a hand. Together we fixed Derek's coat so he didn't look like a victim of a debilitating illness. We also propped a small pillow under the small of his back, so he didn't seem to collapse into the satin. I asked for cosmetics, which Rudy brought quickly.

"You're pretty good at this," he said, taking the case from me when I was finished. "If you ever need extra work I could tell Mr. Barton…"

I shook my head, hoping to hold back a grimace. "Actually I've done a little of this cosmetic work in the past, but it probably helps that I knew Derek. Know how he needs to look."

I thanked Rudy, and he hurried off to replace the borrowed equipment. Probably his boss wouldn't be too happy to find me making little adjustments to his work. But Derek looked better for it; even the assistant saw it.

Just in time, I realized Derek's hair was parted on the wrong side. Hesitating a minute, I took out my own comb and changed the part, tossing the comb into a trash basket when I was done—it was too macabre to think of using it again. I took a dozen pictures, my stomach kneading the whole time, bile floating up and down my throat as I bent over him. He was so small in the coffin. Though all of the men had been young, Derek's death was immeasurably harder to deal with. But I deserved the discomfort and heartache it brought.

"Hope you're not planning to stick around after you're done with him."

I turned to see Inspector Saad standing in the archway. "For the viewing, I mean." He was dressed in a navy suit, his hair still slightly damp from the rain. A maroon tie finished his ensemble. What did these cops get paid anyway? Had he ever worn the same suit twice?

"Mrs. Olsen asked me to stay for the viewing after I finish."

He looked at the camera with distaste. "I thought all the men in your scrapbook were black."

I flushed angrily. "This isn't for that. Mrs. Olsen asked me to take a picture for the family. It's a favor."

"Guess it's catching on. Mantel photos of the dead. You've started a trend." He seemed lost in thought for a minute and I started to return to my work. "Hey," he said finally. "I forgot to mention something back at my office the other day."

"How could there possibly be anything else?"

He walked all the way into the room now, coming to stand over

Derek's body. "Whew, he sure took a beating. I'd forgotten. Mortician couldn't quite cover up the bruises on his throat, could he?"

I adjusted the collar again, trying to pull it higher. "Bill would've done better by him."

Saad nodded. "Whoever strangled Olsen had the strength of a Samson. Squeezed the air out of the carotid, the jugular, the larynx. Plus the trachea. It would take pretty significant muscle to do all that damage." His mouth tightened. "The coroner's almost certain it was one unaided pair of hands too. No ligature. And the poor kid was so skinny, a quick squeeze would've been enough."

"I know."

You could see the delicate bones beneath the flesh. Underneath the makeup, I could see the imprints of fingers still. It was nearly enough to undo me. This was the most maternal I'd ever felt about anyone—and it was too late to act on it, to save him.

"So anyway, I meant to warn you on your way out of the station."

"Warn me about what?" I asked, putting my equipment away and pushing the stepladder back into the corner. "Not leaving town?"

"No, not that." A smile flittered across his face. "You're too much at the scene of the crime for your own good, Miss Hart."

"Half the time *you've* called me in. The other half I've been trying to help."

"That's not what I mean. A damned nasty thug killed the guy that Derek found parts of scattered on Belle Isle. Derek was killed because they thought he knew too much about it—maybe saw things he shouldn't have seen. Who else was involved with those body parts? Who else was on the scene at the time of Derek's death? Who found Derek's body? Who's been in and out of my office?" He stopped. "Get my point? And, as I said, here you are again. You might as well have the words 'next victim' stamped on your forehead."

My hands went numb. "You think someone might try to kill me?"

"You're like the woman in an old murder mystery who goes down the cellar steps after she's heard a loud noise. The 'had I but known' girl." He stopped suddenly. "Yes, someone might try to kill you, Violet. Probably not tonight, but you never know."

"I told Mrs. Olsen I'd stay for the viewing. She's worried there won't be a good turnout."

We both looked at Derek; he looked insignificant and insubstantial in death. His sculptures in the park would probably attract more interest than his life.

"She's probably been worrying about that sort of thing her whole life. The kind of mother who peeked out the window and wept when Derek played alone, when nobody gave him a Valentine or invited him to their birthday party. She'll get over it and you'll be safer out of the fray."

"Look, I have to stay. I owe her that."

"I'll follow you home then," Saad said, shrugging. "Okay?"

"Wouldn't seeing us leave together tip them off? I mean, I'm only mentioned as an area photographer in the newspaper. No names. Maybe no one knows who I am."

His mouth tightened. "You should get out of here right now, Violet. But if you won't, I'll follow you home after the viewing. No one will know I'm doing it." He helped me carry my bags to the back room. "We more or less owe you one for spotting those marks. Least I can do."

"Like you said, they—he—probably wouldn't show up."

"Probably not."

THE CROWD WAS sparse and someone not connected to Derek by family or friendship would've stood out. No one did. They came mostly in ones and twos, said a word or two to Mrs. Olsen, peered sadly at the body, signed the book, and left. I stayed until nearly the end. Despite the suddenness and nature of his death, no one seemed surprised. He'd been headed down this road since puberty.

Inspector Saad followed me home as promised. On the way to the car, he gave me his cell number. "Just in case."

"Think someone might show up at my flat?"

"I doubt it. This sort of person isn't usually skilled at putting the plot points together. Probably has no idea who you are." I took the piece of paper. "And do us both a favor, Violet. Don't show up at the funeral tomorrow. Someone's much more likely to come forward there. Out in the open in a big cemetery isn't as chancy as a tiny space in a funeral home."

I nodded, thinking I'd have to call Mrs. Olsen and give her an excuse other than the real one. No sense having her worry more than she already was. I'd tell her I was ill. Which I was.

CHAPTER 29

*"I photograph to find out what something
will look like photographed."*
Garry Winogrand

FTER THE SCRAMBLED, REM-less sleep extreme fear produces, I got up, climbed into the car, and took off. I'd be damned if I was going to sit around waiting to hear footsteps on the stairs or to see a hand reaching out for me in the tub. So I didn't take a shower and I didn't eat breakfast either. And other than Derek's mother, I didn't call any of the people I'd have liked to call from a landline phone with good reception and a soft chair to sit in. Grabbing my cell, a banana, a camera, and a poorly tossed newspaper, I fled.

My first stop was Fontenel's Funeral Home, which hovered darkly over the empty blacktop parking lot despite the sunny day. The din of rush hour traffic on Jefferson Avenue was only a block and a half away, and I waited impatiently for it to fade. The air smelled bad. The Detroit incinerator was cranking out toxic spew, but it was too hot to sit in a car with the windows closed. I sat, four houses down from Bill's mortuary, for a good hour, watching for the unlikely possibility that

Bill and/or his lady friend might exit through the front door. Oh, yes, I hadn't forgotten her. She ranked pretty high on my lists of worries.

Bill usually kept his funeral-friendly Lincoln in the smaller back lot, but the space was cut off from my view. He and his lady friend could be having sex in the back seat for all I knew.

Watching a house was more difficult than I'd expected. You couldn't do anything *but* watch. Pick up a book, start listening to the radio, dream a bit because you hadn't slept in two days, smoke a joint, bite into your banana, do any of these and you might miss what you'd come to see. I quickly decided I'd never become a private eye. I bet the same people who liked to fish went into that line of work.

I didn't know exactly why I was there, what I expected to find, and what I would do about it should I find it. I just needed to put myself near Bill in the hopes something would disprove my suspicions. Why hadn't I called him last night? Tried to get something out of him? I guess a more surreptitious approach suited me. Maybe Ted Ernst was right and I preferred to live my life behind masks or cameras.

I thought briefly about taking a few photos but getting the proper bead on the house would draw attention. So I sat—waiting and watching. The only upside to my enforced immobility was it gave me more time to think about my father and what to do about that situation. Was it possible my new information would open the door to a relationship? Did I want one? Was it worry about exposure that sent my father into the night or was it only one aspect of his disinterest in his family? Did he see us as an impediment to his career? That'd be my guess. My birth was a good excuse to leave. He didn't seem like the kind of guy who'd be bothered much about color. But as Bunny often reminded me, the sixties were another era.

Nothing was going on at Bill's place. I took a bite of my banana, looking around. A stakeout was worthless here. No activity at all. The door remained closed. Things only picked up once, for about thirty seconds, when a Fed-Ex truck pulled up. But after trotting halfway up to Fontenel's front door, the delivery man checked the address on the package, made a swift right turn, and cut across the well-watered lawn to the house next door.

Bill was almost certainly tied up with the burial of the child killed in the drive-by shooting. I didn't know where or when it would take place. After an hour's wait, I decided my vigil was worthless. Derek's funeral was probably underway, and I wondered if the turnout was any better than the one last night. My whole life was occupied with death now. The deaths I photographed, the deaths I read about, the deaths I caused. Was it the death of my relationship with Bill I was here to witness? And how did my project tie into it?

On a whim, I started the car and drove to the main branch of the Detroit Public Library downtown, parked in a Wayne State University lot for five dollars, and entered the DPL through the main door. Things were a lot easier now than when I'd tried to track my father down twenty years earlier. I put aside the urge to google Howl Heart and instead googled "Cajuan Grace."

Thousands of entries appeared, but his recent death notice topped the list. I clicked the first link and found an article listing Cajuan's survivors: a mother, a brother (Tyrone), and three sisters, (Helena, Bonita, and Athena). I'd bet anything Bill hooked up with one of the women. Why couldn't I remember the name? He'd mentioned her more than once.

I googled the women's names. There were no hits for Helena Grace other than additional cites of her brother's obit. Bonita had apparently tried her hand at acting. She was a featured actress in plays in Ann

Arbor and Detroit in 2003 and 2005. It looked like she moved out to LA in 2008. She'd been in *Fences* last year at the Santa Monica Playhouse. A couple of other small parts were listed. There were several photos when I checked Google images; she wasn't the woman with Bill at Somerset Mall, but she looked a bit like her. It was Athena on Bill's arm. I'd bet.

Athena. The only local Athena Grace was a nurse at Oakwood Hospital in Dearborn. Her resume, posted for a nursing conference in Cleveland last fall, appeared with a PDF file. Athena had presented a paper on new methods of treating pre-diabetic African-American men to a group of practitioners at the conference. I clicked Google images and a photo of a group of nurses standing in the lobby of a hotel, probably the one in Cleveland, appeared. There were two African-American women in the group of ten women and one man. One of the women wore glasses and looked to be in her sixties. The other one looked a lot like the photos of Bonita Grace and a lot more like the woman with Bill at Tiffany's. I clicked the picture to enlarge it. There was little doubt. Given the rest of the evidence, I felt certain. Athena was the woman on Bill's arm.

Athena's knowledge of diabetes probably drew Bill to her. He'd mentioned his diagnosis—or his mother's perhaps—when she stopped by the funeral home, and she'd stepped forward, full of information to give him. Maybe their relationship centered on her medical expertise at first; maybe she was a friend and nothing more. But they hadn't looked like friends coming out Tiffany's the other day. Not at all. I could still remember the way she leaned into Bill as they exited the store. It was an intimate gesture; so friendly, in fact, it made me run away.

That intimacy stung but additionally my mother was with me; I couldn't bear to have her witness my disgrace. A second later and we would've met. I could picture the kind of explanation Bill would've given, and I immediately flashed back on an early scene in my life when I'd come in on my father leaving the house, Bunny shouting out obscenities from the porch, Daisy watching from an upstairs window. I'd only seen my father once or twice in those first years after his departure, bringing inappropriate gifts for his daughters, leaving long before he should, bored with our suburban life.

The next to last time I saw him, five or six years ago, I ran into him playing at a jazz club in New York. Hadn't even seen his name on the bill when I wandered in. If I had, some answers might have come earlier. He didn't recognize me with the lights making the audience disappear, but I easily picked him out. It was an all-black band, except for my father on the trumpet. Or that's what I'd thought at the time—not so strange for a jazz group. After the first set, I ran into him coming out of the restroom; he didn't look twice. Of course if I'd run into him on the street, I probably wouldn't have known him either.

No address was provided for Athena Grace on the resume accompanying the conference paper. I tried a few web address sites, but got nowhere and soon I was back in the car again, driving toward Belle Isle, parking as close to Derek's sculptures as possible, camera in hand, wanting to take a picture of its remnants before it all came down. It was likely to be dismantled quickly now that the cops were done with their investigation. I wanted to take a picture before it was gone.

It seemed I was compiling a record of Derek—why I didn't know. I had a photo of him alive—he'd managed to slip into one of the photos I took of the mounted hands and feet—in fact, he was like an apparition on the print. I'd almost tossed it when I saw it at home the night I developed them. There he'd been with his scarecrow's smile, waving a Salem cigarette around, looking bleary-eyed at his artwork. He looked ghostlike—an omen perhaps. I also had the photos from his viewing, the ones from the prep room.

Easing through the underbrush, I came out on the shoreline. Things had changed a lot in two days—what do they call it—a sea change? Derek's sculptures, or what was left of them, were now encircled by flimsy, orange, plastic link fences—the kind of fence that slumps and doesn't protect anything—just marks it off.

Derek's work, now almost invisible behind the barrier, had been violated with crude additions, vile incursions into his space. People had stuck objects in the holes of the cheap fencing: flowers made of Kleenex, straw, and silk; toys; tiny stuffed animals; crosses; rosaries; baby shoes; pictures of Jesus; a picture or two of people I didn't recognize. Nothing more than debris—yes, that's what you'd call it—and on the face of it not so different from Derek's work. But if Matisse had added a flower to a woman holding a bouquet in a Vermeer painting that would be defacement too.

People had poked dozens of doll's hands and feet into the fence. Mimicking Derek's find, I suppose. The story was too visual for the average nut to pass up. It was the kind of display you saw on bridges over freeways or in roadside memorials. But here? How different *was it* from Derek's own work? Or Tyree Guyton's? Maybe Derek would find it fitting—recognizable. A tribute even.

Someone had also made a fairly professional sign and hung it from the fence: *The Derek Olsen Project.* Evidently its creator also saw the link between Derek's work and Guyton's Heidelberg Project. Even now a few people were here with cameras.

"Would you mind moving aside?" one man called out to me. "I'm taking a few shots for the *Free Press.*"

Well, la-di-da. I was speechless. Derek, in death, had outmaneuvered me in creating edgy work. Despite all I'd felt for him, a frisson of jealousy passed through me. Not nice to admit it, but it was true. But I pushed it aside as I wondered if Derek's sculptures were eventually deemed art, would it be reconstructed, perhaps from my photos, to stand as a memorial? Or was it like those roadside tributes for people killed in car accidents, stuff that disappeared in a few weeks or after the first storm? It'd be nice to think that Derek would be remembered through his work.

"I'm taking photos for Derek's mother," I shot back. "She asked me to come down."

The guy shrugged, unimpressed, and we jockeyed for the best angles for the next fifteen minutes.

As I WALKED back to the car, my cell rang.

"Ms. Hart?" I recognized Joe Saad's voice right away. I could also hear background noise from police headquarters.

"Yeah," I said, looking around guiltily. I was pretty sure I'd promised him to stay away from Belle Isle. Had someone spotted me and my camera?

"I can hear the geese. Pretty, aren't they? Until you look at the soles of your shoes or try to find a clean place to sit." His voice grew indistinct as he spoke to someone in his office. "Excuse me," he said, returning to the line. "Look, good news. You can breathe easier. We have the guys responsible for Derek's death. And the first guy's death too." I could hear him shuffling papers. "Jorge Sanchez was the victim. His brother turned up today and identified him. Or what we had of him."

"So quickly?" I said, exhaling the least constricted breath I'd let go of in days. "You know who did it?" Could it be over this fast?

"They're in the interview rooms right now. Finally lawyering up."

He laughed lightly. "All of them wearing the damned ankle bracelet too. It's a cobra. They should've called their attorneys an hour ago. Or at least before one of them tried to strangle an officer. The guy's hands were as big as a catcher's mitt. A lucky break we picked the right guys up. The gang's new here in the Detroit area, but big in prestige and growing in numbers."

"So it was gang-related? Something to do with cobras—the bracelet, I mean?"

"Yep. Cobra Real," he said, easily affecting a Spanish accent. "One of the bigger gangs in the Midwest and growing deadlier."

"Why did they go after him? Jorge, was it?"

"Jorge had a conscience apparently and came to the police a few weeks ago with the story of a fourteen-year-old girl the Cobras had gang-raped and left for dead. Couldn't stomach it, I guess."

"So they had to kill him?"

"Of course—how else to establish their 'don't fuck with us' ethos. And gangs have a way of signaling their intentions through graffiti. More and more warnings go up on their turf when trouble's about to go down."

"Like war drums?"

"I guess. Anyway, Jorge's initials were all over the place in bombs with a 'K' after his gang name. And the number one-eighty-seven started to appear too in the most recent tags."

"'K' for kill?"

"Right. And one-eighty-seven is the California Penal Code number for homicide. Worst number you can see after a name. He should've come to us for protection. Once the bombs go up, well, it's gonna happen." Anticipating my next question, he said, "Bombs are tagger-talk for graffiti with multi-colored, bubbled letters."

"And Derek Olsen looked like a threat?"

"Haven't gotten them to admit knowing about Derek's death, but we will. The catcher's-mitt-for-hands guy is pretty limited mentally. I think he'll roll over before the day is out. Just have to hope he's not so dumb or crazy that a judge or jury will take pity on him. Anyway," Saad added, "I don't think anyone from Cobra Real linked you with Derek. They seem too unimaginative to put it together—that a woman would come into it at all. I'm not saying you're completely out of danger, but I doubt anything's gonna happen now we've made our case without mentioning your name."

"Thanks for calling. I know you didn't have to."

"Sure I had to. But I'd still be a little careful—at least until we get the case wrapped up tighter. Till we're sure this death squad can be put behind bars or controlled."

"You're not expecting me to testify, are you?"

That idea occurred to me for the first time; I took the photograph showing the marks. I'd figured out what the marks were. Wouldn't they need me to back them up?

He echoed my thoughts. "Might have to testify you were the one who took the photo showing those marks. But that happened only after they were mounted on Derek's sculpture. So what does it mean in the scheme of things," he continued. "We'll see. I think they've said way too much already. Go find your boyfriend and have a nice dinner."

"I only wish."

"So it's like that, huh?"

CHAPTER 30

Detroit Free Press: Two men have been arrested in the slaying of 22-year-old Marcus Denton, whose cash and sunglasses were the motive in his shooting, police said. Witnesses said the suspects pulled out guns and told Denton to empty his pockets and hand over what they believed to be designer sunglasses, shooting him when he didn't immediately act. The shooting took place at the City Party Store in Highland Park. The men are awaiting arraignment in the Wayne County Jail.

(September 2011)

DRIVING AGAIN, I found myself headed for southwest Detroit, curious to see these "bombs" Saad'd mentioned. It'd never occurred to me the initials or words slapped up all over the city were meant to do more than get recognition for a lonely soul. Or, at most, express a sentiment.

Years earlier, a tag on an overpass near my freeway exit read "Eunice Williams, I love you forever." I was taken with the romantic gesture at the time; the thought of the whipped teenager hanging from the railing, spray paint can in hand, was compelling. I shot the tag from several angles, trying to make something of it, but it didn't go anywhere. I'd always looked at the bulk of graffiti as annoying, ugly, pointlessly destructive, derivative—but relatively harmless. Saad set me straight. It could be deadly; the gang equivalent of a newspaper, the throwing down of a gauntlet: a bomb.

"Why don't they put a stop to it?" I asked Diogenes on my cell. "The cops, the city, someone."

He'd refused to come along on the drive through southwest Detroit, so I was talking via cell while I meandered along city streets, driving too slowly for the honking cars behind. Many of the houses had disappeared in recent, or not so recent, years. The landscape looked almost rural. At one point, I spotted a pheasant perched on the rusted chassis of an ancient Oldsmobile. His mate roamed on the trash-filled ground below him, elevating the surroundings through their disregard. They looked like elegant ladies with their skirts hitched.

"I wish you wouldn't do this."

"Do what?"

"Any of the fucked-up stuff you're up to lately."

Di slammed down a pan on the counter in the restaurant kitchen. I held the phone away from my ear. "Lately, having you for a friend is more irritating than parenting an unruly child. You're like a dervish, whirling through this city and stirring things up. Right now though, I'm talking about you driving and talking on your cell at the same time, a more mundane concern than whether one of these gangland snakes will off you, but still, a real worry for a cautious boy like me. Next you'll be texting me while you drive."

"I don't text while I drive. They're going to pass a law against it, right? And it's cobras, not snakes. They call themselves cobras."

"Distinction noted. But I'm gonna hang up if I hear any squeals."

"I used to smoke, drink coffee, and drive—all at once," I said, setting my coffee down. "You never objected."

"People never thought of wearing seatbelts once either. It's called progress. Am I supposed to be impressed with your ambidexterity? And they *do* try to stop the tagging," he said, returning to my question. "They—meaning the police, community groups, schools—try all the time."

I could barely hear him over the continual clatter of pans. Diogenes was preparing a wedding dinner for the pampered daughter of a U.S. Rep and five hundred members of the Rep's closest PAC.

"Don't ask me why I agreed to it. Business is usually slow in late summer and it seemed like a good idea a year and a half ago."

"So what do they do to stop the tagging? The powers that be," I said, returning to the scene in front of me.

"One tactic I read about in the *Metrotimes* was a project called 'Art in the Alley.' Area school kids paint murals over the graffiti."

"Sort of like sticking a daisy in the barrel of a gun."

"Hey, I'm surprised you remember that ad," he said, "being as culturally deficient as you are."

"I always remember a good photo."

"They have a gang squad too, I think. Look, I'm no expert on gang activity, you know. Anyway, what are you doing down there, Violet? Looking for your name on a school fence with—what was it—a one-eight-seven after it? Asking in cash-checking places and liquor stores about Cobra Real? Chasing tattooed guys down back alleys? Playing a Latino station on the radio with your windows wide open?"

"Boy, if you're not the king of the ethnic stereotype. And aren't they your people? I haven't set a foot outside my car. Remember, Saad said I was out of it." I paused to make a left turn and added, "Actually, I thought I *might* take a few pictures. Which *is* what I do. Remember."

I was closing in on the end of the project with Bill. No matter how it turned out, I was stopping after a dozen photos. It wouldn't hurt to start looking around for a new idea. Maybe taking pictures of graffiti would turn out to be another shopping cart fiasco, but maybe not. Graffiti was a show of strength in these parts. Location could make the tags compelling: gritty scenes from post-apocalyptic Detroit. That's what this neighborhood looked like. Except where was the graffiti?

"Did Saad actually put it like that? Did he say, 'Vi, it's okay to drive around southwest Detroit and look for festering trouble. Insinuate yourself into the gangs.'"

"No. But he did say the case was about wrapped up. Probably the danger was past."

"Look if you'll wait till tomorrow, I'll come with you. We can stalk the streets, looking for trouble. Get one of those temporary tattoos, wear muscle shirts to show off, swill beer from those huge bottles while we drive here and there. God, I'm turning myself on."

"Aw, I'm just driving down West Vernor, Di. A million other women are here too. Look, there's one now. Going into a bodega with a baby in her arms, and nobody's tailing her or trying to spray paint. So don't break out in hives over this. I'm Ms. Nobody in this part of town."

I turned off my cell and tossed it on the seat. I needed both hands for what lay ahead.

THIRTY MINUTES LATER, I concluded I didn't know where or how to look for gang graffiti. The stuff I'd seen looked like harmless tagging. Schoolyards, Saad had said—fences, the sides of buildings, railroad yards. The only fences were cyclone jobs. Maybe gangs avoided tagging on the main thoroughfares like Vernor, Fort or Michigan

Avenue, transmitting their arcane messages from the neighborhoods behind the central drags. Secret places for those in the know. And that excluded me.

The recognizable graffiti I saw, and some of it *was* on the sides of houses, was so steeped in symbols and mysterious squibs I couldn't begin to decode it. Either it was hopelessly enigmatic or the work of children. In several places, primitive murals of village life in an alternate universe covered old tags. A street filled with stacks of cement pipes for a new sewer line was heavily sprayed, each cylinder of cement with the same seemingly innocuous O and A, linked by a squiggly, blue line. The O could have meant Olsen, but I doubted it. It looked freshly sprayed and Derek had been dead for days now. I climbed out of the car once or twice and took several photos, although none seemed promising.

It was starting to rain and I headed back to the car. For a grand finale, I swung by Holy Redeemer Church, the heart of Detroit's Hispanic community. An elderly woman was washing the front steps with a scrub brush and a bucket of detergent. It looked like an act of respect or contrition rather than a paid assignment.

I was much too undereducated in tagging to know what to look for. Maybe a trip with Di was worth considering. Maybe I could corral Saad into showing me around—he'd expressed gratitude.

Next, feeling empowered by my trip through gangland, I headed for Oakwood Hospital in nearby Dearborn.

"I'm looking for an Athena Grace," I told the elderly man at the information desk.

"A patient?" he said, poising his fingers over the keyboard and looking through his reading glasses at the screen.

"A nurse."

The flow of people through the lobby muffled my words and he put a hand to his ear. "Personal business?"

"No, it's about her work with diabetic patients. I'm doing a piece on it for the newspaper." I whipped out the press pass I only got to use once or twice a year. "She's done research in that area."

Apparently unimpressed by cutting-edge research, the man gazed at the press pass stoically and nodded, his eyes returning to the screen. "What's the name again?" I told him and he typed it in. "Nope, not at Oakwood-Dearborn anymore. Been reassigned to the endocrinology department downriver. Trenton." He looked up. "Need the address?" Not waiting for an answer, he clicked and a map came off the printer in seconds. He handed it over, looking past me to the next person in line.

I was about to put a foot on the gas pedal a few minutes later when the cell rang. It was Bill. My heart did a little jig as I answered.

"Hi." His voice hovered between warm and cool. "Why was your phone turned off?"

I started to tell him I'd been in a hospital plastered with signs about turning off cell phones, but thought better of it. "Didn't know it *was* off. Sorry. Something up?"

"Usual stuff. You'd have to get right down here though." He paused. "I was late getting to him and now—well, you know the story."

"Be there in twenty minutes. No, wait. I have to go home for the Deardorff. Don't want to use anything else at this point. Damn. Can you give me an hour?"

"That's the outside limit. If I'm not around when you arrive, he's the one in white."

"White? Like a bride?" I took a deep breath, thinking of the finished photo already. "Why white?"

"You got me. Parents picked it out from my wardrobe. Supposedly the suit belonged to a jazz musician, back in the sixties, I think. White satin with pearl buttons. I got it on eBay last year."

I whistled. "Hey, we haven't bumped into each other in a while, Bill." Would he get my euphemism? "Could you hang around for a few minutes maybe?"

"Maybe a few. Got a million things to wrap up."

"I'll be quick."

Maybe there'd be time to tell him. How long could it take to say, "Hey, Bill, I'm partly black." Or "Hey, Bill, I have a contract for you to sign." Or "Hey, Bill, who's this Athena Grace you're hanging out with?"

Bill was waiting in the hallway when I lumbered in with my equipment. "Anything wrong?" I asked. He'd never waited in the hall for me before. He looked antsy.

"Not really. His parents are in there with him. Let's give them a few minutes alone." He herded me into his office. "Two guys murdered their son for a pair of twenty-dollar sunglasses. Thought they might cost as much as two hundred, and how could they pass up getting a nickel bag of coke. Can you believe this rotten world?"

Bill started to put out a hand but then pulled it back. I felt a chill— had I become untouchable? "Look, I've gotta take off." He glanced at his watch. "It's been an hour and a half since I called."

"Traffic. On the Chrysler." I'd flown considering the number of cars on the freeways, the number of lane closures, the accident. "Maybe we can get together tonight? Tomorrow night?"

He shook his head. "I've got Marcus Denton to see to tonight. And tomorrow night—well, I should drive up to Saginaw and see Mom. You know how it is."

"Okay." I didn't believe a word of it. "Maybe later in the week?"

He nodded, relieved. "I'll give you a call once I get past a few of these events."

He was halfway out the door, never having so much as hugged me, smiled, or asked me a question. It was hard to remember what exactly he knew about it'd been so long. What *had* we talked about back in the days when our relationship was going well? Or at least better.

Suddenly, he looked back. "What's this? Number ten or eleven?"

"One or the other," I told him, not sure how many of the photographs were legal. "I'm not keeping an exact count. Bad luck," I added inanely.

"I'm thinking ten. Ten seems like a good place to end it, Violet. Tell Ernst, you're ready."

"I'd planned on twelve," I almost whispered.

He sighed. "But it'll be wrapped up in a few weeks?" I nodded. "Can't say I won't be relieved. No, way more than that." His eyes softened. "I mean it's been interesting at times, and a few of the families have actually taken comfort from the pictures, but still."

"Still, it's not your style."

"Nope." He put his hand on the doorknob. "Good luck with Marcus. I think you'll be pleased." He shook off the words. "Sounds heartless, but what doesn't with this project of yours. That's what tears it for me." He looked at me hard. "If I'd said no early on, would you have stopped bugging me? Would that have ended it?"

Before I could answer, he was gone. I crept back and found Marcus alone in his casket. He was gorgeous. Even in my state of despair over Bill, I could see it. Sunglasses? A monster had killed this man for his sunglasses.

CHAPTER 31

"If I could tell a story in words, I wouldn't need to
lug a camera."
Lewis Hine

"You do realize this is a Looney Tune scheme," Di said, sitting across the table in the only non-trendy coffee shop in Royal Oak, Detroit's hippest suburb for the under-forty set. "A scenario you'd see in a Bugs Bunny cartoon. A plan without parallel even from you."

"Isn't Bugs Bunny a Warner Brothers cartoon?"

I'd reached a level of desperation where ideas like this one came to me unbidden. Desperation had taken my common sense prisoner. I needed to tell Bill about a hundred different things. Have him to myself—alone and uninterrupted. With her out of the picture.

Di's beautifully Botoxed forehead would have wrinkled if it could. He settled for a finger on his chin. "Are you sure this Athena Grace is the only thing standing in your way? God, I love her name."

We'd hunted the streets in Royal Oak until he found this dumpy leftover coffee shop from the nineteen forties on a side street. The coffee served inside the unimaginatively named Coffee Pot bore faint resemblance to the liquid found at Starbucks or its clones. The uniformed waitress poured mud from an ancient percolator, which hissed a doleful warning. She overshot Di's cup, but cleaned it up handily with a sponge smelling of Clorox and grease. The Coffee Pot's only patrons were a pair of portly construction workers and a woman seeming anxious for the bar next door to open.

"Who knows? Anyway, I think I've got every aspect covered," I said, when the waitress had gone. "And you owe me a caper. Remember why?" I was sure he wouldn't.

"I owe you a caper? Do you know how ludicrous that sounds?"

"You've forgotten, haven't you? Remember the time you thought Alberto was having a romp? I sat outside a house in Ypsilanti, camera in hand, for days. Turned out to be his aunt's house or something." I'd forgotten my recent surveillance wasn't the first.

"Oh, right. Six or seven years ago?" He shook his head. "Scared the old lady to death, didn't we?"

I nodded. "Okay, are you sufficiently caffeinated?"

"More of what you told me on the phone? I feel like I'm in a nineteen forties movie with Barbara Stanwyck and Ralph Meeker."

"Who? Well, anyway, pretend you are if it puts you in the mood. Anyway, the first step in my scheme is to have Athena Grace paged at Oakwood-Trenton Hospital. Right?"

He nodded, half-heartedly at best. I handed him the telephone number.

"And when she picks up, identify yourself as Wilson Bluett, an administrator from the Cleveland Clinic. That name ought to make her sit up. Tell her Dr. Singh suggested you call her." I jabbed at the names below the telephone number. "She'll recognize Singh's name. He's a famous endocrinologist in Cleveland. They were on a medical panel together at a conference there last year."

"Where the hell did you get that name? Wilson Bluett? Am I also to be a doctor?"

"Uh, huh. *Dr.* Wilson Bluett actually works at the Cleveland Clinic. I found his name on their website. With any luck, Athena'll be on the road in an hour or two, taking advantage of the deluxe accommodations we're providing."

"We?"

"Well, me."

"You're forking out the dough?"

"I'll tell you about it in a minute."

Di took a sip of his coffee and shuddered. "And all this subterfuge for an evening with Bill? You must be pretty damned horny or desperate to come up with this—what did you call it—caper? And how can you be sure this is the woman who's standing between you and Bill? Hadn't things begun to go bad before she turned up? Maybe it's your pursuit of the gallery of death that did it."

I ignored him. "After identifying yourself as Dr. Bluett, tell Athena the scheduled speaker for a symposium at the clinic is a no-show and you're hunting for a speaker to take his place."

"And why would Ms. Grace be qualified to step in for such an esteemed speaker? I know she'll ask that sort of question." He shook his head and started picking crumbs up off his plate with his finger and eating them. Suddenly aware of what he was doing, he pushed the plate aside.

"Tell her you read a paper she presented at a conference last year and the subject dovetailed nicely with the symposium's topic: 'Caring for Pre-Diabetic African-Americans.' Tell her it'll be a smallish group—a few doctors, lay people, and nurse practitioners—so she doesn't get overwhelmed and say no." Forgetting my opinion of my first sip of coffee, I took a second sip and sputtered.

"And you're booking both a hotel and airline tickets?"

"You can offer her an airplane ticket to Cleveland, Di, but I think she'll probably drive. It'd take much longer to drive to Metro, go through the security hoops, fly to Cleveland, and then taxi in from the airport. I'll make hotel reservations at the Hyatt near the clinic. Say the room will be under her name and she'll be reimbursed for the room and meals when she comes into the clinic in the morning. The speaking fee will be two thousand dollars."

At that moment, it actually seemed that this would take place—much as the script dictated. Even the dicier parts.

"Wow. You pay well at the Cleveland Clinic."

"Does two thousand seem too high? The only speaking fees I could find online were for people like Bill Clinton and Oprah Winfrey. You can't imagine the amounts they pull in."

"How about fifteen hundred? Too high might make her more suspicious than too low." He let out a breath. "I can't believe I'm helping you plan this."

"It should be mid-morning tomorrow before she figures it out. I can see her sitting in the lobby of her hotel in Cleveland, waiting for a car that never comes. Plus she's stuck with the hotel bill in the end. Bitch, she deserves it."

"Geez, Vi. You don't even know for sure she's sleeping with him. I think you've taken a dive into the deep end of paranoia."

I shrugged stubbornly.

"And then what? Won't she come running home to Bill with tales of how she was duped?"

"She'll blame it on an administrative screw-up, or maybe

professional jealously she can't place. No reason to associate me with it. I bet Bill's never once told her I exist."

He was silent for a long moment, beating his fingers on the Formica, various expressions flitting across his face.

"What is it?" I asked worriedly. "Did I forget something?"

He shook his head. "We can try this, Vi. Maybe we can pull it off."

"Great!" I wanted to believe it.

"But I think it'd be much better if you took the leap and found out where you stand with Bill. How long can you avoid admitting what you feel? How long can you avoid asking him what he feels?"

"Pretty long it seems. I don't like to ask a question unless I know I'll like the answer."

"You can't always control things, honey. Not the ones that matter."

"It's worked so far." But I didn't believe this and looked away.

"Call Bill. Tell him you want to see him tonight. Ask him to come up. Keep it simple."

"He's shown no inclination to come over in a long time. Gave me an excuse about going to see his mother when I suggested he come over earlier this week."

"He's been distracted by his mother's illness and his own situation. Give him another chance before you resort to—this." He patted my hand. "Say you need to see him tonight. Look, forget this idea. It's got disaster written all over it. It'll make you look bad if he figures it out— which he will. Like a schemer, or a psycho, or at the least, a desperate woman."

"I still think it could work." I did. Kind of. I wanted Athena far away and feeling as foolish as I'd felt seeing them walk out of Tiffany's.

"I'll keep my script in hand in case it becomes necessary, but I bet Bill will come through for you without the shenanigans. Ask him."

Di looked down at his empty coffee cup. "This whole plan is cheesy. Screwy and cheesy." He waved the empty cup at the waitress. "It might play out in *reel* life, but not in real life."

I still hadn't told Di about my father, and I wanted to...badly. But it seemed like a story I should share with Bill first. Or something I needed to further digest. Maybe Di'd say, "So what?" Was being one-quarter black even worth mentioning in Detroit?

Despite misgivings, a few hours later, I called Bill, fighting back severe nausea as I waited for him to pick up.

"Any plans for the evening, Bill? I know you said you were tied up, but I thought I'd try again." Inspiration hit me on the spot. "They had nice steaks down at Wigley's down at the Eastern Market today." I lowered my voice to a whisper. "It's been a long time, Bill. The guy with the Hitler mustache at Hirt's was asking for you. I picked up those ginger cookies you like. The ones with the lemon icing." The steaks had actually come from my neighborhood Kroger's and the cookies as well, but I knew mentioning the Eastern Market would soften him up. A Detroit booster to the core.

"Bet the last of the tomatoes are showing up about now."

"It's all pumpkins, squash, and mums," I said. "Summer's over."

He cleared his throat. "I guess I can put this other stuff on hold. Sure, baby. I'll be there."

CHAPTER 32

*"It is no accident that the photographer becomes a photographer
any more than that the lion tamer becomes a lion tamer."*
Dorothea Lange

IT WAS A really good thing I hadn't returned the sharkskin dress because I'd need something spectacular to get Bill's attention. Though only a short time had passed since I bought it, it didn't fit as snugly. The travails of the last few weeks had winnowed me down another half-size. When I finished with my makeup and hair, I looked down and thought immediately of Mr. Polifax at Allure Furs. He would've liked this look. I could've sold a few furs for him in this dress—if any of his special clients had let me keep it on.

I called Di for cooking instructions.

"I can't believe you've never broiled a lousy steak," he said. "What the hell do you eat?"

"I don't think many single women fix themselves steaks." My strong preference was for food that didn't require cooking.

"But maybe they might cook one for their family or friends—"

"If only I could find a friend who wasn't always shaking his finger at me."

So Di instructed me on how to broil a steak. His directions included seasoning the meat, but the solitary seasoning in my nearly empty cabinet was salt. Inspiration hit, and I dribbled bottled vinaigrette on the meat and let it marinate, worrying only slightly that the dressing might have expired. I decided it was already too late to check for a date on the bottle so why torture myself over poisoning us. I knew how to make a salad, how to bake a potato. It'd do. Hopefully the main attraction would be me, in and out of the pewter-colored dress.

This was my aim: to win Bill back, to make him love me again. Or want me, at least. And if the evening went well, better than I'd any reason to hope, I might introduce the idea of Ted's contract. And maybe, just maybe, I'd share the story of Howl Heart. Oh, what an agenda I'd set myself.

I wasn't too sure about how the story of my father would go over. Or if I could tell Bill without getting it wrong—fumbling a detail or emotion that suddenly sprang up. I didn't know what he'd think. Maybe he'd be amused. Maybe he'd say, "So what?" Maybe he'd help me work through some complex emotions.

If things were a little iffy, if it seemed awkward between us, the contract could wait and so could the story of my father. My main goal was to have Bill in my corner again—have him want to make love. Love me even. The photographs were secondary. Admitting that was a big step for me. Admitting anything could come before my work was a chilling thought. Where had letting people become important gotten me in the past?

I still had the final photograph to take—and I might take a thirteenth once I had the twelfth. Create a safety net, a margin for error in case Ted rejected one of them; in case it all fell through.

Bill arrived ten minutes early, a good omen. As he stood at the door, his mouth fell open when he saw me. "You didn't tell me I was supposed to get dressed up," he said, looking down at his jeans, his rumpled blue oxford shirt, his running shoes. Remembering his manners, he added, "You look gorgeous, Violet. I'd forgotten how nicely you clean up. I feel like a handyman next to you."

"You *are* my handy man." I almost blushed at my stupid joke but waved him in. "Been so long since you've been up here."

This came out in a whoosh I regretted at once. I sounded like Mae West. Or, even worse, needy. Who likes needy? He started to say something, but I motioned him to the sofa before he got it out, hoping my tone had sounded whiny only to my own ears. Bill sat down hard and a small cloud of dust rose. Hoping he didn't notice this either, I headed toward my makeshift bar.

"I'm not drinking alcohol these days," Bill said. "You know— holding the diabetes off. Athena gave me a regimen to follow. Dropped eleven pounds in three weeks."

I turned around to look and he slid his hands down his sides. "I bet you hardly recognize the new me."

"Your own personal nurse?" I said, sitting down empty-handed, angry again about Athena Grace—wishing the bitch *was* on her way to Cleveland. I should never have let Di deter me. I'd have liked a drink, but it seemed inappropriate if my guest wasn't joining me.

"I think I have some cranberry juice. Club soda, coffee?"

"Sit down with me for a minute. We can talk about food and drink once I've had an eyeful of your lovely dress." He patted the seat. Thankfully, no dust rose this time.

I was surprised he seemed so relaxed, so into me. He hadn't seemed like this in months. It was almost worrisome. But would a man about to break up with a woman appear so calm? Good morticians probably excelled at composure though. I put a hand on his cheek and leaned in for a kiss. He didn't refuse.

"Your own personal nurse, you said?"

He pulled back slowly. "I haven't had a chance to tell you much about her, have I? She's taken my mom and me in hand with this damned disease. Mamma's already feeling better."

An angel apparently. Steaming again, I got up and headed for the liquor cabinet. Like it or not, I was having a drink. It was only wine, for God's sake.

"So how did you happen to meet—Athena, is it?" I managed to say her name as if it weren't imprinted on my brain. I wanted to hear his version of it.

"Cajuan Grace's sister. Remember? Rapper with his own celebrity photographer I buried a few months back? I think you took a picture of him despite the fact we had no contract." He shook a finger and chuckled a bit. "Probably she would've let you take one if I'd worked on her more. Turns out she's a softy." He chuckled in a way that made me want to punch him. "I was cowed by her mother though; one of those stern old biddies running the Baptist Church. Hortense. The only Hortense I ever heard of before her was a cow. But Athena's a softy," he repeated, stretching. "I'm sure I've mentioned her."

Just how soft? And why couldn't he stop talking about her?

"I remember Cajuan," I said, trying to sound casual. Glass in hand, I turned around. "Sure you don't want soda water? It's diet."

"Sure, sure. Anyway, we got to talking one day and it turned out diabetes was her specialty. Written papers on it. Taken part in research studies. She earned a PhD in nursing, you know. I'm sure I told you."

"So you've said." Would his recitation of the wonders of Athena

Grace never cease? "Put you on a diet? What else?"

"She's been up to see Mamma a couple of times." He paused. "She helped me pick a present for her birthday a few days ago. Why are you so interested in her anyway?"

Me? Was it me who couldn't wrestle the name from my tongue?

"I would've been glad to help with a gift, Bill. Why don't you ever ask me?" I was half-relieved and half-hurt. "I'd have liked to help."

Was that why they were coming out of Tiffany's? Had to be.

"I know you would've come along. But she's met Mamma. And they hit it off."

"And because she's black. African-American, like you." *Maybe this was the time to tell him?*

He nodded. "Both of 'em have the same Sunday School kind of taste too. They like tiny pieces of jewelry. Dainty stuff." I tried not to look down at the large onyx pendant hanging heavily between my breasts. "Teensy kitty-cat pin, I got her. With emerald eyes. A garnet collar. Egyptian-looking." He laughed. "Loved it. Exactly what she wears. So anyway, life is looking better now."

"Sounds like you two have become close."

Bill chuckled again. "Ha! You don't need to be jealous, sweetie. It's not like that at all. She's not my type." He paused. "Way too churchy for me. Too much like Mamma. Me, I have a different taste in women."

A deep breath. A soaring feeling.

"Lucky for me. Food or sex first, Bill?"

I'd happily skip over the next ten minutes of planned conversation. Things were going better than I'd dared to hope. Once we were back on solid ground, I might tell him about the contract. And about my father. He'd help me make sense of it, explain my father's action, his attitude. We'd be a true couple, at last. I wanted this—I really did.

"Food's the last item on my mind."

Smiling, Bill rose obligingly, stretched, and headed for the bedroom, stepping out of his loafers as he walked. Within seconds, we had our clothes off and were in bed. Under the scarlet sheets I'd chosen for the night, the sight of him in the mirror was exhilarating. He was sleek, toned. I was whittled down to nothing. Not that I had a fetish about weight. But still we looked nice. Together.

"Hey, you know what I was thinking?" Bill said, as he reached for me.

"What?" I asked, hoping it wasn't the beginning of a discourse.

"I was thinking that not counting the big mirror you got hanging from the heavens, you've got only one other mirror in the whole place. And that is," he continued, "the teensy, worn one over the bathroom sink, half of it blacked out with age. How do you put your cosmetics on?"

I shrugged. "I guess I know where my face is by now." Actually I'd never liked looking at myself. Not since the Allure Fur days. The mirror above us was not for looking at *me*.

He laughed. "Sounds like you don't like your own face. And such a pretty one."

I'd waited months for a compliment and sucked this one in like oxygen.

When we were finished, and it must have been an hour later, I threw on a robe and headed for the kitchen.

"Relax, baby," I said. "I've got dinner under control."

Of course, I didn't, and I was still struggling with how to light the broiler when I heard the sound of the damned treadmill upstairs. Ben had returned from wherever he'd been and was giving his machine a good workout. The thumps seemed louder than before—like he hadn't oiled the stupid thing in months.

"Sorry, Bill," I called out as loud as I could. "Thought we were done with the damned treadmill."

"I'm used to it," Bill called back. "It's our background music, the big drum roll at the end."

We both listened from separate rooms as the pounding grew progressively louder.

"Sheez!" It sounded like Ben was descending through the ceiling. I looked around for a broom to pound out my concern on the ceiling—not that he'd hear me.

"What?"

Bill was saying something but I couldn't hear him.

There was a sort of a roaring sound—maybe from inside an air shaft? But quickly the roar, or more accurately a sort of cracking, splitting sound, grew so loud I knew it had to be inside the apartment. It was like a train coming through the walls. Or, I thought, looking up, through the ceiling. I bolted through the living room in time to see the mirror pull away from the bedroom ceiling, dropping with frightening speed onto the bed. It plunged as if it had been fired, hitting what lay below with ferocity.

Bill lay propped up in bed, his head cushioned by pillows, so his face, which registered only a small look of surprise, was untouched. For a moment, I had hope. It seemed too preposterous to be true—that something like this could happen. Surely he would shrug the mirror aside momentarily, dump it onto the floor, and smile up at me. Laugh at the ludicrousness of the situation. Laugh at the worry on my face.

But the weight of the mirror must've killed him instantly. His right foot quivered for a second, and then went still. I stood frozen, watching helplessly as small pieces of paint or plaster continued to rain on top of the mirror, on top of Bill. His hair turned white from the downpour in seconds—like a terrible aging process had been accelerated by events.

And horribly, the sound of the treadmill continued relentlessly above. Ben didn't know what'd happened, what his treadmill had done. He was probably wearing earphones, listening to his iPod. It was the bolts, mirror, and coat of plaster in my bedroom that gave way, not the ceiling itself. I stood there counting the beats of my heart, the thump of the treadmill; I wasn't sure which. The thumping went on. And on. Still I couldn't move. Only seconds had passed, possibly a minute, but it seemed like hours, days, months.

Breaking loose from my stupor, I raced across the room, managing with considerable exertion to slide the mirror off him. Bill was as motionless as any of the men we'd worked on together these last months. In fact, I never saw anyone more still. I cleared the plaster away as my tears, unfamiliar till lately, fell hard and fast. And suddenly I was screaming, throwing myself on him, and begging him not to be dead. The sound of the treadmill drowned out my screams; no one could hear me.

White dust covered me when I finally rose. Tears stung my throat, which was plugged by another pent-up scream. With enormous effort, I stopped crying. The shaking stopped too.

Like an automaton, I went for the camera, setting it up as fast as I could, pulling over a lamp head, finding a high enough stool to stand on, making the necessary adjustments. My best lighting was at Bill's. The stepladder too. This would have to do.

Bill would need a little makeup, I thought stonily, looking at him through the viewfinder. I walked to the bathroom and grabbed my makeup case, which was still on the sink. Was it only a few hours ago that I had applied my own makeup? I didn't have the range of cosmetics

Bill kept, and the cover-up was a bit too light, although not as far off as I would've guessed. I quickly looked in the mirror in the bathroom as I turned away. The mirror *was* worn and tiny, inadequate for a grown woman; why had this never occurred to me before? My only decent mirror was in the darkroom, a place Bill had never been.

My face was unfamiliar anyway. A harridan stared back: the artist, the professional, the survivor—the one that Hal Hart, Bobby Allison, Ted Ernst, Mr. Polifax and his customers—the one none could defeat but all of them used, screwed, or deserted. I was screaming again, but only in my head.

Bill was naked, and putting clothes on him was too risky; he must be left as undisturbed as possible. Bill's would be my only photo of a naked man. I shot a dozen pictures, several dozen actually, memorizing his body as I'd never done in life. I shot until my eyes were blurry. I shot until I knew I had to move on, to finish up the rest of it.

So I cleaned Bill's face of the makeup, carefully stripping away the evidence of intrusion, making him look like any dead man at the scene of an accident. Afterward, I sat still for ten minutes, composing myself. Then I walked across the room, found the business card near the phone, and called Detective Saad. I knew he wasn't the right person to call; my apartment was not in his district, but I did it anyway. I knew I should have called the cops before snapping the pictures, but what if there hadn't been enough time? What if I'd been denied the most important of all my photographs.

I needed the closest thing to a friend Detroit's finest could offer.

CHAPTER 33

Detroit Free Press: William Fontenel, a prominent Detroit mortician,
was asphyxiated when a heavy light fixture tore loose from a ceiling
and fell on him. Mr. Fontenel, a lifelong resident of Detroit, was
thirty-eight years old and well known locally for the unusual care he
took with preparing the dead. He is survived by his mother, who lives
in Saginaw, Michigan.

(September 2011)

DETECTIVE SAAD HAMMERED on the door about thirty minutes later,
took a quick look around, and called the local police. Both of us
stood aside while a quartet of cops examined the ceiling, the bed,
Bill, the floor above my apartment, my neighbor Ben and his treadmill,
the janitor's supply closet, his ladder, the bolts, the plaster, the mirror
itself—each cop systematically peering into my hidden places.

Or that's what it felt like: a dental instrument probing decaying
teeth. Numbness and grief eventually gave way to anger as I answered
questions put forth from a late-arriving police photographer, lab
technicians, detectives, some cop or firefighter who seemed to
specialize in building collapse. Did they hire engineers for cases like
this or were there men on the squad who knew buildings? Who'd have

thought the city budget of Hazel Park could afford such a battalion? Maybe they'd called for backup from a wealthier neighboring suburb. The tears, which seemed profligate an hour before, had dried up as I came to realize I was under siege and went into fight mode.

"Do they think I did this on purpose? Murdered Bill?" I asked anyone in earshot.

It was incomprehensible. I'd anticipated trouble but not that they'd have the idea I'd set this up to murder Bill. Did they imagine I could drag a twelve-foot ladder in here to loosen those bolts, climbing to the top, calculating the mirror's fall—when and how it would happen? Did they think I made Bill lie on the bed so that the mirror would fall on him when the treadmill began its trek to nowhere upstairs? Was there a way to know for certain it would kill him? Or when? What if he'd turned to reach for his reading glasses as the mirror fell? What if the phone rang and he jumped out of bed? Couldn't it have happened with me in the bed? Couldn't the both of us have been crushed? It was ridiculous.

When I pointed this out, no one seemed impressed by, or even interested in, my logic. In fact, they asked me to step outside so the officers could do their job.

The engineer interviewed me, asking: why hadn't I inspected the bolts for tightness after Ben installed his treadmill upstairs, where had I bought the bolts, and had I specified at Lowes the weight they'd have to secure? How much did the mirror weigh, how had I gotten it up in the first place? Why was it up there? Did I move anything after its fall? Clear anything away? Touch Bill or the bed at all?

"Bill," I said. "I just touched Bill."

They looked at my footprints on the fallen plaster with displeasure. "We can see where you stood," one fellow said.

It was basically, if not technically, true.

The cop frowned. "Well, you shouldn't have touched him. Don't you watch TV?" He looked around the room, saw none, and shrugged. "You're never supposed to disturb the crime scene."

Crime scene? Bill was already a body to them and possibly a murder victim. Wouldn't any woman run across the room to see if her lover had survived? Picked up his arm, checked his wrist, shook him? Moved the mirror away if possible in hopes he was still alive? It wasn't a crime scene. It was the scene of an accident.

The questions fired at me made me feel incompetent, callous, murderous, perverted. The one saving grace was the questions and activities going on in my apartment kept my mind occupied, kept me from sliding into a well of grief.

In retrospect, I should've inspected the bolts, I told the cop who asked, but the walls were thick and I thought the floors and ceilings would be too.

"It's the plaster that tore away, not the floor or ceiling," he reminded me.

We both looked up.

I'd hung this mirror in other apartments, in other cities. It'd had never been a problem before. Yes, I'd bought brand new bolts when I moved in seven years ago, asking the clerk at the hardware store (was it Home Depot or Ace?) for the strongest ones, explaining the job. The lanky black cop evaluated me, surely wondering what went on under that looking-glass, what kind of woman hung a mirror over her bed. Only men were supposed to do that.

"You're lucky he had a ladder high enough," the cop added. "The super, that is."

"He cleans the fans with it," I said, motioning to the ceiling fan on the living room ceiling.

I remembered questioning the mirror's safety weeks ago when it seemed to vibrate over my head. If I'd followed up on that—if I'd been less preoccupied with my pictures of the dead...

"Do *you* think I did this on purpose?" I said, over and over.

Saad and I were standing in the hallway, an alert, rather muscular policewoman hovering nearby in case I should make a break for it. Saad had lost his credibility, the trust of the local cops. Once they'd seen the two of us huddling together on the sofa when they arrived, he'd lost his leverage in the case. Perhaps he had laid under that mirror once or twice too, they were probably thinking.

Saad shrugged, unwilling to choose a side apparently, silent for once. I glared at him, but he was unmovable, offering me nothing.

Ben, from upstairs, owner of the nefarious treadmill, hovered in the stairwell too, dressed in the outfit he apparently ran in: flannel pajama bottoms, a stretched-out striped turtleneck, ballet slippers with vinyl treads on the bottoms. Ballet slippers? Didn't he skid?

"There's a draft from the skylight," he said, fingering the stretched neck when he saw us staring at him. He didn't bother to explain the satiny footwear and I didn't ask. Ben suddenly caught sight of his reflection in a mirror angled to show activity in the stairwell, and he gave it his attention, running nervous fingers through his uncombed hair, adjusting the neck on his shirt.

I watched silently when they carried Bill away, wishing I could cry—if only for the expiation tears might bring. I'd loved him. Loved Bill. Okay, I admitted it. I certainly loved Bill, and this was exactly what I'd always expected would happen should I ever love again. Daisy's death had taught me that.

Saad looked at me critically once Bill was carried past us on the way to the stairs. "You took his picture, didn't you? First," Saad said.

His voice was flat, his eyes black marbles in the darkish stairwell.

I nodded. "How could you tell?"

"I saw beige marks on the sheet you threw over him. Foundation, my ex-wife called it." He shook his head. I was too tired to try to explain the picture was only for me—that I'd never use it in the show. I hoped it was true. It seemed true.

AFTER BILL WAS taken away, I was barred from the apartment while further police work went on. This took several days. The cops removed the bolts, pieces of plaster, my photographs, and bags full of other things (some inexplicable), hoping to find evidence I'd meant Bill harm. Links to the activity on Belle Isle made matters worse. I half-expected to see the treadmill itself coming down the stairs, tagged as the murder weapon.

Within a day, the cops came up with the theory that Bill was giving me a hard time over the use of the photos in a show, so I killed him.

"Ted Ernst told us he'd insisted on the receipt of a signed contract from Mr. Fontenel, disavowing future claims to any profits earned through your work. He said you'd delayed on this to the point where he considering canceling the show."

Ted had apparently been dragged from his gallery and questioned for over an hour, doing me no favors with statements like this one.

"Look, it was insulting to ask Bill to sign a contract. We had a personal relationship beyond the business one. He'd never have asked for a share in any profits. But to placate Ted, I would've asked Bill eventually, and I knew he'd sign it. Bill understood how things worked. It was his idea to have the families sign contracts before we took the photos."

"So none of this bothered Bill? He was onboard from day one?"

I nodded, but wondered if that was ever true. Had I used his feelings for me to get what I wanted. Something he didn't really want. He'd said as much time after time.

None of it made me look good; only good for pinning a murder on. I could feel the officer's eyes boring in, wondering what kind of woman did any of these things: hanging mirrors over beds, photographing dead men, involving herself with Detroit gangs, seducing a bipolar kid.

But in the end, it was too ludicrous to believe I'd murdered Bill to ensure the show would take place. No one saw the procurement of a dozen photographs as a reasonable motive, my artistic pursuits worth taking a life, their value a commodity. There was no real reason to believe it hadn't been an accident. No reason to believe I'd anything but sorrow in my heart. As a method of murder, the use of a falling mirror was too unpredictable, too crazy. No jury would buy it.

"It's pretty damned hard to understand how you could run for your camera after that mirror came down on him," Diogenes said. "I understand the creative impulse, but your actions in this instance elude me." He shook his head. He was with me at Bunny's apartment as I got ready to return home. "I can't believe it was to get the last photo for your show. Tell me it wasn't."

The two of us had come back from Bill's funeral where the majority of the mourners had flashed me cold looks, knowing me from my photo in the newspaper. But I'd gone anyway, gripping Di's arm hard enough to leave a bruise. Thankfully, it was a closed coffin. I didn't think I could manage looking at Bill's face again. As I tried to ignore the chill that swept across the room on our entrance, I kept one thought in my head: Bill knew I'd never meant him any harm and I'd loved him as best I could. How could I not be here? How could I not face these people down? I looked across the room and spotted Athena Grace.

There was a look about her that made me think we might have been friends in other circumstances: Athena had no pretensions; she took her work seriously; she liked Bill.

"I didn't have a single photograph of Bill," I reluctantly told Di. "There, I said it. In all our months together, I never took a picture of him. I tried once or twice, but he hated to have his picture taken. It was my last chance to get one."

The words fell from my lips and I knew in my heart they were true. I took his picture because, like the parents of Rodney—what was his name?—all those months ago, I wanted a record. I needed it. How else could I remember him? Believe he was truly gone? I wanted to make him mine and taking his picture would do that. It was hard to explain it—even to myself.

Di gave this a minute's thought. "Is that picture of Bill something you'd want to stick in your wallet?"

"Of course not. Now, I understand how those families felt now. You're honoring—or acknowledging—the last time you'll see them. I remember what I photograph and I wanted to remember him. Maybe it was selfish or ghoulish, I don't know. It felt right—necessary."

"So you won't use him in the show?"

I hesitated. "He's the best-looking man of the bunch. He's the one who made it possible. I want him to be part of it."

"Oh, Vi." Diogenes shook his head. "It's gonna be seen as exploitative."

"There may not be a show. I'll think about it if and when it's set."

"I don't always get you, Vi."

I shrugged. "That's okay. Neither do I." I looked up. "Di, there's something else. Remember my disappearing father..."

CHAPTER 34

"Images are more real than anyone could have supposed."
Susan Sontag

AN ISSUE OF Detroit's weekly alternative newspaper came out a week later with a story about Bill's death, but more pointedly, a story about me. Unlike the death notice in the daily papers, which changed the mirror to a ceiling light for propriety's sake, this paper told the real story. The headline read, "Shutterfly Proves Ready for Her Close-up."

I was hurrying into the drycleaner's when I spotted the issue in the yellow newspaper machine outside the store. They'd managed to come up with a photo of Derek's obliterated site on Belle Isle and a picture of me. Both of us were plastered across the front page. Luckily Bill's aversion to photographs had kept his face off the front page. There were only mine to use and the paper didn't have them.

The reporter dug up my involvement in several of the recent murders, found out about my photography project, and was now depicting me as Detroit's own angel of death, anxious to take pictures at any cost, out for success in a pathological way. For a minute, I thought the reporter knew about my deathbed photos of Bill too. But that was still a secret—at least to this reporter. The eleven photos that sat in the darkroom were described, but not shown. I guessed the paper couldn't afford a copyright suit.

"For the love of God," Di said via cell, an hour later. "When are you going to return to the anonymity of your recent past? Remember when we were Di and Vi, a couple of pals making good in the city? Now it's something scary every minute. You opened a vault and the demons escaped."

I thought all the way back to the beginning, the day when Bill and I had been doing that crossword puzzle and the clue of Pandora's Box had been on it. Was I Pandora?

"I guess I'd better call Ted. He's probably seen it by now. Why do the arty types flock to that weekly?"

But Ted turned out to be out of town, courting an artist in Chicago, his clerk said.

"He's already working on his spring show. Of course, if your show does the business he expects, he'll postpone it."

Soothing information. But how would my photos play after the newspaper article? Would Ted balk at being part of the "exploitation" of dead black men? This was likely to be his take on it. Or his attorney's.

I debated calling Ted, but decided a day or two's wait wouldn't hurt. Either he'd go nuts over it or he wouldn't. No need to find out which one yet.

"YOU KNOW I'D no business showing up at your apartment when you called me," Detective Saad said later at a coffee shop. "I should've contacted the local cops immediately. You didn't make what'd happened clear on the phone. Certainly it's tested my credibility in the department. If I'd known the circumstances…"

"I shouldn't have called you," I said. "But you're the only cop I know. And besides, I wasn't thinking about what happened to Bill as a crime—it was an accident and I didn't know what to do." I sighed. "Boy, have I said *that* a million times. People involved in a horrific event don't always read it the same way a cop does. My god, I was in a state of shock."

If I hadn't been, I'd have contacted an attorney instead of a cop before opening my mouth. If I hadn't been in shock, I also might not have taken the pictures of Bill.

He looked at me strangely, reading my mind. "Yet you still took those pictures of him before you called me."

I looked around, wondering if anyone could hear our conversation. "Yes, and I've told you why I did it several times now." I shoved the coffee aside. "So hang me."

"If I'd pointed out the makeup on that sheet covering him to any of those cops, you'd have spent another ten hours or so being questioned."

"Oh, who's to say it wasn't from me. I was under that sheet minutes earlier."

"It was tucked right under his chin." He took a sip of his coffee. "I hadn't counted on you finding new ways to knock men off. Hey, I'm sorry," he said a second later, slapping a hand on his mouth. "A lousy thing to say." He removed his hand and added. "My ex-wife's always telling me I'm an insensitive pig."

"So why'd you invite me out for coffee today? It can't be that you want my company. Not a woman as dangerous as me. A callous bitch."

"Well, I do enjoy your company, but you're right, that wasn't my reason."

"So?"

"Cal Black, one of my colleagues, spotted you in Southwest Detroit last week taking pictures of tags. You can only follow your photographer's nose so far in Detroit without getting spotted."

"I take pictures. That's it." I thumped my fist on the Formica and his coffee overflowed. "And I don't take the kind of photographs you find in *HUM* magazine. Except for hire, of course.

"You can't be so naïve that you don't know such activity can get you into trouble? Why can't you play nice and take pictures of girly stuff? Why are you so attracted to dangerous subjects?"

"Why are you?"

He wiped up spilled coffee with a napkin and shrugged. "I would've thought you were smart enough after Derek's experience to know gangs are nothing to fool around with."

"I wasn't photographing people—only their tags."

"The two are never far apart. Find another subject."

"Is this an official police order?"

"No. Call it a request from a friend."

We talked a little more and then he grabbed the tab and headed for the cash register.

CHAPTER 35

"Photography is the story I fail to put into words."
Destin Sparks

"WANT ME TO go with you?" Di asked.

"That'll make me seem weak. He must have seen or heard about the article by now. I don't know why he hasn't called."

I was pacing again, having spent the day planning and discarding various strategies for dealing with Ted.

Ted was unlocking the door when I arrived. He gave me a quick glance and pushed open the door. "Come in," he said unnecessarily since I was right on his heels.

He swept across the room and immediately began making a pot of coffee. I could tell from his movements he was very angry.

"Look," he said when the machine started making noises, "it was bad enough when the police hauled me in for questioning. But I could let that pass because it became clear after a few minutes it was an accident. The project wasn't threatened by such a mishap. Nobody knew about it except the cops."

"It took the police days to recognize…" I started say, but he waved it away.

"The newspaper article effectively crashed and burned the whole project. Nobody's gonna get past the scenario the article outlined. That you—well, the both of us—are exploiting the deaths of black men. Two white people, I might add."

Should I tell him I was not strictly a white woman? Would that raise or lower my street cred?

He poured two cups of coffee and handed me one. I was sick of coffee and didn't move. He set it down on the table. "I can't jeopardize the future of this gallery—my future—by seeming to use other people's tragedy for my success. Fuck, Vi, this is Detroit. Now that the whole project's been framed in racial terms, there's no going back or forward. I'm sorry." He shook his head, almost ferociously. "I'll be lucky if I survive the mention of the gallery in the story. Damned shame."

"So where does that leave me?"

I didn't know why I asked him this. He'd never shown himself to be altruistic in the past, never been at all interested in me. "Any ideas about where I could go for a show?" He glared at me. "Well, I do have to make a living. I sunk months into this job."

"I imagine that gallery in Soho might still be willing to show your work. New York's a million miles away. Even if they've heard about the article, they'd probably see it as a bonus. Or wouldn't much care." He smiled slightly. "New York doesn't know Detroit exists."

"No kidding—I lived there for a few years. Would you call them? Give me an introduction at least?"

He shook his head. "You're on your own. I need to steer clear of you and your business. I'm not going to let you drag me down with you a second time. You seem to have an unerring instinct for making bad choices." He walked over to his battered desk and opened a drawer. "But here's Alan Richter's card. I told him about you months ago, forwarded the first two photos you did along. He liked them. Remember? So give him a call." His voice softened momentarily. "I know this all seems unjust, but maybe it'll work out for the best. Your work might be too big for Detroit anyway. Too tied to hard times." He smiled slightly. "Locally, it's more of a reminder of what's happening—what people see every day on the news—than a piece of art. It may just be too personal too. People are going to recognize these men."

"Is that so bad?"

"Who knows, maybe later I'll regret letting you get away."

I was back in the car in ten minutes, shaking and angry, my usual state nowadays. Too big for Detroit! A few months ago, he'd ripped my work from his walls with nary a kind word. But I took the card home and set it on the counter, looking at it for the next day or two. Then I picked up the phone and called the gallery.

"Ted told me about your project a few months back," Alan Richter said, remembering immediately. He'd answered the phone himself so clearly the gallery wasn't a big or busy one. "And I'm not in Soho, Ms. Hart. I'm in Hell's Kitchen. The gallery in Soho wasn't mine; I was an assistant there. They're calling Hell's Kitchen Clinton now. We're at Forty-eighth and Tenth."

I pictured the neighborhood west of the theater district, wondering if it'd changed over the years. "So where do we go from here?"

"Well, let's start by you emailing me your files. Ted sent me one or two a few months ago, but I'd like to see the whole group. But I have to warn you, the earliest we could do this is next summer." I heard him snapping on a light switch. "Let's see. I'm booked through June. If it works out, maybe a July-August show."

"Next summer?" Would the earth still be here?

"Think it over," he said. "But let me know if you're going to send me those photographs. My clerk's quick with the delete button since a virus infected us a few months ago. We don't open any files we don't recognize."

Next summer? The words kept running through my head.

And I'd no guarantee. Hell's Kitchen was no more promising than Ferndale—or at least it hadn't been when I lived in New York. There was a long line of ifs between a show in New York next summer and now. Would the photos make any kind of splash in a city as big as New York? Was it what I wanted—a splash? Did I want to mess with New York again? The photos were about Detroit. They deserved to be shown here. The men deserved it even if I didn't. It was personal.

ONCE AGAIN, I lined the twelve photos up across the tables, seeing Bill among the others for the first time. He was naked, and so the shot was only from the chest up. His nakedness seemed as elegant as any costume. His skin looked luminescent, especially in black and white. There were subtle differences, of course. The angle was different, the lighting more subdued, slight shadows on the walls, the look of a body not prepared as skillfully, not embalmed. But he looked fine.

Weeks later, and I still couldn't believe Bill was gone, that I was inadvertently responsible, that at some point, I'd fallen for him hard. If I'd let him do what he wanted to do, what he'd planned to do that night—he might be alive. Perhaps the mirror would've fallen on me; maybe I'd be dead. If I had quashed the idea he had inadvertently presented me with all those months ago, he'd be alive and perhaps Derek as well.

This was good work. I knew it was—but waiting nearly a year—hell, a year! Maybe I could find a gallery in Chicago or Toronto—out of the fray, but not with the tight schedule of a New York spot. I'd like to get it over with now—get it over with and go on to the next thing—whatever it was.

Heading for the kitchen closet, I took the local phone directory off the shelf. Nowadays, it covered less territory, but there were a dozen or more galleries only miles away. I'd been to most of them—for other artists' shows or to try and sell my work. Photography wasn't as popular as big oily canvasses right now, not as popular as multimedia displays, installation art, computer or digital work. A few new galleries caught my eye, but eventually I slammed the book shut, went into the bedroom, and threw myself on the bed. The plaster above the bed had been redone and I stared up at pure, smooth white. I'd never have the nerve to hang more than a light fixture up again.

Later, I picked up the phone and dialed a number I'd kept in my wallet for years. I knew it by heart though. "Hal Hart? Dad?"

"Violet?" he said, his voice sounding old and only faintly familiar, but oddly not surprised to hear from me. "Is it Bunny? Is she okay?"

"Mom's fine. I'm calling about me."

"You?"

"I know, Dad. *I know.*"

He sighed heavily, but it sounded like a sigh of relief. "Oh, Violet," he said.

I WAS HEADED toward Belle Isle a few weeks later. It was a bright early November day, better than any I could've hoped for. Stan, the porter, was waiting outside the DYC.

"You wanted the drinks tent, right?" he said. "Checked it out last night and set it up this morning. Nice and clean. No mildew, no stains. Like you asked for." He jiggled the change in his pocket, waiting for a response.

"Thanks. The other tents are too big."

I didn't want the *crowd*, if the term wasn't too optimistic, to seem small, the space too big. I'd found, over the last weeks, that art shows were difficult to plan for—especially Belle Isle's first; you never knew who might show up. Most of the flyers I circulated might have found their way into the trash after Monday's storm. I'd also posted information on Detroit's many Internet sites—if anyone read them—on various Facebook pages and Twitter, and in the free newspapers.

"You wanna follow me over there?" Stan said, getting into his Jeep. "'Course you know where it is. Right?"

Nodding, I climbed back into the car and followed him to a parking space near Derek's former site. I walked, pulling my super-sized portfolio on wheels behind me. Parts of the site looked undisturbed, but most of the grisly items were gone. The drinks tent, used at outdoor weddings, was already set up. It was fairly small, but again it'd be better if the tent looked crowded.

"Want me to help you set 'em up?" Stan asked. "The pictures?" He rubbed his hands together enthusiastically.

"Thanks, but I have a couple friends coming to help. I wasn't sure if you'd have the time."

"Well, if they don't show, you got my cell. I'll be tooling around here today, tidying up for winter. We don't have any other special events scheduled." He looked curiously at the first package I was about to unwrap. "Are you showing pictures from weddings you photographed on the island? Drumming up business?"

"Not this time."

If he saw what was in the packages, he might not be so willing to help, so solicitous. A taste for cadavers was probably acquired. I'd only won over the DYC director after a week of haggling, offering to photograph their annual ball for free, offering to help them with their next brochure. He was none too happy about it even now, but here I was. The weekend weather was supposed to be perfect. Good for football or cider mills, the forecaster said. Maybe one of the last warmish weekends this year. Thanksgiving was only a few weeks away after all.

"Hope it goes well," Stan said, starting up his Jeep. "Be nice to see the island put on a big event. Detroit could use something special."

"Me too," I said, hand-visoring my eyes and immediately flashing to Bill's face on my bed. "I could use it too." The sun nearly blinded me. "But let's not get our hopes up." In my whole life, had my hopes ever been up?

I unzipped the attaché holding the placards to accompany each of the bodies, ones giving the date and cause of death but not the name. The priest had been right. It wasn't photojournalism to make it clear how these men died. It was necessary. I took their pictures because of the way they died. How could I ever have thought of denying it?

It'd struck me for the first time last night that almost none of the men had a spouse or partner. Parents, friends, siblings, but few wives to mourn their loss. Except for Pete Oberon, the firefighter, and the bartender, Willis Dumphrey. I thumbed through the contracts to be sure of it. Did being alone make you more vulnerable to death at a young age? Did wives help bar the door to death?

Derek Olsen's photograph was on top. I'd decided to include him only a week ago.

"I hope you'll include Derek. I'm sure he'd want to be part of it," Susan Olsen said, surprising me when we'd had lunch. "I know it sounds odd, but I'm certain of it. Does his being white matter?"

I shook my head. His death was in keeping with the others. He was part of the project—black or white.

"Maybe you'll get a bigger crowd than you think," Stan said, breaking into my thoughts now. "I can get a bigger tent up in a couple hours if need be."

Stan wanted to be part of it too. Detroiters wanted to be around if something good was about to happen. Good wasn't the normal for Detroit.

I smiled. "Let's wait and see. Seems like bad luck to think too big. I'm the pessimistic sort."

In the distance, I saw Di's Mini Cooper rounding the bend. "Oh, here they come now. My help."

"In that toy car?" Stan said. "You might need a burlier man than what's inside that little vehicle for this job."

"Don't worry," I said, heading out to the road to meet them. "I'm used to taking care of myself."

EPILOGUE

Detroit City Paper; November 1, 2011

Raising the Dead
The Photographs of Violet Hart

The days of photographing majestic, snow-capped mountains may be gone. Perhaps such photographs no longer hold our interest or tell our story. Artists, or photographers in this case, are forced to look in other directions for their subject matter. Some choose to photograph children dressed as animals. Others take pictures of naked people, tattoos, or car crashes. Fresh subject matter is not easily come upon in our selfie, YouTube, digital age.

In the case of Violet Hart, a Detroit photographer, pictures of dead, young black men captured her interest. Apparently no local gallery was brave enough to mount her show, however, because she's done it herself, saving the cost of a middleman, but marginalizing public access and ultimately the response. Finding one's way to a white tent on Belle Isle takes more work than cruising galleries in tony suburbs. You'd be a fool not to seek her little tent out, however. This is a show that reveals today's Detroit more effectively than photos of its bombed out buildings, its assembly lines, or its celebrity musicians and athletes.

Although the twelve black (and one white) men Ms. Hart has photographed are not named, the cause and date of their deaths are provided. All of the men died over the last eight months. I wonder if Ms. Hart knew how quickly the number of photographs would mount. The causes of death encompass the sorrows of our age and city with great effect.

Will anyone buy these photographs? Is it an unseemly subject, inappropriate to some? Should anyone be allowed to exhibit photographs of young dead men, many who've died tragically? Well, their families say yes and have given their approval to Ms. Hart's exhibition. Few people denied her a photograph once they saw her work. It is that remarkable.

The art community should be behind Violet Hart too because her exhibit is splendid. Each of her subjects is imbued with a dignity they may or may not have possessed in life. And the mortician who dressed them, William Fontenel, now deceased and tragically one of Ms. Hart's final subjects, put these young men on the path to stardom by dressing them so movingly, with such panache. Ms. Hart's artistry is evident in every photograph; her technique superb. I haven't been as moved by a photo exhibit since I first saw the work of Helen Levitt many years ago. These pieces belong in a museum—and I hope they find their way there.

Even though summer is over, make your way to Belle Isle quickly.

The autumn leaves make a fitting carpet, the wind blows in from the Detroit River, the boats are disappearing from their moors. Winter will come quickly now and the exhibit will be gone. New York calls.

Amanda Rush
City Paper Arts Reporter

THE END

ACKNOWLEDGMENTS

My heartfelt thanks to my husband, Philip, who read this book countless times, always assuring me it was a worthwhile project. Boundless gratitude to Anca Vlasopolos, who encouraged me with her enthusiasm for the story. Appreciation goes to my children, friends, and the writing groups who have supported me on the long road to publication. Special thanks to Clair Lamb for her invaluable editorial assistance. So too, Robert Hensleigh, who educated me on the Deardorff camera and other aspects of photography. Thanks to Dorene O'Brien, Dennis James, and Barbara Grossman who read SHOT and offered encouragement. To Jason Pinter, you made it happen.

But most of all I want to thank the City of Detroit for providing me with a rich, fascinating, unique, and mercurial source of inspiration.

I began writing SHOT IN DETROIT in 2007, long before the recent (and hopefully permanent) resurgence began. Over the four decades before this, Detroit went from boasting the highest rate of home ownership in the nation to suffering the highest rate of home foreclosures. Many scholars date Detroit's entrance into the Great Recession to about 2001 so that by 2007-08, an overwhelming number of Detroiters were threatened with or had already experienced the loss of their home. Many had also lost their job, their family, their self-esteem. School population plummeted as families who could afford to leave did, depopulating a sprawling city that made the provision of city services even more difficult. In 2007 only 25% of Detroit students entering public high school graduated.

Although I spent 45 years living within a mile or two of city limits, my life has been one of comparative privilege. I have never experienced what so many Detroiters endure: poverty, crime, illness, decay, neglect, despair, and worst of all, hatred. This concerned me daily in writing this book. Did I dare to even try to imagine the life many Detroiters live? As an older white woman, can I be credible and not give offense in writing about what I only know as an outsider? And the concern grew as my central theme: the death of young black men appeared more and more in the news. How could I talk about the idea that black lives matter without being either self-serving, callous, or cavalier?

I hope I have succeeded in a small way in capturing something of what went on in Detroit in 2011. Most, but not all of the deaths of black men discussed in SHOT IN DETROIT, were similar to ones that actually took place. The central premise: that of a female photographer taking photos of dead black men mirrors a photographer in Harlem only in the broadest strokes. Everything personal about Violet Hart and Bill Fontenel in this story is strictly fictional and written with the greatest affection.

You will find many Detroiters who despair for Detroit but never one who doesn't care about it. It's that kind of town.

Patricia Abbott, February 2016

ABOUT THE AUTHOR

Patricia Abbott is the author of the acclaimed novel *Concrete Angel*, and has published more than 100 stories in print, online, and in various anthologies. In 2009, she won a Derringer Award for her story "My Hero". She is the author of two ebooks of stories: *Monkey Justice* and *Home Invasion* (through Snubnose Press). She is the co-editor of *Discount Noir* (Unteed Reads). She makes her home in Detroit.

Visit her online at pattinase.blogspot.com and follow her on Twitter at @Pattinaseabbott